THE BURN

Also by James Kelman

'And the Judges Said . . .' Essays
The Busconductor Hines
A Chancer
The Good Times
Greyhound for Breakfast
Not Not While the Giro
An Old Pub Near the Angel
Translated Accounts

THE BURN

James Kelman

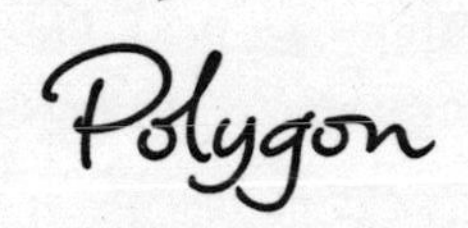

First published in 1991 by Secker & Warburg.
This edition published in 2009 by Polygon,
an imprint of Birlinn Ltd

West Newington House
10 Newington Road
Edinburgh
EH9 1QS

www.birlinn.co.uk

9 8 7 6 5 4 3 2 1

ISBN 978 1 84697 053 5

British Library Cataloguing-in-Publication Data
A catalogue record for this book is available on request from the British Library.

Typeset by Palimpsest Book Production Ltd,
Grangemouth, Stirlingshire
Printed and bound by tbc

Acknowledgement

Stories from this collection have appeared in
Bête Noire, Cencrastus, Chapman, Guardian, New Statesman & Society, Not Poetry, Short Tales from the Nightshift, Writing Together

This collection of stories could not have been finished easily without the hospitality of my wife's family and relations, and our friends, in the town of Lawn, Newfoundland.

For Peter Kravitz

Contents

Pictures	1
A walk in the park	15
A situation	26
Cronies	74
Fr Fitzmichael	77
Street-sweeper	79
Margaret's away somewhere	88
A Memory	89
A player	92
Naval History	99
That thread	113
From the Window	115
Sarah Crosbie	123
That's where I'm at	125
the Hon	128
Unlucky	130
A woman and two men	144
Lassies are trained that way	148
Real Stories	162
A decision	168
the chase	173
it's the ins and outs	176
The small bird and the young person	192
the Christmas shopping	193
events in yer life	196
by the burn	242

Pictures

He wasnt really watching the picture he was just sitting there wondering on things; the world seemed so pathetic the way out was a straight destruction of it, but that was fucking daft, thinking like that; a better way out was the destruction of himself, the destruction of himself meant the destruction of the world anyway because with him not there his world wouldnt be either. That was better. He actually smiled at the thought; then glanced sideways to see if it had been noticed. But it didnt seem to have been. There was a female sitting along the row who was greeting. That was funny. He felt like asking her if there was a reason for it. A lot of females gret without reason. The maw was one. So was the sister, she gret all the time. She was the worst. Whenever you caught her unawares that was what would be happening, she would be roaring her eyes out. The idea of somebody roaring their eyes out, their eyes popping out their sockets because of the rush of water. Or maybe the water making them slippery inside the sockets so they slipped out, maybe that was what it was, if it was anything even remotely literal. No doubt it would just prove to be a total figure of speech: eyes did not go popping out of sockets. There was a sex scene playing. The two actors playing a sex scene, the female one raising the blanket to go down as if maybe for oral intercourse, as if maybe she was going to suck him. Maybe this is why the woman was greeting along the row; maybe she once had this bad experience where she was forced into doing that very selfsame thing, years ago, when she was at a tender age, or else just it was totally against her wishes maybe. And she wouldnt want reminding of it. And look what happens, in she comes to see a picture in good faith and innocence, and straight away has to meet up with that terrible ancient horror

or else she enjoyed her feelings of anguish and had come along because of it, a kind of masochism or something, having heard from one of her pals about the sort of explicit – and maybe even exploitative – sex scenes to expect if she did. That was the director to blame anyway. In the pictures he was involved in something like this usually happened, and there was usually violence as well, like in this one murder. And people would end up in bad emotional states. Was it right that it should be like this? It was okay for somebody like him – the director – but what about other folk, ordinary folk, them without the security, the overall security, the ones that actually went to watch his fucking pictures! The thought was enough to make you angry but it was best to just find it funny if you could, if you could manage it. He nodded and started grinning – it was best to. But it wasnt funny at all in fact it was quite annoying, really fucking annoying, and you could get angry about it, the way these bastards in the film industry got away with it.

And there was that female now, her along the row. He felt like shouting to her: What's up missis? Something wrong?

God Almighty but, the poor woman, maybe there *was* something bad up with her; he felt like finding out, maybe he should ask, maybe it was some bastard in a chair nearby, maybe wanking or something because of the sex scene, and here was the woman within perception distance – listening distance – having to put up with it, and it maybe reminding her of a terrible time when she was younger, just a lassie, and was maybe forced into some sort of situation, some kind of similar kind of thing. So fucking awful the way lassies sometimes get treated.

But it had to come back to the director, he it was to blame, it was this movie making the guy wank in the first place, if he hadnt been showing the provocative sexy scenes it wouldnt be fucking happening. There was a lot to be said for censorship.

If a censor had seen this he would have censored it and then the woman maybe wouldnt be greeting. But no, it was more serious than that. Definitely. It was. She was definitely greeting for a reason, a real reason, she had to be – it was obvious; it had just been going on too long. If it had stopped once the scene changed then it would have been different, but it didnt. And the woman actor was back up the bed and her and the guy were kissing in the ordinary mouth-to-mouth clinch so if the oral carry-on had been the problem it was all over now and the woman should have been drying her tears. So it was obviously serious and had nothing to do with sex at all – the kind that was up on the screen at least. Maybe he should ask her, try to help. There were no attendants about. That was typical of course for matinée programmes, the management aye worked short-handed, cutting down on overheads and all the rest of it. This meant attendants were a rarity and the audience ran the risk of getting bothered by idiots. Once upon a time a lassie he knew was a cinema attendant. She used to have to walk down the aisle selling ice-creams, lollipops and popcorn at the interval; and they tried to get her to wear a short mini-skirt and do wee curtseys to the customers. But they obviously didnt know this lassie who was a fucking warrior, a warrior. She quite liked wearing short mini-skirts but only to suit herself. If she wanted to wear them she would wear them, but it was only for her own pleasure, she would please herself. She used to get annoyed with the management for other reasons as well; they used to get her to wear this wee badge with her name on it so it meant all the guys looked at it and knew what it was and they shouted it out when they met her on the street. Heh Susan! Susaaaaan! And then they would all laugh and make jokes about her tits. It was really bad. And bad as well if you were out with her if you were a guy because it meant you wound up having to get involved and that could mean a doing if you were just one against a few. She was good too, until she fucked off without telling him. He phoned her up one night at tea-time and she wasnt in, it was her flatmate. And her flatmate told him she had went away, she had just went away. She had been talking about it for a while but it was still unexpected when it happened. Probably Manchester it was she went to. He had had his chance. He could have went with her. She hadnt asked him, but he could have if he had wanted. It was his own fault he hadnt, his own fault. She had gave him plenty of opportunities. So it was his own fault. So he never heard of her again. It was funny the way you lost track of folk, folk you thought you would know for life; suddenly they just werent there and you were on your ownsome. This seemed to happen to him a lot. You met folk and got on well with them but then over a period of time yous drifted away from each other – the same as the guys you knew at school, suddenly yous never even spoke to each other. That was just that, finished, fucking zero. It was funny. Sometimes it was enough to make you greet. Maybe this is what was up with the female along the row, she was just lonely, needing somebody to talk to God he knew the feeling, that was him as well – maybe he should just actually lean across and talk to her. Could he do that? So incredible an idea. But it was known as communication, you started talking to somebody, your neighbour. Communication. You took a deep breath and the rest of it, you fucking just leaned across and went 'Hullo there!' Except when it's a male saying it to a female it becomes different. She had the hanky up at the side of her eyes. She looked fucking awful. He leaned over a bit and spoke to her:

Hullo there missis. Are you okay?

The woman glanced at him.

He smiled. He shrugged and whispered, You were greeting and eh . . . you alright?

She nodded.

I couldnt get you something maybe, a coffee or a tea or something, they've got them at the foyer . . .

She stared at him and he got a sudden terrible dread she

was going to start screaming it was fucking excruciating it was excruciating you felt like stuffing your fingers into your ears, he took a deep breath.

There wasnt anybody roundabout except an old dear at the far end of the row. That was lucky.

Maybe there *was* something up with her right enough. Or else maybe she was fucking mental – mentally disturbed – and just didnt have anywhere to go. Genuine. Poor woman. God. But folk were getting chucked out on the street these days; healthy or unhealthy, it didnt matter, the powers-that-be just turfed you out and they didnt care where you landed, the streets were full of cunts needing looked after, folk that should have been in nursing homes getting cared for. She was maybe one of them, just in here out the cold for a couple of hours peace and quiet. And then look at what she has to contend with up on the bloody screen! God sake! In for a couple of hours peace and quiet and you wind up confronting all sorts of terrible stuff in pictures like this one the now. Maybe censors were the answer. Maybe they would safeguard folk like this woman. But how? How would they do it, the censors, how would they manage it? No by sticking the cinemas full of Walt Disney fucking fairyland. Who would go for a start? No him anyway, he hated that kind of shite. Imagine paying the entrance fee for that, fucking cartoons. He leant across:

Ye sure you dont want a coffee?

She shut her eyes, shaking her head for a moment. She wasnt as old as he had thought either. She laid the hand holding the hanky on her lap and the other hand she kept at the side of her chin, her head now tilted at an angle. She kept looking at the screen.

I was going to get one for myself. So I could get one for you while I was at it . . .

She turned to face him then; and she said, Could you?

Aye, that's what I'm saying.

Thanks, you're a pal.

Milk and sugar?

Just milk.

He hesitated but managed to just get up, giving her a swift smile and not saying anything more, just edging his way along the row. He had to pass by the old dear sitting in the end seat and she gave him a look before holding her shopping bags in to her feet to let him past, and he nodded to her quite briskly. He walked up the aisle and down the steps, pushing his way out into the corridor. Thick carpets and dim lighting. He grinned suddenly, then began chuckling. How come he had nodded at the old dear like that? She was as old as his grannie! God Almighty! But it was to show her he was relaxed. That was how he had done it, that was how he had done it. If he hadnt been relaxed he would never have bloody managed it because it would have been beyond him.

Cinema 2 was showing a comedy. He had seen it a week ago. He wasnt that keen on comedies, they were usually boring. He continued past the corridor entrance. There was an empty ice-cream carton sitting on the floor in such a way you felt somebody had placed it there intentionally. Probably they had. He used to have the selfsame habit when he was a boy – thirteen or something – he used to do things to make them seem like accidental events. If he was smoking and finished with the fag he would stick it upright on the floor to make it look like somebody had just tossed it away and it had landed like that as a fluke.

He used to go about doing all sorts of stupid things. Yet when you looked at them; they werent all that fucking stupid.

What else did he used to do? He used to leave stuff like empty bottles standing on the tops of stones and boulders, but trying to make it look like they had just landed that way accidentally. To make folk imagine alien things were happening here on planet Earth and they were happening for a reason, a purpose.

He was a funny wee cunt when he was a boy. Looking back you had to admit it.

The woman at the kiosk passed him the change from the till;

she was in the middle of chatting with the cashier and didnt watch him after she had put the money on the counter so he lifted a bar of chocolate, slid it up his jacket sleeve. One was plenty. He took the two wee containers of milk and the packet of lump sugar for himself.

It was raining outside. He could see folk walking past with the brollies up. And the streetlights were on. It would soon be tea-time.

He didnt take the chocolate bar from his sleeve until along the corridor and beyond the Cinemas 1 and 2, which were the most popular and had the biggest auditoriums – but there were usually cunts talking in them, that was the drawback, when you were trying to listen to the movie, they held fucking conversations. He had to lay the cartons of coffee down on the floor, then he stuck his hand in his side jacket pocket, letting the bar slide straight in from the sleeve. He was going to give it to her, the woman. He wasnt that bothered about chocolate himself. And anyway, in his experience females liked chocolate more than males. They had a sweet tooth.

That was one of these totally incredible expressions, a sweet tooth. What did it actually mean? He used to think it meant something like a soft tooth, that you had a tooth that was literally soft, made of something like soft putty. When he was a boy he had a sweet tooth. But probably all boys had sweet tooths. And all lassies as well. All weans the world over in fact, they all liked sweeties and chocolate, ice-cream and lollipops, popcorn.

She was sitting in a semi-motionless way when he got back to the seat and it was like she was asleep, her eyelids not flickering at all. Here's your coffee, he said, milk with no sugar, is that right?

Ta.

He sat down in his old seat after an eternity of decision-making to do with whether or not he could just sit down next to her, on the seat next to hers; but he couldnt, it would have been a bit out of order, as if just because he had bought her a fucking coffee it gave him the right of fucking trying to sit next to her and chat her up, as if he was trying to get off with her – which is what women were aye having to put up with. The best people to be women were men because of the way they were, the differences between them, their sexuality, because they could get sex any time they like just about whereas men were usually wanting it all the time but couldnt fucking get it – it was a joke, the way it worked like that, a joke of nature, them that wanted it no getting it and them that didnt want it having to get it all the time. The bar of chocolate. He took it out his pocket and glanced at it; an Aero peppermint; he passed it across, having to tap her elbow because she was staring up at the screen.

Here. It's a spare one. He shrugged, I'm no needing it. I'm no really a chocolate-lover anyway, to be honest, I've no got a sweet tooth, the proverbial sweet tooth. He shrugged again as he held it to her.

Oh I dont want that, she said out loud, her nose wrinkling as she frowned, holding her hand up to stop him. And he glanced sideways to see if folk had heard her and were maybe watching. He whispered:

How no? It's alright.

Oh naw pal I just dont eat them – Aero peppermints – any kind of bar of chocolate in fact, being honest, I dont eat them.

Is it a diet like?

Aye. Thanks for the coffee but.

That's alright.

You're no offended?

Naw. I'll eat it myself. On second thoughts I'll no, I'll keep it for later. He stuck it back into his pocket and studied the screen while sipping the coffee which was far too milky it was like water. Funny, how they said something was coffee and then sold you a cup of fucking water with just a splash – a toty wee splash – of brown stuff, to kid you on. Total con. They did the selfsame thing with tea, they charged you for tea but served you with milk and water and another wee splash of brown, a different tasting one. You couldnt trust them. But it was hard to trust people anyway, even at the best of times. You were actually daft if you trusted them at all. At any time. How could you? You couldnt. Cause they aye turned round and fucked you in some way or another. That was his experience.

The film would soon be done, thank God. It was a murder picture, it was about a guy that was a mass-murderer, he kills all sorts of folk. A good-looking fellow too, handsome, then he goes bad and starts all the killing, women mainly, except for a couple of guys that get in his way, security men in the hostel, it was a nurses' hostel, full of women, and a lot of them fancy him, the guy, the murderer, he gets off with them first, screws them, then after he's screwed them he kills them – terrible. And no pity at all.

But sometimes you could feel like murdering somebody yourself in a way, because people were so fucking awful at times, you helped them out and nothing happened, they just turned round and didnt thank you, just took it like it was their due. His landlord was like that, the guy that owned the house he stayed in, he was a foreigner, sometimes you helped him out and he didnt even thank you, just looked at you like you were a piece of shite, like you were supposed to do it because you stayed in one of his fucking bedsits, as if it was part of your fucking rent or something.

He was sick of the coffee, he leaned to place the carton on the floor beneath the seat. He grimaced at the woman. She didnt notice, being engrossed in the picture. To look at her now you would hardly credit she had been greeting her eyes out quarter-of-an-hour ago. Incredible, the way some females greet, they turn it off and turn it on. He was going straight home, straight fucking home, to make the tea, that was what he was going to fucking do, right fucking now. Hamburger and potatoes and beans or something, chips. He was starving. He had been sitting here for two hours and it was fucking hopeless, you werent able to concentrate. You came to the pictures nowadays and you couldnt even get concentrating on the thing on the screen because

because it wasnt worth watching, that was the basic fact, because something in it usually went wrong, it turned out wrong, and so you wound up you just sat thinking about your life for fuck sake and then you started feeling like pressing the destruct button everything was so bad. No wonder she had been fucking greeting. It was probably just cause she was feeling so fucking awful depressed. About nothing in particular. You didnt have to feel depressed about something, no in particular, because there was so much of it.

The bar of chocolate in his pocket. Maybe he should just eat it himself for God's sake! He shook his head, grinning; sometimes he was a fucking numbskull. Imagine but, when he was a boy, leaving all these dowps lying vertical like that, just so somebody passing by would think they had landed that way! It was funny being a wean, you did these stupid things. And you never for one minute thought life would turn out the way it did. You never for example thought you would be sitting in the pictures waiting for the afternoon matinée to finish so you could go fucking home to make your tea, to a bedsitter as well. You would've thought for one thing that you'd have had a lassie to do it for you, a wife maybe, cause that's the way things are supposed to be. That was the way life was supposed to behave. When you were a boy anyway. You knew better once you got older. But what about lassies? Lassies were just so totally different. You just never fucking knew with them. You never knew what they thought, what they ever expected. They always expected things to happen and you never knew what it was, these things they expected, you were supposed to do.

What age was she? Older than him anyway, maybe thirty, thirty-five. Maybe even younger but it was hard to tell. She would've had a hard life. Definitely. Okay but everybody has a hard life. And she was on a diet. Most females are on a diet. She wasnt wearing a hat. Most females were these days, they were wearing hats, they seemed to be, even young lassies, they seemed to be as well; it was the fashion.

The more he thought about it the more he started thinking she might be on the game, a prostitute. He glanced at her out the side of his eye. It was definitely possible. She was good-looking and she was a bit hard, a bit tough, she was probably wearing a lot of make-up. Mostly all females wore make-up so you couldnt really count that. What else? Did she have on a ring? Aye, and quite a few, different ones, on her different fingers. She shall have music wherever she goes. Rings on her fingers and rings on her toes. Bells on her toes. She had black hair, or maybe it was just dark, it was hard to see properly because of the light; and her eyebrows went in a high curve. Maybe she *was* on the game and she had got a hard time from a punter, or else somebody was pimping for her and had gave her a doing, or else telt her he was going to give her one later, if she didnt do the business, if she didnt go out and make a few quid. Maybe her face was bruised. Maybe she had got a right kicking. And she wouldnt have been able to fight back, because she was a woman and wasnt strong enough, she wasnt powerful enough, she would just have to take it, to do it, what she was telt, to just do it. God Almighty. It was like a form of living hell. Men should go on the game to find out what like it was, a form of living hell – that's what it was like. He should know, when he was a boy he had once went with a man for money and it was a horror, a horror story. Except it was real. He had just needed the dough and he knew about how to do it down the amusements, and he had went and fucking done it and that was that. But it was bad, a horror, a living hell. Getting gripped by the wrist so hard you couldnt have got away, but making it look like it was natural, like he was your da maybe, marching you into the toilet, the public toilet. Getting marched into the public toilet. People seeing you as well, other guys, them seeing you and you feeling like they knew, it was obvious, him marching you like that, the way he was marching you. Then the cubicle door shut and he was trapped, you were trapped, that was that, you were trapped, and it was so bad it was like a horror story except it was real, a living hell, because he could have done anything and you couldnt have stopped him because he was a man and he was strong and you were just a boy, nothing, to him you were just nothing. And you couldnt shout or fucking do anything about it really either because

because you were no just fucking feart you were in it along with him, you were, you were in cahoots, you were in cahoots with the guy, that was what it was, the bad fucking bit, you were in cahoots with him, it was like you had made a bargain, so that was that. But him gripping you the way he was! What a grip! So you had to just submit, what else could you do. You had to just submit, you couldnt scream nor fuck all. Nothing like that. Men coming into the urinals for a pish, no knowing what was going on behind the door and him breathing on you and feeling you up, and grabbing you hard, no even soft, no even caring if he had tore your clothes. What the wonder was that nobody could hear either because of the rustling noises the way he had you pressed against the wall and then you having to do it to him, to wank him, him forcing your hand and it was like suffocating, forcing his chest against your face and then coming over you, no even telling you or moving so you could avoid it it was just no fair at all, all over your shirt and trousers, it was terrible, a horror story, because after he went away you had to clean it all up and it wouldnt wipe off properly, all the stains, the way it had sunk in and it was like glue all glistening, having to go home on the subway with it: broad daylight.

For a pile of loose change as well. How much was it again? No even a pound, fifty stupid pence or something, ten bob. Probably no even that, probably it was something like forty pee, he just stuck it into his hand, some loose change. What did prostitutes get? what did they get? women, back then, nine year ago. It was probably about five quid if it was a short time; a tenner maybe if it was all night. That was enough to make anybody greet. But you could spend your life greeting, like his fucking sister. Because that was the thing about it, about life, it was pathetic, you felt like pressing the destruct button all the time, you kept seeing all these people, ones like the woman, the old dear at the end of the row, plus even himself as a boy, you had to even feel sorry for him, for himself, when he was a boy, you had to even feel sorry for yourself, yourfuckingself. What a fucking joke. A comedy. Life was a comedy for nearly everybody in the world. You could actually sympathise with that guy up on the screen. You could, you could sympathise with him. And he was a mass-murderer.

He glanced at the woman along the row and smiled at her, but then he frowned, he glared. You shouldnt be sympathising with a mass-murderer. You shouldnt. That was that fucking director's fault. That happened in his pictures, you started feeling sympathy for fucking murderers. How come it wasnt for the victims. They were the ones that needed it. No the actual perpetrators. That was probably how she had been greeting, the woman, because of the fucking victims, she was a victim, and that's who it was happening to, the fucking victims. He wanted to go home, right now, he wanted out of it, right fucking out of it right fucking now it was a free country and he wanted to get away home for his fucking tea. He glanced along at her, to see what she was doing. She was still holding the carton of coffee, engrossed in the picture. The old dear as well. It was just him. He was the only one that couldnt concentrate. That was that nowadays, how he never seemed able to concentrate, it never fucking seemed to work any more, you couldnt blank it out. He kicked his coffee over. It was a mistake. But he was glad he had done it. He wished they had all fucking seen; it would sort them out, wondering how come he had done it, if it was meant; he got up off the chair and edged his way along to the end of the row, watching he didnt bump into her as he went; she never so much as glanced at him, then the old dear moving her bags in to let him pass, giving him a look as he went, fuck her, even if he stood on one of them with eggs in it, bastard, he just felt so fucking bad, so fucking bad.

A walk in the park

She was coming towards him and he hesitated, she had yet to see him. But then he stepped out the close and he smiled the welcome while taking her by the arm. Beyond the park gate they continued round the corner and along in the direction of the main road. He said nothing to her. He noticed when she became aware of the fact. He glanced at her, seeing a certain look on her face; she was trying to hold it to herself, but she didnt succeed and she frowned at him and stopped walking: Is there something up? she asked, but she smiled to make it sound less dramatic.

Naw, no that I know of.

She studied him.

I'm just no feeling very talkative.

Mmm. She smiled, I dont really believe you.

Is that right? Well it's quite straightforward. He laid both his hands on her shoulders. He was about nine inches taller than her. He stared at her without smiling, then he relaxed and grinned. But she didnt. And she wasnt going to again, not until she knew there was something to warrant it.

Ach, he said, christ, I dont have any cash.

Oh.

Aye oh.

So what are we going to do?

I dont know.

I've hardly got anything either. Did something happen?

Happen? What d'you mean?

She looked at him.

Sorry. Naw, nothing happened. I'm just skint. People are skint these days you know.

Why are you being sarcastic?

Oh fuck sorry, sorry.

And now you're swearing. Are you worried about your son?

Naw.

Did the doctor come?

He stuck his hands into his trouser pockets, sauntered a few steps forward then turned to her: Doctors dont come these days, that's how they sell invalid chairs with fucking caster wheels on them! Sorry . . . Christ! He turned away from her again, stared into the shop that sold antiques. It was a shop she liked to look into. He saw her reflection in the window. For some reason he felt very angry. He still had his hands in his trouser pockets; now he brought out his left one and rubbed his brow and left eye. When she reappeared beside him he put his arm round her. Ach, I'm just no in a cheery mood. I'm sorry, too much on my plate . . .

It's okay.

He nodded then sighed. Where can we go?

I dont know.

They stood staring at each other for several moments. Then she said: The library?

Nah.

A walk in the park?

Uch naw.

We could go into town.

Into town?

See the shops . . . Dont look so excited.

He glanced at the antiques in the window: What about this shop here, can we no just look in it?

. . .

Ach, sorry. But I mean it'd just be a case of walking about.

Well that's better than nothing.

He sighed again.

What is it?

Ach nothing. Nothing.

Is something wrong?

No.

She studied him.

He shrugged and stepped away from her. I mean if you really want to go into town . . . I mean, if you do it's fine, just say.

It was only a suggestion.

Aye, fair enough, I know. He sniffed, gazing along the road, and wondered if she did have any cash. And if she did and it was enough to take them both for a coffee then how come she was not offering. Economics entered everything. It had caused the collapse of his marriage. At least it had as far as he was concerned. Who knew about the wife, she went her own way, had her own thoughts, you never knew what she was thinking. You never knew what anybody was thinking, that was the problem, the same applied everywhere. She was looking at him. He said, Do you want to go up the town?

She didnt answer.

Eh?

No.

He grinned suddenly and touched her arm. Give us a smile!

She didnt smile.

I'm sorry, I'm just . . . Ahh! He shook his head. He rubbed his hands together and blew out sharply, Bloody cold! Time we were going somewhere.

Did he let you down, the guy that owes you the money?

Yeh.

I might've known.

He was supposed to meet me but he never turned up.

Mmhh.

I thought he would.

Did you?

Now it's you that's being sarcastic.

Oh I'm sorry . . . She smiled, reached up and kissed him on the mouth, thrust her tongue inside.

They looked at each other as they parted.

Well? she said.

What about your sister?

I cant ask her.

Definitely?

No.

He nodded.

I cant.

Ah well. He turned abruptly: Christ . . . ! I'm gasping for a fag! He grinned: I says I'm gasping for one no I'm going to smoke one. There's a big difference you know!

I dare say it'd improve your temper.

He smiled at her. He liked her, he really did, he really did bloody like her. He wanted to put his arms round her and hold her, he wanted to give her a cuddle, a real cuddle, he wanted to hold her and give her a really big cuddle.

When she raised her right hand and touched his chin with her fingertips his eyes closed. She cupped both hands round his face. He opened his eyes and said, Let's walk.

Yeh.

They walked hand in hand, firmly. It was a thing he liked about her, how she held his hand, it was always so tight and he felt like it meant she was wanting to make sure of him, that he was there and that they were together. It was some time before either spoke. She said, I know you've got a lot on your plate.

It's okay.

You have though.

Ah well so have you, so have you.

Not so much as you.

He shook his head. I disagree. And he felt her grip on his hand tighten, and it sparked the muscle in his cock. He only had to look at her, that was the problem. I'll end up getting an erection, he said.

She smiled.

I cant help it.

She withdrew her hand and dug him in the ribs.

It's no my fault! He grinned.

Ssh. And come on! She took his hand.

Right, right! Will we go through the park?

If you want, it's up to you, I'm no the boss.

Ah well neither am I.

No but just decide.

Can you no.

Tch!

I want a rest. I spend my life making decisions. That's how I like being with you!

You trying to say I'm bossy! She grinned.

They crossed the road into the park, past the line of red sandstone villas – Victorian, four bedrooms maybe plus lounge, dining room, kitchen and bathroom; with probably an extension built out the back garden – maybe even with the attic kitted out into a wee annexe bedroom and play area for the kids. And kids liked that kind of space, the adventure of it, even going to bed in itself, that became exciting. One of his wife's aunties lived in a big house. Not a great big house but big enough, big enough to get a bit of privacy. Wee rooms to go and sit in, empty rooms, ones that had fireplaces and standard lamps, you could sit there and read a book, on your own, really good; the sort of place you dreamed about owning, plenty room, not tripping over one another; you could keep cats if you wanted, cats and dogs, all the pets you felt like – plus the privacy, that much space you could go away and be by yourself, you could be alone, you could just sit and think, work things out.

She broke the silence. She spoke without turning her head to him: Was your wife down at the weekend?

She was, aye.

Did you see her?

Well I had to to give over the wee yins.

Yeh . . .

Christ! It really is freezing! His shoulders moved as though in a shiver. He saw her watching him now. What about your boyfriend? he said.

What about him?

That's what I want to know, what about him?

Nothing.

Nothing?

Nothing.

Great. Life is so wonderful.

Dont complain.

I'm no.

It could be worse.

Could it?

It could be worse, of course it could.

Aye, I suppose so . . . He shivered again. You no cold?

No, because I'm wearing a coat. Which is what you should be doing, but you arent.

Glasgow macho . . . aye. He put his arm round her then his teeth started chattering; and he laughed, exaggerating the noise of it till eventually she also laughed. He pointed out the red sandstone villas. I'll get one of them and fill it with servants. To hell with the social conscience, I'm sick of it.

So am I!

I'm going to become a smug capitalist.

She laughed. She linked arms with him as they continued on over the brow of the hill.

I was reading John Maclean this morning, he said.

I havent read him.

What a life he had! How they treated him as well! Bloody disgraceful. Sick. The authorities, sick.

Mm.

A woman was walking along towards them, leading two small terrier dogs on leashes, they both had tartan jackets tucked round their bodies. Caricatures, he said, *Sunday Post* specials.

Yeh. Who's pulling who eh?

He smiled in answer.

The path stretched beyond a clump of trees for about quarter of a mile. There was nobody about. Two other directions were possible. The woman with the dogs had taken one of them.

Will we go the long way round, he asked.

What?

Will we go the long way round?

I dont care.

D'you just want to go the short way?

I'm no bothering. Then she added: I thought I smelt smoke on your breath?

Ha, I wish to God you had! That'd mean I was a cheery smoker, a cheery dier of cancer!

Have you no been smoking then?

Naw.

Honestly?

Well I've had a couple.

Ah.

A couple.

D'you mean two?

Aye.

Honestly?

You and your bloody honestly!

D'you mean two?

I said yes didnt I!

That's all?

That's all.

Good . . .

It's bloody hard but know what I mean? He shook his head.

When he saw she was still looking at him he asked her the time. She unlinked her arm to pull back her coat sleeve. Quarter to three.

Christ!

Time passes.

No half!

When you're enjoying yourself.

He put his arm round her again and he kissed her on the side of the mouth. She turned into him. But quarter to three, he said, moving from her slightly, that's hellish I mean you'll have to go back soon.

No for a bit yet.

Naw but soon.

She shrugged. Not for a bit.

He nodded. She smiled suddenly. I once smoked you know and it was in a park.

What! You! My God! Smoking? I cant bloody believe it!

It was no laughing matter either!

Whereabouts? No in here?

Whiteinch.

Whiteinch! What age were you?

I was thirteen; we were over watching the boys play football.

My God!

D'you know where the pitches are there?

Naw, no really.

Behind the pond. You walk towards your left, if you're coming from the dressing rooms it's your right.

From the dressing rooms?

Where the boys played football, where they got changed. They had to change in there before going to the football pitches to play.

Aw aye, now we're hearing the awful truth I mean did you watch to see if you could see anything when they were changing! Is that what yous were up to!

Tch.

He laughed.

We werent that bad!

A likely story! So tell us about the smoking then, did it make you sick?

Yeh, it did, it did!

Ha ha!

She punched him in the ribs and he let her go, stepping away from her, still laughing: I might've known. Females, you cant handle it!

That's right, we're no macho enough . . . It was bloody awful but, I thought I was going to pass out. We had two cigarettes and we smoked them one after the other, sharing them between us, taking draws each.

You and the boys?

Me and my two pals. Lassies . . .

I see, mmhh, on you go, but I warn you, I'm taking all this down to use in evidence at a later date.

And I mind as well how they were all soggy. Bits of the tobacco was in your mouth. Uch! It was awful. Disgusting.

Bits of tobacco? That means it was plain fags.

What?

Fags without tips?

I cant remember.

Must've been, if they were all soggy like the way you're saying. Hell, you must be older than you look.

Shut up.

Naw but honest, no kidding.

I think somebody had stole them off their dad.

God, thieving as well! What next! Dont tell me – with all these boys about!

You've got a dirty mind.

He smiled, but only for a moment. He looked at the grass.

A joke, she said, want to hear it?

Aye.

She let go his hand and walked on a pace, stopped and turned, trying to keep her face straight: You're laughing already! he said.

Because it's funny.

He chuckled.

If it wasnt I wouldnt tell you it.

Ah but it puts me under pressure.

Charlie's daughter told me it.

Charlie's daughter?

I knew it already. You probably know it yourself.

Naw I dont.

You will when you hear it.

Tell me then.

After a moment she said: What's yellow and very dangerous?

I dont know.

Shark-infested custard!

Christ!

She smiled.

Where do they get them!

Och it's an old one, I think I heard it at school myself.

Aye. He turned from her and stared along the path. There was a group of people in the distance – teenagers; they had a ball. He sighed.

What's up? she had touched him on the elbow.

Och . . . He smiled for a moment, then gazed into her face; she was just so bloody beautiful. She was. And he was just fucking . . . hopeless, he was just fucking hopeless. He couldnt bloody cope, that was the problem, he couldnt bloody cope, with life. The expression on her face had been serious; she relaxed now and smiled for a moment, she gripped his hand tightly, put her other arm round his waist and spoke his name, but he shook his head in answer.

Dont worry. She whispered, Things arent as bad as that.

Och I know I know.
Well then.
Yeh. Yeh.
She was staring right into his eyes.

A situation

Different incisions seemed to have been cut into the wall and from inside one of them an insect was peering at him. The insect reminded him of a flea, the curved part of its body, even down to its blood tan colour. The middle finger of his right hand began to drum on the edge of the table, he was frowning. What if for every incision one such insect was lodged? Mind you, they were so minute, these insects, that he was not afraid. He could ignore them easily. Or else he could get a spray gun and blast them all to smithereens. But what was the use of fantasising. He was not going to do anything. He couldnt do anything. He was stuck fast on this wooden chair, surrounded by everything hostile you could possibly conceive of in the universe. And as well as that it was like he could hear a scraping noise coming from somewhere too so no wonder he couldnt concentrate. Or was it just his ears? The finger drumming stopped but he continued frowning at the insect. Its toty brain would be working overtime. Who is this giant staring at me? Is he going to kill me? Somebody as big as him could squash me in a tick! Will he leave me alone? Forget all about me? Because if he does then I can continue crawling up the wall. Or down the wall; maybe it was going down the wall. Or else burrowing deeper into the hole, the incision. Maybe it and its relations, its ancestors – bearing in mind that each day is probably a lifetime and thus you have a state of affairs where four weeks ago is prehistoricity:

the world of the insect is of an eternity undreamt by man.

He shook his head to clear the brains into some sort of order, some sort of cohesion, so that he could think properly, he had to think properly. Life wasnt as good as all that just now. Not at present. But he couldnt afford to get more panic stricken than he currently was. On top of all the studying he had to meet the girlfriend in next to no time and he had had sex with her sister less than four hours ago. It was the sort of factual statement you had to present so coldly to yourself, so coldly. What was that bloody insect doing? Maybe burrowing deeper, trying to find a way of escaping out through the damn wall. That reminded him of himself. He spoke aloud: Make it big enough for the both of us, me as well as you. He could imagine hearing the insect's voice in answer. It would of course be squeaky, in keeping with its size. Unless it was an ironic bass baritone. Why ironic? Because of its size obviously. And what was that scraping noise, was it the actual burrowing sound? Surely no. But where was it coming from? He stared hard at the wall. It was just a wall. As walls go it was simply one of them. It was neither up nor down. Walls are walls, the prison bars make them. That was a line from somewhere, a poem or a song. Prison bars make them. Prisons do not a prison make, walls and bars, cells. He had never been in a cell, a jail; it was an experience he hadnt had. And didnt want. Not at all, why should he? Why should he want to end up in a cell? He had never done anything remotely worthy of such a crime, charge, jail, that sort of castigation.

Nor do insects have heads wherein brains are tick-tocking thus they do not worry about minor tragedies, only the major ones such as food and sex, the impetus for survival.

He sighed so loudly he glanced immediately over his shoulder to see if he had been heard, sitting there alone, in his poky wee room, feeling oh so tired, drained and exhausted. It wasnt his fault he had slept with Jeanette. He was up in her flat to give her some advice on something and she just more or less offered herself. She did. She offered herself to him. Probably the pair of them had had a big fight or argument or something, her and Deborah. Mind you, as far as he had been given to understand they were always the best of pals. They seemed to get on fine the gether. He gazed at the wall. It was actually covered in these incisions. Tiny toty wee holes. Oh Lord. Lordie Lordie. Lordie Lordie Lordie.

The A4 folders. Ah dear. All the A4 folders, and the trade brochures.

A4 folders and trade brochures. Life was a series of A4 folders and trade brochures. Cardboard and glossy paper. Pens and pencils. Stamped addressed envelopes and gummed labels, invoices.

His eyes had just about closed there. God. But he was knackered. He was. He was drained and exhausted, feeling like a quick forty winks. He needed it. Plus it was a good way out of a problem, to sleep on it.

But this was a genuine tired feeling with a genuine real cause. There had been no time for rest and recuperation after the Jeanette performance because her own boyfriend was coming home and he had had to get out fast, fast. Which was not as bad and decadent as it sounds. She was wanting to dump the bloke, she really was – she just didnt fancy him any more, but found it difficult saying the magic words of release. He was hell of a clingy Benny – Benny being her boyfriend's name. Poor old Benny. The two males had met on a couple of occasions, plus they had gone out on a foursome once with the sisters, to a pub up the town. It hadnt been a great success because the two females had had an awful lot to speak about – family stuff and that kind of thing – whereas the two men had had nothing at all, they had just sat there, not even any music to listen to, having to discuss football and general things about society. Except later on when the women went off to the *Ladies*, Benny had confided. Insecurity and an inferiority complex with women. These were the guy's problems. Imagine confiding in somebody who was a stranger to you! My God. Even the insect was laughing at that one. He could see it poking its napper out the incision on the wall again. He put his thumb up and squashed it. It made him wince. It was awful. His stomach felt queasy. It was just an insect and he had squashed it with his thumb. Why worry? But why do it why did he do it, why did he do it? Why did he do it, in the first place, take away its life? The stain of it on his thumb, a brown brackeny coloured substance. Here he was having just had illicit sex with his girlfriend's sister

fiancée's sister. She was his fiancée's sister. Deborah was his fiancée:

and now into the bargain he had squashed a living creature. And God would rightly be angry. Nobody likes their creations getting killed.

And what was that when you come to think about it but blasphemy, talking about God like that, in that tone of voice.

So here was now the third mark against him this day.

But he was a male and the sexual needs of the male are so horrendously hard to contain. Everybody knows that. And he had let himself fall into her web. Jeanette was a spider. She drew him in in that willowy winsome way and then let him have it, her bending down like that in front of him etcetera etcetera, an old trick which he was delighted to have played on him let us be honest, let us be good and damn honest about it he thought she was an extremely sexy lady and always had done since first they had been introduced. So what now what now. Killing a creature for no reason, just a silly absentmindedness. But wanton all the same. He had killed one of God's creatures through an act of wanton absentmindedness. Yes He would be angry with him and would make him fail tomorrow's test and he would then be forced into a life of continuous penury. He would have to go out working the road for a living instead of just training other folk to do it. That is what happened when you crossed the Lord.

That was him blaspheming again. Upon this day he had committed what amounts to adultery, and murder, and blasphemy. There was no fun in the thought. In fact it demanded an honest appraisal of himself, his entire life. If he couldnt manage an honest appraisal then the future was definitely bleak. He was doomed, he was doomed to become an ordinary salesman, a cynical salesman, somebody who held no truck for half measures and had absolutely no compunction whatsoever in destroying people who were customers, they would destroy all the resources of the world if they could get away with it, all on behalf of the selling racket. It was so bad. And yet it was the corollary of the downward spiral. It began with minor atrocities like the destruction of insects and the destruction of love, both earthly love and spiritual love. And the mark of the beast was on his thumb. And he needed rid of it. He got up and went to the toilet and washed his hands thoroughly. If he had had a bath he would have bathed. If he had had a shower he would have showered. He had neither of these facilities. Jeanette had both in her flat. It belonged to the two of them, her and her boyfriend, and they were able to bathe together and play sexy games. He would have wanted the same sort of fun and nonsense. But he and Deborah didnt do it, they didnt play sexy games. There was something that wasnt just right for it, something between them. Something that seemed to stop such an enjoyable interlude from happening. Plus his room was only big enough for what his grandpa used to call a jawbox, a sink in the wall, and this was where the diverse functional uses for water were put to the test, from shaving the chin to washing the socks through the doing of the dishes, given that the owners of the property were so totally greedy and so directly opposed to the whole concept of cooked food where tenants were concerned, so he didnt have that much crockery, and there was nary a pot and nary a pan, and normally a rinse of cold water was ample for everything. There was a bathroom. But it was outside on the next landing, shared by folk upstairs and down, including wheezing old McAllister who spat into the washhand basin there and never sluiced it out properly and you could always see the tell-tale signs. Plus there was always sticky things on the linoleum floor and even if you were having a bath you felt like wearing shoes. The idea of Deborah and him getting up to anything in there was beyond imagination. Deborah!

Lord, oh Lord, Lord please help me, have mercy, I am a soul in need of succour.

Two other women shared Deborah's flat with her and it was really short on privacy. Nice women, but they were never out the place if you were sitting watching television. So there was never any.

But most of all it was his fault! The pair of them should have been married by now and then they would have had privacy and everything would be fine, fine: and none of this would have happened. It wouldnt have. It wouldnt have happened if they had been married. But they werent married because she had said no to his first proposal and he hadnt made a second. That was six months ago. She had said no the first time so that was that, he hadnt asked her again. And maybe he never would, they would just have to wait and see. Everybody. That included his parents and her parents and all their acquaintances and everybody else they knew throughout the world, them all, they would all just have to wait. You cannot just go about refusing things and expect life to remain the same. If and when he and Deborah were ever to share a flat together they would no doubt instal a proper bathing service. Of course they would. Once he got round to asking the question again and if things worked out then that sort of pleasurable life facility could be taken for granted. But he was not going to ask the question just now, he was just not going to. And anyway, things were too upside-down at the moment, he just didnt know where his head was with all this product study and memorising he was having to do. The job was driving him nuts.

And what would happen now with her sister oh Lord Lord what was now going to happen now, now, after that please God please God oh please God.

It was all so amazing. Life. Life was so amazing, it was just so incredibly amazing.

But for heaven's sake he was so sick of this poky wee room where insects crawled out of the wall and stared at you as if you were an object of derision; or an object of contempt, of horror even. As the killer of one's fellows

bearing in mind that the insect he had murdered was probably about to copulate and be responsible for the birth of a million eggs, a hundred thousand of which would survive to become fully fledged members of the beetle race. It was like committing genocide. He needed coffee. Coffee coffee coffee. The caffeine was good for him. His adrenalin. It would assist him in thought and he did require assistance in just that direction, because he needed to think, to think to think to think, he needed to bloody think, he needed to think. These bloody test questions required consideration. If he did not consider these bloody test questions with the utmost bloody care he would wind up failing tomorrow and therein lay his doom, to exist for all eternity as an ordinary guy on the road, and he would grow into a tired and clapped-out old chap with ulcers and heart attacks. And God would be angry because he hadnt put his talents to good use.

The idea of sitting snugly in a toty wee cavity though, secure on three out of four sides, and then coming towards you is something in appearance similar to a meteorite, it getting huger and huger as it rushes towards you. And you are mesmerised by it. All you can do is stay stuck fast in your cavity; and then glulp, you're squashed. It doesnt bear thinking about. He didnt want to think about it. He had no time to. He had to do his studying. All the A4 folders.

And in less than half an hour for heaven's sake in would come Deborah.

And what would happen if she expected to stay the night he would not be able to have sex with her because of his condition, the way he was now, at this moment, at this moment in time. Because Deborah would know! She would know! She would guess. She was too percipient! Percipient? That isnt even a word.

Dictionaries dictionaries dictionaries. Plus the fact he wouldnt be clean, he would have to go and have a wash. That is what he would do, he would go and have a wash.

He went to the sink and put on the kettle for a cup of coffee then cleared the dishes and made space for himself, taking the trousers down to his ankles and setting the towel over them between his feet. Nor did he wish to think about Jeanette who was a very sexy lady and her thighs.

The water was freezing! My God!

In fact he *was* slightly tender around the genital region. He hadnt been aware of it till now. To tell the truth he was a wee bit sore; a wee bit sore.

The cold water now quite soothing.

Yes and it *was* adultery. A fiancée was as good as a wife any day of the week so who was he kidding there was just no way out of it in that direction as far as the morals went.

Plus vanity. That is what it was, vanity. Otherwise they would now be married, a married couple.

But she had refused the first proposal and he was not giving her a second chance, arrogant vain bastard that he was. So conceited. So damn conceited. But it was her own fault. If she hadnt fancied the idea then it was nothing to do with him. He had tried to persuade her but she was resolute. So how could it be him to blame? It couldnt. It wasnt his fault at all, if he had proposed and she had deposed, deponed, said no,

Yes it was. It was. Of course it was. You have to be honest in this life and not fool yourself and here was one occasion he was not about to: it was him; he was to blame, for the transgression in question. Pride. Plus now another three of them, transgressions, another three transgressions oh Lord three more of them, transgressions. Sex and murder

and what was the third?

blasphemy for heaven's sake imagine forgetting that which some would say was the worst most grievous charge of all.

Certainly ministers of the church would say so. Mind you, they were biased; making out blasphemy was the worst was just an unsubtle way of asserting how important they were themselves. It put them a cut above lawyers for instance because look at the judge they had to intercede with: the good God Himself! Then they would shove adultery next in line because of the taboos and how it affected so many more people than murder. Quantity is what counts. No matter the business you're in. The more souls you save the better. And far fewer people get affected by murder in comparison to the vast multitudes who get directly affected by sex, including most especially themselves, the clergy.

But there's no time to think of that though even worse if it had been priests and the involvement was with the Roman Catholics, and he had been one of them, a Roman Catholic. But no time to think of that either. And look at that the purplish red patch on the right testicle there a purplish red patch; that was odd. What was that about the purple red patch on the right testicle? Unless he had been scratching, but he hadnt been scratching, not that he could remember, not like this, to have had this effect. My God. It wasnt so good. Probably it had just kept rubbing against Jeanette's thigh. Was that it? Jeanette's thigh. Rubbing against Jeanette's thigh, soft upper. If that was it. It was so

But she had fancied him, it wasnt the other way about; so dont go blaming him, it wasnt his fault; if you're going to blame somebody blame her. Okay he had looked, but who wouldnt? It was her made the actual move, the first actual move. He shouldnt have allowed it though, his fiancée's sister. How come she had done it; there must have been a feud, they must have had a fight. Oh God he didnt feel good he just didnt feel good he needed to sit down quickly, quickly. He was just a bit dizzy. Just feeling a bit dizzy. Black dots in front of the eyes, plus whitish, a whitish

If he hadnt reached the chair he would have fainted, he would have fallen down. Probably it was a castigation, a punishment, a retribution, a righteous chastisethment. He had been bad and now he was getting made to suffer. Murder, adultery and blasphemy. Plus of course the pride of vanity. The vanity had been first and then

what was the time what was the time! Deborah had left her house she had left her house. She had been away seeing her parents today. She was now getting the train. She was at the station and getting the train. Her parents lived nearby a railway station, so it was good and convenient. The train let her off in the city centre and then she got a bus from behind St Enoch's subway station straight to his place. Who in heaven's name was St Enoch? Where had he come from? Was he even a man! She would be here in half an hour. Unless she was late oh please God make her late if she was just late for a little bit, to let him think straight and get his mind on things and how he was to handle what he would say to her because he had never been what you would call a good teller of tales, teller of lies, of fibs, i.e. never any good at it, at telling them, so he needed out of selling, out of the selling racket all together, he was no good at it, he wasnt, it wasnt his forte; he would be much better at training others, if he could just get onto that training course. He would be good at it. He would be good. He would try so bloody hard. Plus his memory was fine and it was a memory you needed.

The A4 folders spread out on the table. All the mumbo jumbo. Because frankly this is what it was, a load of mumbo jumbo, and high time somebody informed Head Office of the fact. He should actually just burn it all and run away. He had no chance of passing tomorrow with flying colours. He didnt, he just didnt have any chance. He was doomed to lead a life of terrible distaste, a guy for whom life will never ever be a time for fun, trying to survive on the road and failing failing failing thus back on the broo and having to face up to the people down at the DSS office, how they would just ignore him and humiliate him all day long because here he was seeking handouts from a decent Government agency like them. Why had he thought so badly of them! They were just doing a bloody job same as him if he was doing it, he would just be doing a job, it wasnt his bloody fault

Oh God, he just wasnt any good at it it was all his own fault, how in the name of heaven had he left college why had he been so bloody damn daft and absolutely stupid and damn stupid naïve that's what he was oh God, he just wasnt any good at it, he wasnt –

I'm not. I am not any bloody good at it. Please help me. I am having to face up to those who hate me. They dont mean to but they do. I do not blame them because they sin, because they sin against me. Please to help me overcome, amen.

He wasnt any good at it. He would be better if he was doing something different. Or else out of it altogether. It was best he resigned in advance. If only he could have made better use of his education and stuck it all out instead of leaving when he had, if he had stuck it through to the bitter end. But even if he had gone in to the Post Office bank like his dad had advised him to do: and so strongly. That was his experience talking. If he had just listened to him, but he hadnt, he just hadnt bloody listened because he had wanted bloody out, because he had hated the place and he just couldnt get his heart in it he just couldnt like it at all, what he was doing there, what they were asking him to do and all that stupid damn studying for no reason, it was all just bloody nonsense and difficult and even if it had been difficult and had a purpose but it didnt, it was just for nothing, graphs and statistical analysis, and nobody ever talking to you, it was like they all knew each other from years ago, except him, he was a sore thumb, he was a sore thumb, or else he would have done it properly, he would have stuck in and just managed it, he would have concentrated hard, hard.

How come he had not bloody done it when he had the chance! He was just a damn fool. He had always been a damn fool. His dad knew it, he knew it; you could tell by the way he looked.

And probably mum secretly agreed although she made excuses for him. And Deborah knew it as well, she did, it was bloody obvious, he was just a damn bloody fool. She would maybe forgive him his trespass if he told her truthfully, if he explained it, all he had to do was explain it and then she would see because it was her sister, her own sister: it was her led him into the spider's web and trapped him and it was just male sexuality and her breasts and stockings and her thighs.

And there was just no possibility of her staying the night for heaven's sake that just wasnt on. How could it be it couldnt be it just was beyond anything, even having washed.

The thing about Deborah of course her character trait it wasnt so much her temper but her stubbornness, how stubborn she was. It was just so bad; she had to learn to control it, she really did – otherwise it would definitely cause her problems in life. Maybe that had something to do with Jeanette, the way Jeanette had acted with him, if she had maybe been upset by Deborah if they had had a fall-out, and this was her taking revenge, seducing him, her sister's fiancée, the future brother-in-law. But had it been on the cards you could say it had been on the cards. Things had been

Well it was that selfsame very sister's own fault. It was, it was her own damn fault, damn and bloody blast. Her own mother had even referred to that awful bloody stubbornness which was surely something because normally they stick together mothers and daughters

At that moment a loud chap-chap at the door just about gave him a heart attack, he nearly toppled over, having returned to the sink, the trousers still at the ankles but he very quickly got himself ready and glanced into the mirror to see he was okay, steadying himself, he closed his eyes for some moments because life, because

he wasnt good he just wasnt good, he wasnt, he felt so bloody, so damn the chap-chap at the door again. He walked forwards and turned the handle. It was a small elderly old woman. It wasnt Deborah. His head craned over her. He felt like the Blackpool Tower and she was a wee midget. She spoke to him; what she said was something like, I'm your neighbour up the stairs if you mind son myself and my husband moved in last week.

Pardon?

You gave us a wee hand up with our suitcases and our bags.

Yeh, yeh.

If you mind the housing put us in after we got decanted out our own place.

Aye aye, that's right that's right, yeh . . . He stared at her then stepped out and peered sideways. He said, Go on, the coast being clear. Go on, he said, yes, what is it?

The woman studied him, evidently thinking he was being uncalled-for abrupt and hostile to her.

Sorry. Sorry sorry sorry. He didnt mean it at all. He really didnt. I've got a sore head just now, he told her, I'm studying for a test tomorrow for my work. It's an in-house thing and it's really

He frowned at the woman: what the hell was he telling her for! He said: What is it you want, is it something you want?

My husband would like you to come up the stair a minute, he would like a word with you.

Pardon?

If you wouldnt mind. He's just awful worried the now about something and he'll no tell me . . . And onto her face appeared a kind of – what look? a something look, it would have flummoxed you. He stared at her and then glanced away in case something bad happened. And she said, You know how he's an invalid.

Aw aye, yeh, that's right, an invalid – he's got a walking stick or whatever it is one of these three-angled triangular frame things whatever you call them, sorry, I mean . . . Is he wanting me to do something?

He'll tell you himself.

Yeh but missis it's just I'm so busy the now, I'm just so busy, I've got all this, God, stuff I'm studying and having to learn, to memorise, for the morrow morning, first thing . . . And he was about to fling back the door and show her but no, no, she was the last person he wanted to see inside his room, the last person, somebody like her, unspotted, untainted, such a fresh old lady with her invalid husband who never had had a bad thought in her entire life, who had never ever periodically once upon a time ever felt or saw, thought or spoke an evil word, deed or action please the Lord.

The woman nodded but she took him by the elbow and he was powerless to refuse because how do you know it might well have been a chastisethment, something like that he was suffering and had to endure as a penance: but then he frowned at her a moment later and tried to pull himself clear because she could be a malevolent demon or something it seems stupid but who knows who knows the way things were and how life was turning against him, old-age pensioners plus her being a woman and maybe the wrath of a female because of what had just so lately taken place – he glanced down the stairs. I'm waiting for my fiancée, he said. He shrugged and smiled for a moment; We're getting married, I'm just having to pass this wee test first, for my promotion, and then after that we'll be putting the mortgage down for a house, a flat, a wee room and kitchen or something, a place of our own . . . He grinned at her.

You'll just be a minute, she said. Honestly. It's because you see my husband gets agitated sometimes, he gets things on his mind and they'll no let him go. She then made a brandishing motion with her right hand as if an indication of it, of how the things went inside her husband's mind: He's a worrier. He never used to be. Telling you son he was aye about the most relaxed man you could meet, but no now. Us being stuck in this lodging house just makes it worse.

Yeh . . . He stared at his arm as she held it, leading him across the landing and up the stairs to the room directly above his own and therefore likely to have very similar walls and incisions; she held the door open for him to enter. The odour of something like ancient bodies filled the doorway. It wasnt a vile stench although he breathed in and out through his mouth to avoid it. The invalid husband was waiting. He had his three-angled contraption there which he was leaning on from the inside; he wore a dark-brown serge suit with outsize lapels and quite smartish-looking although it was creased as if he had been sitting in a certain way for too long, maybe like he had fallen asleep, dozed off, his bad leg resting maybe up on a stool, and further when you looked at the suit you could see it was greasy, shiny.

Here he is, said the woman.

What's your name young fellow? asked the invalid.

My name's eh . . . He paused. He was wondering why he should be giving his name to a complete stranger. He couldnt remember helping him up the blasted stair last week with no blasted suitcases either – neither him nor his damn wife, this old woman and her quasi-humble politeness. Edward Pritchard, he said, emphasising the two ards as he used to do many years ago when he was in primary school, about eight years of age or something and thought such a remarkable poetic feature just had to be a personal and secret message from Jesus setting him apart from his fellows, it was pathetic, pathetic – as if he had any reason to be famous, because all he was cut out for was what he was about to receive for his sins, sent out on the road as a working sales for the rest of his days, whenever he could bloody get a damn job and lump it, just bloody lump it, he was never going to be anything special, nothing, he wasnt going to amount to anything really at all, these silly stupid dreams, none of it was worth a damn, because he had ruined it all, his entire life, and that was that, he was finished, it was over, he was never going to make it at all, you would be as well laughing at the very idea, because he was a malcontent who committed transgressions in the name of the Lord and was therefore doomed.

You go away Catherine, the invalid commanded.

His wife looked at him as if she was trying to figure out what he was thinking.

Go a message, he said. I want to have a word with the young fellow. The invalid had taken one of his hands off from the contraption now and was waving at her to leave and you felt you hoped he wouldnt fall down and hurt himself his hands were so shaky. What could he want maybe it was a male problem or something to discuss or else to give him a hand in some way, shave him or something the old guy because he needed a shave he looked like he hadnt shaved for a couple of days, and if his hands were suffering from too many twitches

The old woman was now pulling on her overcoat, a quite smart one for rainy weather, pink and grey and her legs were short. Some people had funny short legs thank the Lord it wasnt him he couldnt imagine it, walking down the road having to step over puddles, big puddles with your wee toty stride, how could you manage it it would be so bloody difficult you had to admire her, she was so strong in the face of the world, that was a trait though in old women he found, they were so brave, his grannie was like that; plus his other one who was now dead; they had come through the mill – this old woman especially with her invalid husband, having to take care of him what the hell did he bloody want! My God he didnt even look worried, no really. And when the door closed behind his wife he started gesticulating. Sit down! he commanded, imperious old bugger, glancing roundabout and then manoeuvring his way to a chair nearby the window. He got himself seated and sighed deeply. And he looked at Edward.

Edward wanted to have something to say but there was nothing, there was nothing at all and his brow became furrowed.

See young fellow what it is, I've got a confession to make and I dont want Catherine to know.

Edward felt his head go funny at this but he kept his eyes open and concentrated hard.

Poor old sowel she's got enough on her plate, she works hard and she looks after me you see, she looks after me. The invalid breathed in sharply, then sighed. Edward had been watching him very attentively and he too breathed in sharply but via his nostrils and it was terrible. The smell was a fuisty one of dirt, and it was definitely coming from the old bloke. A fuisty smell of dirt – or excrement! Shit, old shit. God! Maybe he needed his bum cleaned and was too proud to tell his wife. Oh dear. Oh dear. Edward just couldnt cope with that, he couldnt, he just couldnt cope with it if he was maybe not able to attend to himself for heaven's sake did they not have home-helps, had the government stopped home-helps now and strangers were getting called in to wipe folk's bums, old invalid people who couldnt manage it theirselves and were wanting to hide it from their nearest and dearest so the neighbours, now having to get called in. He ran his hand across his forehead, opened his eyes widely.

You see young fellow I've got this confession to make. What's your name? No, dont tell me, it's best I dont know. Now pay attention: before they invalided me out my job of work I used to be involved in what some people would call malpractice; some other people would call it sabotage and other people again, well, they would call it something else all the gether. What I used to do you see was the spanner-in-the-works carry-on; I used to stop the line. Understand me? That was what I did, wherever it was I was working, I used to bring things to a halt – I tried to anyway. That's the shape my politics took and that's the shape they were; and I cant help it and nor did I ever want to help it, and I've never wanted to change things neither. But as a way of living my life so to speak what it means is I've aye had to do what my conscience tells me. There's no an in-between. Now . . .

The invalid stopped there and he studied Edward as if wanting to make sure who it was he was telling all this.

But Edward's face was expressionless.

Now the last place I worked in was a firm by the name of eh Gross National Products which, as you probably guess, is a made-up name. I dont want to tell you the real one because you never know you might be a police informer.

Edward smiled after a moment, shaking his head.

The invalid's hands started waving about furiously: But never mind that never mind that – and never mind me neither because I get nervous and I get agitated.

And the way he pronounced 'agitated' sounded funny although Edward didnt acknowledge this. And the old invalid was looking at him with maybe a bit of impatience or something maybe just wanting to know who it was he was confiding in, because how do you know who you're talking to in this world you dont, you just dont know, it could be anybody; it was the very same when you were out on the road trying to talk your way into some office or garage or factory. Even when you were down at Head Office with the other sales-teams you werent free, you had to watch it; you had to say nothing and keep your distance while at the same time try not to appear too stand-offish because that was bad points and you knew they were always watching and taking notes – especially if your figures werent that good, if they had been on the decrease, during the last four-week period even although the area he had to work was nothing like the density of other areas, and you would expect such things to be taken into consideration, but no, they were treated like they just didnt matter, which was a strange way to run a business. But the selling game was a funny business. That's exactly what it was, a funny business; the way it operated.

which happened to me, said the invalid.

What

something that I ended up doing as well and it's caused me a lot of pain and suffering, a hell of a lot . . . The invalid smiled, he waved at his contraption: I wasnt always pushing one of them about you know.

Edward nodded. What is it you call it?

But the invalid just gave an impatient shake of the head and continued talking: Now what happened you see, I've got to fill you in, I was keeping a low profile because they were after me, I'm talking about the bigwigs, they were out to get me. And they were using a fellow who was a mucker, a pal. Mind you he was a waster the same man, if I'm to be honest about it, and you dont like saying that about anybody never mind when he's your mate. But this yin was the sort that winds up changing colours, he joined the enemy, he was a turncoat. That happens a lot in this life: traitors.

Edward stared hard at the old invalid, concentrating on each word he spoke, noting the way his head twitched this way and that, he looked like he was wanting a place to spit into:

Bad bastard that he was. And to think you took him into your home and gave him your hospitality. And his wife and mine became friends too and my Catherine, poor old sowel, she used to look after their weans like they were her own. But that was who it was, the very one they sent to get me. They had chose him because they knew we were close. Ahh! It's a world of conspiracies out there.

Pardon?

But I soon knew the situation anyway. Too many ears to the ground young fellow . . . You probably dont know that yet but you will soon enough. Wait till you get to my age, then you'll find out. The invalid winked and tapped the side of his nose. Then he smiled, waved his hands in a dismissive gesture. But there's much more you've got to understand and I'm no wanting to get us bogged down in the petty stuff. Come and sit next to me so I dont have to bellow.

I'm fine here though.

No but I want to tell you a secret young fellow, and walls have ears.

What?

The invalid squinted at him: I thought you'd have kenned that by now, you being a student and aw that.

But I'm no a student, replied Edward, frowning, I'm in the selling game. I'm just studying for a work test, it's a kind of I dont know what you would call it, mainly it's product memorising I've to do. I think it's what's known as a Re-training Schedule. In reality it's to do with regrading, if you dont pass it you stay where you are. And that's like a demotion. In fact it is a demotion. In fact, this test isnt really to pass onto greater things at all, it's just to avoid the pit.

The pit?

Yeh.

The old woman says you were a student.

Did she? I wonder how she thought that.

She'll have keeked in the letter-box and seen you at your lessons.

Pardon?

Cause that's how she does it. She's good so she is. You just wouldnt have heard her at all but what she'll have done she'll have lifted your letter-box and just looked in to see what you were doing. The invalid chuckled. I aye wished I'd had her for a partner at the 'spanners'! She would've been rare at it – better than me. And I would say I was one of the best though as a masculine model my limitations were there, they had to be. Masculine models and limitations masculine models and limitations. These facets we are born with – faculties I mean – man. Man is born with definite limitations. We attempt to set out and change the world but then we get bogged down in the microcosmic ephemera of getting to B from A. You have your goal. You go to college and you take a wee look about. You think the road ahead is signposted – not so much signposted as like the conditions are set for you. You find a lass and the two of you set out as partners in the face of a hostile and aggressive world; and that includes your parents. Because the harsh truth is that most parents hate their children, just like Romeo and Juliet, wherefore art thou, they hate them actively and discourage them from doing the things they want, if you want to change the world you're no allowed to, they dump you down so you have to take what you're given, and then you end up with things you dont really want but are just settling for and it isnt your fault at all because you are doing your best, trying your damndest to please and to settle down properly with your loved one in your nest, when you are married, when you are given the proper chance, the nettle, grasping that opportunity

Edward had a look on his face, it was a smile, his eyelids were closed and he shook his head. An overwhelming sensation of relief. Utter and total relief. Oh Lord, Lordie Lordie, it was so good sitting there, just sitting there, so good just sitting there – here, I find it so relaxing, he said, opening his eyes and grinning at the invalid: I just wish I had a cigar! But no, honest, being serious about it, it's just so soothing, for my head – and for my brains, giving them a rest like this, not having to worry about things, you see my fiancée eh was coming, she's about due to come.

Ah . . . ! So you've a fiancée, that's even better. That shows you're responsible. I like to see responsibility in a young fellow. What's your name?

. . .

You're no going to tell me eh?

I told you before.

Did you?

Yeh, it's Edward Pritchard, I dont mind you knowing at all.

The invalid nodded, and he said slowly, Edward Pritchard. He pursed his lips. My name's Robert Parker, Bobbie – like the boy who used to play for Falkirk or was it the Hearts? – big right back if you remember, I think he got a cap for the Scottish League team, maybe even the full national one.

Edward shook his head.

Before your time I dare say. The invalid continued speaking: There's a confession I need to make you see. I need to make it because I've got a feeling something impending is going to happen . . . I dont know like it's as if maybe you think you're about to get knocked down by a lorry or a bus or a taxi –

Pardon?

Well you see sometimes they go careering down the road and they dont see you if you're an invalid, you're walking that slow they fail to take you in on their line of vision. And you cant but take a stride without doing so with that very reckoning and you're darting a look this way and that or else trying no to, you just keep your face fixed to the front and try no even to listen for the roar of the engine – the thing that's coming to mow you down.

My God!

Yeh.

That sounds like an awful nightmare. Edward's left hand went to his face and he covered then rubbed at his left eye.

It's like they think you're a pillar or a post.

Surely no!

Aye! The invalid waved his hand, then signalled the need for silence and he whispered, Come here till I tell you. You're no a religious young chap, are you?

I believe in God if that's what you mean.

Do you? The invalid sat back on his chair and he studied Edward.

Well I hope I do I mean I hope I do . . . And I'm no ashamed of it. I used to be an agnostic. But no now, I'm back to believing. Edward gazed at the invalid and suddenly felt very sad. His parents were getting old and no doubt they would be dead eventually, just like everybody else, his good old grandpa as well. And it wasnt long since Deborah's grannie had died, he remembered the funeral quite vividly, the two sisters taking charge of doing the food, and they did it really terrific, rolls and different scones and things, bowls of nuts and crisps – better than if they had gone for a meal in a hotel.

My parents are churchgoers, he told the invalid. But I'm no. When I was a boy I was, but I've no been for years apart from when my fiancée's grannie died last March. I felt a hypocrite . . . Edward stopped and frowned: Did I though? Maybe I didnt. Maybe I just thought I should have felt a hypocrite, because that's . . . He glanced at the invalid: I've been involved in some things recently that I think really are sins, to be honest, I dont mind telling you Mister Parker and I can only hope I'll be forgiven, I hope nothing's going to get held against me although if it does I'll no complain, if I've to suffer a chastisement. If I can only make up for it, maybe by doing my test properly tomorrow, if I can only manage that.

He punched his right fist into his left palm and cried: That's all, that's all I want!

You will pass it, the invalid said.

What!

You will. You'll pass your test and you'll get your promotion.

Edward stared at him and was immediately suspicious. Somewhere there was a line between making a slight fool of somebody and genuine fellowship and good company like the way at the fortnightly sales-team talks when the guys made jokes about one another and you didnt quite were sure, you never quite

You just couldnt laugh. But the jokes always seemed to be so damn unfunny. How was it possible to laugh? Edward could hardly even smile let alone throw the head back. It was terrible. He hated it.

The invalid was speaking:

Somebody that's as diligent a studier as you, he's the kind that deserves to succeed. And you will succeed. I'm convinced of that.

Edward coughed to clear his throat. Ah but I'm no that diligent, he said, my concentration's nil . . . He wet his lips and swallowed, his mouth seemed to have gone dry; then he glanced sideways for some reason but everything was fine, fine.

The invalid was frowning at him: Although with me mind

you there's aye the wish that a young fellow like yourself could one day take up the cudgels where me and the muckers left off. But these battles have finished, just like the days they happened in are finished, and the kind of future that sorts itself out on the past isnt the kind of future we fought for – and I'm no a supporter of such things – none of us were, no in the slightest. You understand me?

Edward hesitated.

Ah you will young fellow you will. And now if you'll no come to me then I'll come to you.

And so saying the old invalid got himself up onto his feet with the aid of the contraption and he made his way over to sit down on the chair next to Edward and Edward hoped so strongly that he wouldnt put his hand on his knee because he hated that being done he just couldnt stand it, couldnt cope with it and knew his face would just get so crimson, so awful crimson

And the invalid whispered: Now young fellow, my confession, afore Catherine comes back; when I worked in whatever you call it, Gross National – which is twelve years ago now – the country was in a state of economic decline, everything was to pot. You're a bit young to remember that eh?

Edward felt nauseous, he felt sick sick sick, he needed to vomit, he needed to spew, to spew. He clamped shut his nose by squeezing it with his right thumb and forefinger. He breathed out loudly, clearly, to prepare for the refreshment of his lungs, breathed deeply in; he opened his eyes and stared at the frayed carpet on the floor. His room was better than this, it was bad, but not this bad. But maybe the old couple had something special that made it better and evened things out, although the light was terrible, and the walls and ceiling were just as crappy looking and it was so heavy an atmosphere – that dull yellow everywhere and it all so damn unhealthy and just damn bloody ungood.

But Lord Lord Lord was it a smell of shite right enough? Ohhh. But it might just have been sweat, the old invalid male having been using such tremendous exertions in merely getting to B from A about the room, even toing and froing re the cludgie. So he was bound to get sweaty.

Always he had to think the worst about folk, that was his problem; even with Deborah for heaven's sake how come he was always blaming her for everything? And he was. No matter what it was he blamed her. It was just so uncharitable and wrong. Pride. That's all it was. Conceited buggar. Pride.

but the pong from this old bloke sitting next to him he felt like he was going to keel over off the chair, he would topple over onto his doom and he would just die here in this room with an ancient stranger as a companion, somebody who could have devised an unheard-of method for removing fresh limbs from a young person's body in order to weld them onto an elderly sick person, an invalid – spare-part surgery, and here he was about to become a human trunk with no limbs like that horrible story he had once read about a man getting mutilated by evil slavers for some purpose he couldnt remember, set in the Sahara region, and these armless and legless beggars in third-world countries who have to get wheeled about in bogies in an effort to pay off loans to the IMF and the World Bank. God he was so cold now, cold, he was so cold. No bloody fire, why was there no bloody fire, rabbiting on like this about all these factory incidents from a forgotten past and all his gesticulations it was so difficult to even listen because of it.

You did your best.

. . .

. . .

Still silence. Had he finished? What did he mean 'you did your best'. Edward was almost scared to look up from the carpet. But he managed it, and found the invalid staring straight at him. It was such a strong stare. You would like to have looked at this stare but it would have been a stare-out contest if you had and he would have lost. He was no good at that kind of thing. It reminded him of these facetious mock-ups they had to play out at the monthly inter-district meetings. Awful, so awful. You felt so self-conscious and not just for yourself but for them as well, all the other sales-persons. He was the only one seemed to have that kind of response. Then there was that funny sadistic aspect about it. He just wasnt into it, and not the humiliation side either. It wasnt something he enjoyed at all. These games were just a kind of psychology. That's all they were. And he didnt have the mentality needed if you were ever to excel at them. It was a certain kind you required. And he didnt have it. The other blokes did have, they had the right sort of make-up, they were the right mettle, it was him that wasnt, that was how he had to get out from it.

Plus he couldnt reach a closure anymore. That was the real truth, he couldnt close a sale, he just couldnt close a sale. And that meant he was a goner because if there was one thing you needed in the selling game it was the closure knack, how to close a sale, how to stop talking and point the customer's pen at the dotted line. He had been great for the first few weeks. He seemed able to sell anything to anybody. No now. He was rubbish now. A dumpling. That's the truth, he was a dumpling.

But he could train others. He could definitely train others. He knew what the correct procedure was; and his product knowledge was good – all of that side of things.

But talking to potential customers, he couldnt bloody manage that either, the theory yeh, but not in actuality, when face to face with them, as individual human beings. What was that poem by William Wordsworth?

Jeanette had just happened to flash her breasts at him and he was a goner – then also her stockings, he knew she wore stockings and not tights when she was bending.

The invalid was looking at him.

What is it?

I was just saying to you when the old woman comes back

we've got to speak about other things, maybe the facilities in this place.

Pardon?

I'm meaning when Catherine comes back, she's a habit of sneaking up on you. If she does then just you should start talking about the facilities here – I mean what you're supposed to do for grub and so forth because you're no allowed to cook in your room as far as I hear. That right?

Edward nodded.

Start talking about that then. Because it's a hell of an irritation, especially to her. No me so much cause I'm no what you'd call an eater, but she gets all het up about it and you cant blame her, poor auld sowel, she's used to an oven and a cooker and what have you. So if you start talking about the facilities you see I dont want her knowing what I'm going to tell you. I want that to be a secret between me and you. The invalid gazed at Edward then sighed. And he sighed again.

But it was like there was something underhand going on and Edward couldnt put his finger on it. Was it like a form of sarcasm against him? It was. It was actually like a form of sarcasm. Just the way all this was happening, like it was all falling into place. And he was a culprit.

A lot of different things, nothing you could just put your finger on.

Such an incredible cheek really. You had to just sit there with your mouth hanging agape. Then you felt like getting up and letting him see you knew what was going on. Edward smiled to himself, shaking his head. But imagine his dad hearing about it! What would he do! It was like a slur being cast on him, not just him, his entire family.

He glanced sideways at the invalid who was now gazing round the four walls in a very intentional and deliberate way. He gazed at the window in particular – as if expecting a snooper to be hanging outside on a painter's platform. And then he started talking but it was so difficult to hear him properly with all his wavering and his gesticulating plus as well the terrible terrible fuisty pong that came from him. He seemed to be speaking about a horrendous and wicked horrible incident in a factory, something bad and evil he had been involved in that drove somebody out their mind and destroyed them, and killed somebody else, an accident or something, and related groups and even families as well as different industrial stresses were involved, and it was turning to centre on one of these wee boyish kind of apprentice lads that everybody's supposed to like – naughty and full of devilment etc. etc. It was just so awful and impossible to hear. In fact Edward was going to leave right now. His head was spinning. It was too much. How was he supposed to cope with it, it just wasnt bloody feasible when he was supposed to be studying because either one thing or the other but not both; that was too much, too bloody much, just too damn bloody much. Damn and bloody blast. Edward stared at the invalid.

What happened you see I was working in this place where a spanner had just been tossed.

A spanner had just been tossed. He stared at the wide lapels on the invalid's jacket; there was a stain down one of them.

a very big spanner, one of the biggest seen in this country for quite a number of years – me and a couple of blokes working the gether for it, a team effort – and I reckon it must have cost maybe one point seven five million for final rectification see young fellow because we had it worked so the bigwigs never found out it was deliberate – no even that it was an accident.

If it was an accident . . . ?

No, said the invalid, that's that I'm saying. I'll tell you something you'll maybe no quite understand except maybe you might: you see they never found out that it happened at all. You get it? They just thought there was something wrong with the entire works, and I'm no talking about safety measures because safety measures dont make that much difference as well you'll know, but just that a general improvement would need doing, right the way through all their factories – and I'm here meaning across the whole of what you call the 'free world';

It's a hoax!

That's how it cost so much to put right you see because you're talking Thailand, Indonesia, India, Zambia, Kenya, Korea, Vietnam, Scotland,

It's a hoax!

Denmark, the Irish Free State, Wales, Pakistan, Australia, Iceland, Sweden – wherever GNP Plc used to exist it no existing now of course because it was taken over by a big conglomerate back in the time of the conspiracy trials. Then it went itself in the Throgmorton Crash if you mind, and you had the Makgas Consortium stepping in, government funding and CNI money, headed by a noted patriot – though you understand young fellow that the patriot's real name is something different to anything I might tell you so what's the point of me telling you anything at all. Unless you rather you heard everything, but that sort of information isnt classified I mean it's freely available elsewhere and if you would rather hear than no hear then you should go and check it out, you'll find most of it down the Advocate's Library.

Edward looked up from the floor. He looked the invalid in the eye. As much as you could tell he was the real mccoy. You would never know for sure of course. But how could you know anything for sure in this world since it was full of illusion. His dad used to tell him as a wee boy that if ever he found himself in dark trouble it would pay to tell the truth and if God really was there – and we knew that He was – then everything would turn out fine. Because He would look after you.

That was the route Edward would have taken way before he left off being a believer. And now he was back to it again he knew the course of action was right. It was right and it was good. But it was difficult. Telling the truth as an adult male was different from telling the truth as a boy.

After a moment he said, It's a world I dont know Mister Parker. I wish I did but I dont. I've never really been able to get the hang of it – it's like the international news in the quality Sunday papers, all these places and names you can never remember, they go hazy as soon as you look at them. I'm sorry. Honest. My mind's good at some things but no at others. I wish it was different: I wish I could just bloody I mean it's concentration, it's just concentration, I dont seem able to concentrate beyond about five minutes at any given point – even when I was at college it was the same, I think there's something up with me.

The invalid was watching him and he had a frown on his face.

Edward cleared his throat before continuing: I just do my best at my job of work without hurting too many people, although you've got to appreciate about it that being on the road, what I do, as a sales rep what you've got to do, anybody, you've got to gyp folk because that's the nature of the game, salesmanship, you have to gyp people into buying stuff they dont like. Silly buggers. How come they buy all that junk! I've never been able to work it out. Even my own mother, with all her experience through having a salesman for a son, this guy comes to the door a week ago and he sells her some insurance that's more or less useless, in fact it's absolutely useless, it's no good at all, if I'd had been there I'd have bashed him one on the jaw. Bloody stuff! I went through it to check. Rubbish! Absolute rubbish! And I mean

The invalid stopped him from talking by waving his hand. Young fellow, were you the lad that helped me up the stair the other day?

Edward couldnt answer because this was part of the hoax and it was a trap question.

Were you?

Your wife says so but you'll have to work it out for yourself, it's no good asking me because how do you know about me you dont know nothing quite honestly, quite frankly, when you come to think about it. She says it was me, she says it was but I wouldnt actually believe her, how do you know, she might be lying, just because she's elderly and small and acts like she's the epitome of truth and wisdom therefore she has to be a paragon, but how do you know the devil hasnt entered her soul and she's only there to draw us all into evil ways?

He stopped speaking. Then he said, I obviously only mean that as a for instance; I dont really think it – I mean how could I! Obviously I couldnt.

The way the invalid was staring at him, his eyes set, set fixed and firm.

Look, said Edward, I'm just trying to be honest. I dont know anything about industrial sabotage or industrial injuries, I dont know anything at all, if somebody has to suffer a terrible horrendous agony just in order that others might go free, that's just the same as happens to other people – it happened to Jesus Christ, He had to be crucified, so maybe it was like what you're saying, for the sake of the good of mankind as a whole, if that's what you're talking about, about somebody having to get killed instead of something else. Well there's other sins people have to atone for, it's no always just your own. I think that's a mistake a lot of folk make, especially males like us, men, I think we're very often mistaken at the very root of our own existence as human beings.

The invalid was squinting at him. He shook his head: I'm no following your drift.

Well look I mean you asked if I believed in God. I do, I really do. I stopped it for a while but now I'm back to having the faith. I feel on my best behaviour because of it and having everything to overcome. The world's just such a big place I find with people suffering the wide world over. I find it hard. You help the one person are you supposed to help them all? And then how are you supposed to keep on living your own life into the bargain? Cause nobody helps you. Know what I mean? That's all I'm saying, it's no because you're selfish, you just dont have the power or the control except maybe a wee minuscule slice, and then you wind up getting squashed, just like a wee beetle – that's what happened to a friend of mine . . . when we were at college, he started to get involved in charity work for foreign countries and then he ended up in trouble.

You're misjudging yourself young fellow.

Pardon?

I was beginning to guess that just after you came in. But there again it's my own fault; I tend no to get things right either.

Edward scratched the side of his head.

And then you see I've got to trust whoever she trusts; my missis, I have to rely on her for my character judgments. Of course it's this bloody thing here . . . ! He shook his head, staring at the contraption. If it wasnt for it I'd be able to give more time to things, I'd be able to do my own thinking when it comes to getting things done, and that's what's important. Ach . . . The invalid's head drooped and he sighed.

Edward nodded, he studied the frayed bit of the carpet, how its wee threads were spread so very haphazardly and you could just reach down and straighten them out, get them into a neat wee row. This was a memorable meeting but it wasnt nice at the time. He would always take pains to remember that. It was a promise. He had promised, and he would do it. Even when he would tell a friend about how all this had happened he would make sure he added on about it not being nice when it happened, actually was happening at the time; it was very uncomfortable – not even the chair was good to sit on and plus as well you had the very proximity of the old man, how him being an invalid meant you got this old smell which was really quite fuisty and you hate to say it but almost nearly what you would call a stench, when you came to think about it, like as if he hadnt washed or perish the thought cleansed himself the last time he visited the toilet etcetera etcetera though you dont like saying that because he was a genuine and good old guy that you had to respect for his integrity down through the years, him being involved in politics in an active way on the factory floor, you had to really respect him. There was the door! Deborah! Deborah . . .

Oh Lord Lord Lord.

Edward had started up from the chair, he glanced this way and that; but whosoever was outside on the stair landing must have continued on to some other destination. He relaxed, settled himself back on the chair again.

Where was she though? She was late. Usually she was on time, she was quite a precise person. In fact that was quite a good thing about her and fitted in with him; they were quite alike in that sense, him also being a person who was quite precise or tried to be. That side of things was fine but not an especial plus, not in the selling line, it was definitely not an especial plus in the selling line: you could be as late as you wanted as long as you knew how to close a sale.

Deborah:

He really thought she was a great lassie, really great. It was just she didnt have the best of manners. This bad habit she had of – it was like not having a sense of humour maybe, to do with that – quite a nasty tongue even, in some ways, you had to admit it. Even her own mother said it about her, and that was something surely. And maybe as well, and it was terrible to say, and it wasnt a criticism at all but just if she maybe just learned to wear better clothes, a wee bit more stylish, if the truth be told, maybe like Jeanette who was called Jinty by people. You couldnt call Deborah anything like that. She didnt like him calling her Debbie for instance and Debs just sounded stupid

Edward got to his feet.

Because it was time to go. It really was time to go. He had all these bloody things to learn before morning came, never mind prepare his head for her, get his head right, get things sorted, get the things worked out because of

God, he just didnt know what to do, he didnt, he didnt know what to do. He had no idea. He just had no idea. He was in a terrible state, situation, it wasnt something he didnt know how to get out, what he could do, and she would be here she would be here, she would be here, she would be here

Just sit down a minute, the invalid commanded.

Edward shook his head.

Just for a minute.

I cant, I just cant.

You can.

I've got to go.

I've a need to tell you something. It's a kind of confession.

Edward gazed at him.

I've got to talk things out with you.

But you've done that already, have you no?

No.

I thought you had.

Look young fellow talking it out in that certain way I'm meaning *is* a confession; that's what a confession *is*. And I'll know when I've done it, because you always do, once you've made it you know you've made it. Your mind feels easy.

Edward paused. He was looking to say something. There was something he was to say and he was looking to say it, it was maybe to do with guilt, because he knew about that, a wee bit at least. Although he was so much younger that didnt mean he didnt, because it was a thing you could feel even as a boy.

The invalid was waiting to speak.

Sorry, said Edward.

The invalid frowned and made a gesture with his hand: You see I'm no able to speak unless you're willing to listen, you've got to be able to hear what I'm saying but you're no always willing to do that.

Yeh but Mister Parker I'm sorry eh it's just that my fiancée's due at any minute.

The invalid glanced at the door, then said, She'll know where you are, Catherine'll tell her.

Will she?

Aye, she'll be back soon herself . . . And again the old invalid glanced at the door.

Edward nodded; he sniffed, breathed in deeply and raised his head, at the same time making a gulping noise like as if his adam's apple was stuck, then the tears started in his eyes and he was blinking to keep from crying.

What's wrong?

Jees I'm just in awful trouble Mister Parker, awful trouble.

Sit down a minute.

Yeh but I'm just in so much trouble.

Sit down a minute then. Sit down. Maybe we can share it. Sometimes you share a problem you swop it, and in the swopping it gets lost.

Edward had his face in his hands.

Dont get yourself into a state . . . He leaned forwards, grasping Edward's right shoulder: Edward's a king's name by the way, did you know that?

Edward shook his head.

Come on, at your age it cant be that bad, it'll be a personal thing, personal things are easy. Just sit down a minute and tell me what it is. I was going to tell you mine so you can just tell me yours – see! if you tell me I'll tell you, that's what I mean by a swop.

Edward dragged the cuff of his sleeve across his face, wiping his eyes as he sat down.

I'll take on your problem if you'll take on mine. You hear me out and then I'll hear you out.

Yeh but . . . Edward now rubbed quickly at his eyes with the palms of both his hands.

In that way you see we'll both have things into the open, we'll have shared what's troubling us . . . If I start worrying about your problems you start worrying about mine. You get it?

Edward shifted on his chair enough to see the door. She was

coming along the street, he knew it. There was no time at all now. He was sunk. What was he going to say to her because he couldnt think of anything, and he wasnt clean. What could he do? He hadnt given it any thought, none, none, he was just relying on something, chance maybe oh more than that more than that he had been praying, he had prayed for assistance, because he needed help, help, he needed help, help help help help please the Lord, oh God but he needed help from Our Father who art in heaven, hallowed be thy name, thy kingdom come, thy will be done

Edward closed his eyes and he put his hands next to each other, not clasping them.

I slept with my fiancée's sister, he said. He raised his head, opening his eyes, but not looking at the invalid. I slept with her. I didnt mean to. I dont know what to do about it. I just dont know.

Mm.

I've never done it before, never, it just bloody happened it was just bloody out the blue, I think maybe it was me with my head full, all the worries I've had cause of this damn test, my job, the whole lot.

Mm.

Edward gazed at him. I just didnt mean it, it just happened.

Aye it's a difficult one that.

Is it?

Questions of loyalty young fellow, they're aye difficult.

Yeh, Edward sighed.

And she doesnt know?

What?

You're wife's no found out?

It's no my wife it's my fiancée; I'm no married.

Aw.

Edward paused, I suppose they're the same really anyway, if you're married or engaged. I am wanting to get married to her. In fact I actually asked her and she said no.

She said no?

Yeh. I asked her. Hh, she didnt want to.

Aw.

I dont know how. I thought it was good you know I mean I thought it was fine, but it wasnt, she just said no. It was a shock.

Oh well, aye. Had you been planning it for a while?

No, no really, I just actually popped it out one night. I hadnt thought of it happening, her saying no. I suppose it's ego, you just dont think of it, you always think it's you, you always think you've got to make the decision. And that's that. Then you find out it isnt, the other people have got their own minds, and what they say for themselves you dont find out till you've asked . . . Eh . . . I know this is a personal question Mister Parker but I was wondering . . . I'm only meaning how it's as though here we are meeting up with each other at a time when we need a way out of a problem.

Edward paused. The old invalid had his hand raised and was waving:

Mine isnt really a problem, he said.

Oh.

It's different to that.

I see.

But on you go anyhow and say what you were saying.

Edward wasnt going to but then he resumed talking. I dont mean like fate, he said, us meeting, because I know God doesnt arrange things just for our benefit in that way I mean that's even a bit like blasphemy to think that, I'm thinking more in the way you get led along a road, it's like how you see a road in the country going over a hill in the distance where the fields look rectangular with their hedgerows and you're going to a village to do a bit of business and there's no avoiding it even although you hate the very idea because the road leads you there and you know you're to have to grit your teeth but you're used to that because that's what you do all the time when you meet these clients even if they're old and valued ones I mean you're always gritting your teeth anyway and then having to go and do it because that's the way things are, you've always got to go straight in and start off the chat as if it was the first time in your life. But maybe things are going to happen to you along the way. Maybe you start to get a blind panic settling in cause that can happen too, that can happen too – it happens to me, sometimes. There's all kinds of trials and tribulations. You see in some ways today has been awful bad for me. I'll no bore you with all the sorry details, it's just personal stuff mainly, and maybe that kind of thing's best not to get aired. You have to remember I'm younger than you I mean you know what like it is nowadays anyway, folk just dont talk about serious things, they dont want to, they only talk about things like television and videos and football, rock bands, that side of things, media personalities and high financiers, big businessmen, big fat-cats who work down the Stock Exchange in London, all these big high financiers who get the great big sums of money.

facilities young fellow

What you were saying there a wee minute ago . . . The invalid was staring at Edward. About the facilities, mind? Just tell us about them.

There was something in the invalid's gaze and he turned swiftly to see Deborah. Deborah and the old woman. Both standing there just in from the doorway.

Deborah smiled briefly.

Hiya . . . Edward continued to sit, then he coughed and made to rise from the chair but didnt. For one split second he felt so comfortable and nervous at the selfsame moment he wanted to rush straight across and take her by the hand and drop to his knees and ask her to marry him right there and then but something was stopping him and he felt like bursting out crying again because he seemed to have failed he seemed to have failed and it was in so dramatically and so suddenly and in so unforeseen and unexpected a way it was just so amazing and so ultimately stupid, it was just stupid, there was just something so up with him, something so just

He was telling me about the facilities Catherine. Some funny rules they've got in this place! Eh young fellow?

Oh yeh, yeh . . . He raised his head and looked directly at the old woman, and he tried to swallow saliva but his throat was as dry as a bone.

Tell us again, asked the invalid.

Yeh, said Edward.

They're strict eh?

Yeh.

Tell her about what people do.

Edward nodded. You mean the other tenants or just me myself?

Just how you all get by for your meals and the rest of it.

Edward addressed the old woman: Some people I think just eat cold stuff; cheese and slices of cold meat, tins of beans unheated, that kind of thing. Bread and butter. Or chips or maybe kebabs or pakora from the carry-out shop.

She nodded.

Other people have got an electric kettle and what they do is boil eggs and cook things preserved in salted water, like these wee hot-dog sausages you can buy out Presto's and sometimes I think some of them heat up these wee fish done in tomato sauce – pilchards.

He's talking about himself, said Deborah, giving Edward a look, and then he makes a cup of tea without rinsing out the kettle so it's all tomato sauce left inside – even vinegar sometimes.

Edward avoided looking back at her she sounded so honest and good, he felt so badly sick, so badly sick. And he had to say something they were waiting. She's just saying that, he said, and smiled, she's just saying that.

And he twisted a little bit on his seat as if he was trying to glance at her somehow like he was not able to the way he was at present and he saw her frowning and puzzled. And he cleared his throat at the invalid and he carried on speaking about maybe even soup could be done in your kettle, he said, especially if it was really clear and no full of vegetables. As long as the owners dont find out, what they dont know wont hurt them.

Mm . . . The elderly woman grimaced from him to her husband: If he was fit and healthy we wouldnt be in this state. We would have a proper cooker with an oven and I could make proper meals. She was looking at Deborah now: You see he was on the injured pensioners' income supplement but they took him off it because it'd become a condition, so that's us now until he gets better, if he ever will. And he's the only one that says he will, cause the doctor says he'll no.

That's bloody appalling, said Deborah. She glanced at Edward, shaking her head.

Edward stared at the carpet.

It's bloody appalling.

He raised his head and peered at Deborah, his eyebrows sticking out in front of his eyes, the hairs, as if he was getting old before his time, bushy eyebrows. He said to the old woman: I'm sorry missis I'll have to go back down the stair now because I've got my studies to attend to.

He's got his test tomorrow morning, said the invalid.

Did you tell him about your cousin Jim?

No.

You should have.

Och he's no wanting to hear about him.

It's only because things are so rushed, said Edward, plus as well I was thinking of setting my alarm early, so's I could get up and do an extra bit of studying the morrow morning.

You'll pass young fellow so dont worry.

I hope so, Edward said, smiling but feeling hopeless. And he knew his forehead was falling, falling flat – how it would be flat and he would droop there to everybody, them knowing his state, and he stood up and stepped to the side of Deborah, speaking while he passed: Will we go then?

Alright.

I thought you would feel like something to eat . . . Do you? he said to her.

Do *you*?

Well if you do.

Deborah sighed.

I'll maybe pop down later then like we agreed, called the invalid.

Pardon?

Maybe the back of nine, when you're knocking off for a coffee. Or else will you just come up here?

Eh

Well I'll just pop down then?

Eh, what about I mean . . . ?

It'll be alright. I just have to rest now and again. Have you got a chair?

Yeh

He's a stubborn old besom, said his wife. You know you're no supposed to be walking too much!

I'm only going up and down the one flight of stairs Catherine.

Aye well you're no supposed to.

Edward grasped Deborah's arm but released it at once.

That was a bit rough, she said.

Sorry.

The elderly woman had opened the door for them. He ushered Deborah out then followed. 'Bye, he said.

The door closed.

It was a hard grip, said Deborah.

I didnt mean it, sorry.

She nodded.

So where did you meet Missis Parker?

On the pavement. Outside the front close.

Mm . . .

Why?

Oh nothing I mean it was just, a bit strange.

What were you talking about when we came in? it seemed interesting. You just switched subjects; one minute you were talking about fate and big business and then you went to making tins of soup in your electric kettle.

We were having a conversation. Edward shrugged. That's all – it wasnt really strange. Just me. It was just me.

How d'you mean?

He looked at her. Och, nothing. She was somebody he didnt know but knew as well as anybody in the whole world. There she was in front of him. How she had been a minute ago with the elderly couple. Then there she was with her family. He didnt know her at all. She was just the way she was, whatever that might be. Then her and her sister, how they would also be together, that kind of faith maybe or loyalty. Something. They would have it between them. And it was now broken. He had broken it, he had come between them. Before him it was fine. Now it wasnt. He wanted to lift her up and protect her from all the dangers and pitfalls. If ever she was to get a happy outcome to her life she needed some advice, guidance, she needed to have her faith restored as well, once the truth came out. He felt abased in front of her. Plus she had a certain look in her eye. He could easily push her in the back when she was going down the stairs.

Did you get a sleep? she said when they reached his landing.

No. Did you?

I did, yes, eventually. Did you see my sister?

Yeh.

Was it alright?

Yeh.

Can you help her?

I think so.

Edward that's good.

Yeh.

It is, she'll be so relieved.

Aye . . . He grinned at her. If they went out for a meal it would be fine they would just be fine and the things to talk about, different things to do with different things. He gulped for air. He needed to open the door to the room because now she was waiting for it and he hadnt done it yet. I'm just worried about the test, he said.

Well you shouldnt be.

But it's important.

I know it's important but it's not that important.

It is for me.

Yes I know it is.

I've got to treat it seriously, he muttered, getting the key into the lock, it's important, important for me . . . Oh God! He sighed. Life eh? Life. He smiled. An old couple like that too, imagine getting put out their house because of arrears, would it no sicken you? It's appalling, you're right what you said up the stair. Edward turned and frowned at Deborah: Or else do you fancy going out for a meal?

Out for a meal?

We could go for something to eat, I'm starving, quite hungry. He pushed the door open and entered, waited for her then shut it afterwards. He sighed again. All the stuff on the table. He walked to it and shook his head and he smiled. Ach I dont know Deborah, sometimes I feel as if I'm just making no headway at all. He breathed to get air he was going to faint, and he had got to get a chair onto the seat to sit down oh God, the Lord my God.

Edward!

Oh m'God.

What's wrong?

So bloody bad.

Edward.

His face down on the table the smell of the paper. I'm so God awful

Are you alright?

No, no, I'm no, I'm no feeling good I'm no feeling good I'm no feeling good

What's wrong?

Aw Jesus

She put her arms round his neck and shoulders. You're shivering . . .

He peered upwards from the table. There was a smudge on the wall where he had killed the insect. It was funny how your life went. He was in the tennis league as a boy. He had quite enjoyed it. Him and the others used to have masturbation contests some nights. But if it was possible to give all his woes to this old invalid then that would be that and he would have given them to him and that would be him okay again, like a new start was being made and he would never ever ever again in his whole life ever think of straying again because it was just sex, it was sex, male sexuality and he was sick to death of such things trying to take over your life, trying to dictate the terms of life to you, as if you had no say in the matter and were there just at the beck and call of your erections, any woman who wanted to flash herself at you, and you were finished.

Oh God God God. And it was like it was going to be as if the old guy with the bad legs had been sent down here to help him in his hour of need. That was what it had been like. Edward raised his head and glanced at Deborah's wrists. Because there was something in how that old guy had looked, a sort of honesty, as if there were no clouds surrounding him at all. What like was it it was something

He didnt want to think, he didnt want to

The kind of thing that was difficult.

She wasnt the usual kind of woman how could you say she

was, she wasnt. What like was she with her sister? Her smell. Deborah had a smell. It was a smell of skin, how her skin gave a smell that was different. His shoulders were now weak. How they were weak. He also felt cold. One time with the tennis league from school camp they were on this what they called 'manoeuvre', pretending to be commando troops and Bob Finlay had cheroots from Holland he had stolen off a prefect and they had all smoked them. My God was that bad! So terrible and bad and maybe the worst queasiness he had ever experienced. You had to grow up and get involved as an adult, a man, you had to get to be a man, like that old invalid and the troubles all over the world what a span of mind he had, somebody that kept going in spite of his handicap and did all the things he did. Edward just to be honest felt he would never have coped with being shut in, stuck in offices with crowds of folk in shirts and ties and smart outfits and all the pecking orders.

Your memories just come. We dont have any control. The good Lord made us with memory boxes. Inside each one of them as well is the Voice of Conscience. And the Voice isnt your own. As well as that it's in touch with everybody else's. It was part of how the Voice could say what was right and wrong. It had the insight because it had some sort of ghostly communication with everything.

The door opened and Deborah came in. She hadnt been holding him. She must have gone away when he wasnt looking. Now she was back again and holding a cup. Drink this, she said, it's just water. He took the cup and she held it to his mouth as he turned his head to sip it, her face staring at him. You look bad. He closed his eyes.

I feel like a bad sinner he rushed on and gazing straight at her, It's a feeling all day maybe I'm working too hard, no sleeping enough. He stared at her. I dont get on with Jeanette you know I was meaning to tell you that. She's your sister but I dont. I just dont. And I cant help it.

What? What d'you mean?

I dont get on with her and dont want to see her again, that's all. It's like there's something wrong, wrong. He sipped the water then lifted the nearest folder and flicked at a page. He said, D'you want to get something to eat?

But what are you saying about Jeanette?

Nothing.

Yes you are.

I'm not, honest.

You dont get on with her? You're saying you dont get on with her.

It doesnt matter.

It does.

It doesnt.

But it does Edward, it matters, if you dont like my sister.

I dont, it's just – I dont not like her at all, it's just

Just what?

It's just . . . He sighed. I thought we were going for a curry.

Well I didn't know what we were doing.

D'you not want to

Edward, for God sake!

She had taken her coat off. And the kettle was going. He stared into the cup of water. There *was* something wrong with him. He *wasnt* a good man. It was as plain as the nose on your face. He just hadnt *seen* it before. He hadnt *seen*. It had *always* been there but he just hadnt looked. Other people had seen but he hadnt. They all knew it. Except him.

Oh Christ

She had pushed him on the shoulder. What's up with you! she cried.

I'm sorry. I'm sorry. I'm just no well, leave me alone.

What's wrong?

There's nothing wrong, I'm just

She was staring at him.

My head

She was so staring at him.

My head

Her mouth going *what's wrong, what's wrong*. It's my head I've just got a sore head it's so bloody sore and my insides, wracking and dry I'm just all dry inside and I need water. He gulped a mouthful from the cup and it shook in his hand and he put his other round it steadying it, getting it firm but his hands were shaking it maybe he needed food, maybe that's what it was.

But was it him?

Fine

What?

Deborah smiling

What is it? he said, he smiled. It wasnt me, he said, it was her, it was her. If she claims about me, it was her – because

because it was her seduced him, it wasnt him, he didnt seduce her, that was the so bloody unlucky thing about it, the whole business, because he was the man, that's how it went, that was the trials and tribulations of it, just being a man, the maleness; it was so unlucky it

he gestured at the A4 folders. I just dont know what to do with my life.

That's fine but tell me?

I killed an insect earlier on

I dont want to hear about a bloody insect Edward I want to hear about what you're saying about Jeanette!

But Deborah I just squashed the thing, the wee soul, I just actually killed it, in cold blood, just like you would I dont know I was going to say kill a beetle, that's how bad it is for the poor wee creatures. It's become a byword for it all, death and destruction and just wanton brutality, even the way you sell your equipment to people, how the guys just gyp people into buying rubbish they dont want. The whole thing, it's just so awful, it's terrible and wanton and just goes against everything God stands for. People dont want that sort of life. They dont. They dont want it. It shouldnt be forced on us.

You're no listening!

I am

You're not.

I am! It's just the way things are. You take the way I live my life just as an ordinary man; this is an average day and I've committed awful sins. Just like wanton brutality. And I feel so awful . . . just so bad just so awful bad.

God Edward what's wrong with you?

Nothing. He stared at her. She had leaned to gaze into his face and she had placed each hand on his shoulders.

You've not been eating and now your stomach's in knots because of the work you've been doing for tomorrow morning's test.

Yeh, he smiled and laid his right hand on top of her left hand while it still lay on his shoulder. Aw Deborah, he said, aw Deborah.

Cronies

For three long days and three long nights we drank together, me being there simply because I had nowhere else to go, nobody else to be with, not a soul, not in the whole world; and the other strictly because it was business, and the business lay in the undermining of the other, his crony, me. And not that he was going anywhere either as it happens, although this information is irrelevant, him being a sort of a businessman first but a human being second, and the business in hand was in being here with me, his crony, so-called.

The rest of the company found the thing a spectacle, an incident worthy of the greatest attention. On the one hand it was amusing but on the other there was this sordid undercurrent, them being in the know about the nature of the business. But me and him, as far as ordinary onlookers were concerned, we were the greatest of pals, even if it now seems likely we neither of us understood one word the other was saying.

There was something about it all made the rest of the company wax lyrical, a bad sweet kind of thing. You would have thought the one was not being undermined by the other, that this other was not in the business of undermining me. But the real reason for this false lyricism lay in the rest of the company wanting to consolidate their own fraternity. And meanwhile this barely disguised actual assault on fraternity was continuing right in front of their very eyes, it was quite disgusting, it just deserved contempt, the strong one seeking out the intimacy of the weaker, i.e. me. Plus over their bottles of beer and tumblers of whisky or vodka.

Then it became noticeable he was drawing in for the final assault, his friendliness was gradually being thrown off for the disguise it was, not so much in any outward display of violence but in an absentmindedness that accompanied each one of his actions. It was almost as though he who was to be undermined, and I mean by that myself, that I had become a habit, one more habit, of a tired businessman, if you could call him that; speaking personally I would say he was just an inveterate snob, and that was how he adopted such a nomenclature; the truth is he wasnt a real businessman. He was playing a double game. In the first place he wanted not to be seen as a businessman since most of his associates and acquaintances were socialists or if not socialists as such as least were all in hostile positions toward reactionaries or toryness or whatever, shade or hue. But then again in the second place he wanted everybody to secretly think of him as a businessman, maybe subconsciously; and that because to be a businessman was to be in a position of power.

And above all this was his real goal, power, as witness his assault on myself, someone the world presumed to be an old and trusted crony.

The day the company finally shattered began from him entering the room and the victim, myself, already seated at the table, rising to not so much greet him as wave him into the empty seat facing me. But he just stared at me and he grinned, and when he grinned it was a horror because it was so internalised. I read the signs and I was greatly taken aback, I gaped up at the ceiling as if I was looking for a religious emblem but the rest of the company, they were staring really hostilely at me and I couldnt fathom it out. You have to remember that until the businessman's strong interest they had been more than willing to abuse me for a scapegoat, more than willing, and at this moment there was nothing quite so obvious. I wanted to shout to them about how it had all happened only this short span of time, how three long days and nights were so short. It was a mortifying experience and it was me that was the martyr.

Fr Fitzmichael

Outwith the Palace Grounds the sudden reversals were being met by widely differing though often violent retorts. But the worthy Fr Fitzmichael continued to perform his duties in a no less perfunctory manner: at 3.24 a.m. he was awake and set for his first of the day; the second was followed by the third and the fourth. When that time for the sixth had arrived he was to be seen sheltering beneath the large tree near to the Boundary. November is a dismal month. A month of the Spirit. A dismal month requires Spirit. In order that we may progress into the next, more than usual attention is to be given over to entities whose design is Spiritual. Fr Fitzmichael then stretched his arms, he was reclining with his back against the gnarled trunk of the tree; a trio of ants had appeared on the tips of his toes. With a smile he leaned to cuff at them with a flick of his over-garment. Such things are we brought to. The condition being a Triumvirate of Hymenopterous Insects on the tips of one's toes. Hello. His *call* to a passing Brother was greeted with an astonished raising of the eyebrows. He waved. November. A month of the Spirit. Spirit and Dismality are equidistant. The Brother hurried off in the direction of the Palace. So, it would seem the Game is to be up. Fr Fitzmichael's smile was benign. The attention of the Superiors shall be brought to bear heavily. So it must be. The tree contains ants. One enters the Palace Library to peruse the books of one's pleasure. One enters the Palace Grounds to be confronted by unimaginable entities whence from pleasure is to be derived in the month of the Spirit. Take an acorn. Place it in the palm of one's hand. Squeeze.

Squeeze. Examine the acorn before throwing it onto a heap of soggy leaves. See it bounce. Upon soggy leaves an acorn can bounce in November.

Street-sweeper

The sky was at the blueyblack pre-heavygrey stage of the morning and the gaffer was somewhere around. This is one bastard that was always around; he was always hiding. But he was somewhere close right now and Peter could sense his presence and he paused. It wasnt a footstep but he turned to see over his shoulder anyway, walked a few more paces then quickly sidled into a shop doorway, holding the brush vertical, making sure the top of his book wasnt showing out his pocket. This was no longer fun. At one time in his life it mightve been but no now, fuck, it was just bloody silly. And it wisni funny. It just wisni fucking funny at all. These things were beginning to happen to him more and more and he was still having to cope. What else was there. In this life you get presented with your choices and that's that, if you canni choose the right ones you choose the wrong ones and you get fucked some of the time; most of the time some people would say. He closed his eyes, rubbed at his brow, smoothing the hair of his eyebrows. What was he to do now, he couldni make it back to the place he was supposed to be at, no without being spotted. Aw god. But it gave him a nice sense of liberty as well, it was an elation, quite fucking heady. Although he would have to move, he would – how long can you stay in a doorway! Hey, there was a big cat watching him, it was crouched in beside a motor-car wheel. Ha, christ. Peter chuckled. He was seen by a cat your honour. There he was in a doorway, having skived off because he had heard about a forced entry to a newsagent shop and thought there mightve been some goods lying available to pilfer.

Objection!

Overruled.

Ah but he was sick of getting watched. He was. He was fucking sick of it. The council have a store of detectives. They get sent out spying on the employees, the workers lad the workers, they get sent out spying on them. Surely not. The witness has already shown this clearly to be the case your Honour. Has he indeed. Aye, fuck, he has, on fucking numerous occasions, that's how come he got the boys out on strike last March.

Ah.

Naw but he's fucking sick of it, he really is. High time he was an adult. Here he is forty-seven years of age and he's a boy, a wee lad – in fact, he is all set to start wearing short trousers and ankle-socks and a pair of fast-running sandshoes (plimsolls for the non-Scottish reader). What was he to do but that is the problem, that is the thing you get faced with all the bloody time, wasnt it just bloody enervating. But you've got your brush you've got your brush and he stepped out and was moving, dragging his feet on fast, dragging because his left leg was a nuisance, due to a fucking disability that made him limp – well it didni *make* him limp, he decided to limp, it was his decision, he could have found some new manner of leg-motoring which would have allowed him not to limp, by some sort of circumlocutory means he could have performed a three-way shuffle to offset or otherwise bypass the limp and thus be of normal perambulatory gait. This was these fucking books he read. Peter was a fucking avid reader and he had got stuck in the early Victorian era, even earlier, bastards like Goldsmith for some reason, that's what he read. Charles fucking Lamb, that's who he read; all these tory essayists of the pre-chartist days, that other bastard that didni like Keats. Why did he read such shite. Who knows, they fucking wreaked havoc with the syntax, never mind the fucking so-called sinecure of a job, the street cleaning. Order Order. Sorry Mister Speaker. But for christ sake, for christ sake.

Yet you had to laugh at his spirit I mean god almighty he was a spirited chappie, he was, he really and truly was. But he had to go fast. There was danger ahead. No time for quiet grins. Alright he was good, he was still doing the business at forty-seven, but no self-congratulatory posturing if you please, even though he might still be doing it, even though he was still going strong at the extraordinarily advanced age of thrice fifteen-and-two-thirds your honour, in the face of extraordinarily calamitous potentialities to wit said so-called sinecure. Mister Speaker Mister Speaker, this side of the House would request that you advise us as to the appertaining set of circumstances of the aforementioned place and primary purpose of said chappie's sinecure so-called. Uproar. A Springburn street. Put on the Member for Glasgow North. The Member for Glasgow North has fuckt off for a glass of claret. Well return him post-haste.

But the goodwife. Has the goodwife a word to say. Yes, indeed. The goodwife would bat him one on the gub. She thought all this was dead and buried. She thought the sinecure was not deserving of the 'so-called' prefixed reference one iota, i.e. sinecure *qua* sinecure in the good lady's opinion.

She wouldni think it was possible but, it's true, she thought it was all over as far as the problematics were concerned. Pussycats pussycats, I tought I saw. But there you are, getting to the doddering stage, being spotted by a crouching cat, so much for his ability to cope, to withstand the helter skelter, the pell mell, the guys in the darkblue and the bulky shoulders. Bejasus he was getting fucking drunk on the possibility of freedom, a genuine liberty, one that would be his prior to deceasement. What he fancied was a wee periscope from the coffin, so he could just lie there watching the occasional passersby, the occasional birdie or fieldmouse:

he was into another doorway and standing with his back pressed into the wall, eyes shut tight, but lips parted, getting breath, listening with the utmost concentration. Nothing. Nothing o christ why was he an atheist this of all times he felt like screaming a howsyrfather yr paternoster a quick hail mary yr king billy for christ sake what was it was it a fucking footfall he felt like bellowing, bellowing the fucking place down, it would show them it would show them it would display it, it would display how he was and how he could bellow his laughter in the face of the fucking hidebound universe of them, fucking moribund bastirts – was it the gaffer? He pulled the brush in, held it like an upright musket of the old imperialist guard, India or Africa yr Lordship.

Carol thought it was all dead and buried. She did, she truly truly did. His eyes were shut and his lips now closed, the nostrils serving the air channels or pipes, listening with the utmost concatenation of the earular orifices. Not to scream. Not to make a sound. Another minute and he would go, he would move, move off, into the greying dawn.

He was safe now for another few minutes. It was over, a respite o lord how brief is this tiny candle flicker. Peasie Peasie Peasie. For this was his nickname, the handle awarded him by the mates, the compañeros, the compatriots, the comrades: Peasie.

It didni even matter the profit but this was the fucking thing! Maybe he got there and the newsagent turned out to be a grocer for god sake how many cartons of biscuits can you plank out in some backcourt! Fucking radio rental yr Lordship. Mind you the profit was of nay account, nane at all. Neither the benefits thereon. If there were benefits he didni ken what they were. He shook his head. Aright, aright me boy, me lad. There was a poor fucker lying on the grun ahead. There was. Peter approached cautiously. It was a bad sign. It was. If the security forces martialled, and they would, then they would be onto him in a matter of hours, a couple of hours, maybe even one; he would need a tale to tell. Diarrhoea. Diarrhoea, that saviour of the working classes. He had to go to the loo and spend some several minutes, maybe thirty, unable to leave in case the belly ructured yet again. But the body was a bad sign. Poor bastard.

Peter knelt by the guy. He was still alive, his forehead warm and the tick at the temple, a faint pulsing. But should he drag him into a close-mouth No, of course not, plus best to leave him or else

but the guy was on his back and that was not good. Peter laid down his brush and did the life-saving twist, he placed the man's right arm over his left side, then raised and placed his right leg also over his left side, then gently pulled the left leg out a little, again gently, shifting the guy's head, onto the side: and now the guy would breathe properly without the risk of choking on his tongyou. And he would have to leave it at that. It wisni cold so he wouldni die of frostbite. Leave it. You'll be alright son, he whispered and for some reason felt like kissing him on the forehead, a gesture of universal love for the suffering. We can endure, we can endure. Maybe it was a returning prophet to earth, and this was the way he had landed, on the crown of his skull and done a flaky. He laid his hand on the guy's shoulder. Ah you'll be right as rain, he said, and he got up to go. He would be though, he would be fine, you could tell, you could tell just by looking; and Peter was well-versed in that. Yet fuck sake if he hadni of known how to properly move the guy's body then he might have died, he couldve choked to death. My god but life is so fragile; truly, it is.

And he was seen. The pair of eyes watching. The gaffer was across the street. The game's a bogie. He looked to be smiling. He hated Peter so that would be the case quite clearly.

Come ower here!

Peter had walked a couple paces by then and he stopped, he looked across the road. Guiseppe Robertson was the gaffer's name. Part of his hatred for Peter was straightforward, contained in the relative weak notion of 'age'; the pair of them were of similar years and months down even to weeks perforce days and hours – all of that sort of shite before you get to the politics. Fucking bastirt. Peter stared back at him. Yeh man hey, Robertson was grinning, he was fucking grinning. Ace in the hole and three of them showing. Well well well.

Come ower here! he shouted again.

He wasnt kidding. Yeh. Peter licked his lips. He glanced sideways, the body there and still prone; Robertson seemed not to have noticed it yet. He glanced back at him and discovered his feet moving, dragging him across the road. Who was moving his fucking feet. He wasnt, it had to be someone in the prime position.

The gaffer was staring at him.

I'm sorry, said Peter.

It doesni matter about fucking sorry man you shouldni have left the job.

I had to go a place.

You had to go a place . . . mmhh; is that what you want on record?

Aye.

The gaffer grinned: You've been fun out and that's that.

As long as you put it on record.

Ah Peter Peter, so that's you at last, fucking out the door. It's taken a while, but we knew we'd get ye.

You did.

We did, aye, true, true true true, aye, we knew you'd err. So, you better collect the tab frae the office this afternoon.

Peter gazed at him, he smiled. Collect my tab?

Yes, you're finished, all fucking washed up, a jellyfish on the beach, you're done, you're in the process of evaporating. The gaffer chuckled. Your services, for what they're worth, are no longer in demand by the fathers of the city.

That's excellent news. I can retire and grow exotic plants out my window boxes.

You can do whatever the fuck you like son.

Ah, the son, I see. But Guiseppe you're forgetting, as a free man, an ordinary civilian, I can kick fuck out you and it'll no be a dismissable offence against company property.

Jovial, very jovial. And obviously if that's your wish then I'm the man, I'm game, know what I mean, game, anywhere you like Peter it's nomination time.

The two of them stared at each other. Here we have a straightforward hierarchy. Joe Robertson the gaffer and Peter the sweeper.

Fuck you and your services, muttered Peter and thereby lost the war. This was the job gone. Or was it, maybe it was just a battle: Look, said Peter, I've no even been the place yet I was just bloody going, I've no even got there.

You were just bloody going!

Aye.

You've been off the job an hour.

An hour? Who fucking telt ye that?

Never you mind.

There's a guy lying ower there man he's out the game.

So what?

I just bloody saved his life!

Robertson grinned and shook his head: Is that a fact!

That means I've just to leave him there?

Your job's taking care of the streets, he's on the fucking pavement.

Mmhh, I see.

It was on the streets, past tense.

Aw for fuck sake man look I'm sorry! And that was as far as he was going with this charade, no more, no more.

It doesni fucking matter about sorry, it's too late.

It'll no happen again yr honour . . . Peter attempted a smile, a moment later he watched the gaffer leave, his bowly swagger, taking a smoke from his pocket and lighting it as he went. Death. The latest legislation. Death. Death death death. Death. Capital d e a

He continued to watch the gaffer until he turned the corner of Moir Street.

Well there were other kinds of work. They were needing sellers of a variety of stuff at primary-school gates. That was a wheeze. Why didnt he get in on that. My god, it was the coming thing. Then with a bit of luck he could branch out on his own and from there who knows, the whole of the world was available. Peter cracked himself on the back of the skull with such venomous force Aouch that he nearly knocked it off Aouch he staggered a pace, dropped his brush and clutched his head. O for fuck sake christ almighty but it was sore. He recovered, stopped to retrieve the brush.

It was bloody sore but christ that was stupid, bloody stupid thing to do, fucking eedjit – next thing he would be cutting bits out his body with a sharp pointed knife, self-mutiliation, that other saviour of the working classes. O christ but the head was still nipping! My god, different if it knocked some sense into the brains but did it did it fuck.

Who had shopped him? Somebody must have. Guiseppe wouldni have been so cocky otherwise. One of the team had sold him out for a pocket of shekels; that's the fucking system boy no more street-sweeping for you. Yes boy hey, he could do anything he liked. Peter smiled and shook his head. He glanced upwards at the heavy grey clouds. He felt like putting on a shirt and tie and the good suit, and get Carol, and off they would go to a nightclub, out wining and dining the morning away. He liked nightshift. Nightshift! It was a beautiful experience. My god Robertson I'd love to fucking do you in boy that's what I would fucking like. But he had no money and he was eighteen years short of the pension. And he was not to lose control. That was all he needed. The whole of life was out to get you. There's a sentence. But it's true, true, the whole of life. Who had shopped him but for fuck sake what dirty bastirt had done the dirty, stuck the evil eye on him, told fucking Robertson the likely route. Och, dear. I had a dream, I had a dream, and in this dream a man was free and could walk tall, he could walk tall, discard the brush and hold up the head, straightened shoulders and self-respect:

the guy was still lying there.

Ohhh. A whisky would be nice, a wee dram. Peter carried a hipflask on occasion but not tonight, he didnt have it tonight. Ohhh. He paused, he stared over the road, seeing the guy in that selfsame position. Perhaps he was dead, perhaps he had died during the tiff with the gaffer. Poor bastard, what was his story, we've all got them, we've all got them.

Morning has bro-ken.

Margaret's away somewhere

Of course Margaret wasnt the sort of woman you trusted. She had that way of looking at you as if she was wondering how she was going to con you this time and if she could just take it for granted she would get away with it or else did she have to work out methods of escape afterwards. It put you on your guard. And I mean everybody, even the paperboy or the milkboy, when they came to collect the money at the end of the week, they were wary as well. You couldnt help watching her. Even if you were talking to somebody else, if you were standing somewhere where she was, if you were talking to somebody, in the post office for instance, you were always watching her at the same time, so that your eyes might meet and she could go surprised, a bit taken aback, as if she was having to think to herself 'Did he see me there?' but then she would give a wee self-possessed smile and you would give her one back. It was funny the way she managed it, because the truth is she would have won as far as that particular exchange is concerned. And if ever she had to actually say something it would nearly always be a 'What was that?' and this made you know she hadnt been listening to a word you said, this because she rated you so low there was nothing at all you could say would ever interest her, whereas probably you thought she had been waiting for you to speak to her all the time. It wasnt easy being in her company and you were always glad to see the back of her, I mean relieved. But it didnt dawn on me she had disappeared till a long time after – I mean when you told me about it, about how she hadnt been around for a while, it hadnt dawned on me.

A Memory

O mirs! And a slice of square sausage please!

Beg pardon?

I squinted at her. A slice of square sausage – she didnt have any idea what I was rabbiting on about. A piece of absentmindedness, I had forgotten I was in fucking England. But too late now and impossible to pretend I only said 'sausage' and that maybe she had misheard the first bit, something to do with 'air' or 'bare' maybe, 'scare', 'fare' – sausages are excellent fare I could have said but structured as excellent fare sausages, although the strange syntax would probably have thrown her.

Square sausage? She was frowning, but not unkindly, not hostilely, not at all, this lass of not quite tender years.

It's a delicacy of Scotland.

You what . . .

It's actually a delicacy, a flat slice of sausagemeat approximately 2 inches by 3, the thickness varying between an eighth of an inch and an inch . . . making the movements with both my hands to display the idea more substantially.

The girl thinking I am mad or else kidding her on in some unfathomable but essentially snobby and elitist way. It's fine, I said, just give me one of your English efforts, these long fat things you stuff full of bread and water – gaolmeat we call them back where I come from!

She was still bewildered but now slightly impatient.

Glasgow sausage manufacturers could earn themselves a fortune down here eh! Ha ha.

Yeh, she said, and walked off to the kitchen to pass in my order.

But at least she had answered when spoken to and not left me high and dry. When you think about it, imagine having to take part in such a ridiculous conversation! And yet this is how so many parties have to earn a living. One time I was aboard a public omnibus and dozing; it was a nice afternoon and the rays from the good old sun streaming in the window there. An elderly chap of some seventy or so summers sat nearby. The bus was fairly empty. The driver, a rather brusque sort of bloke I have to confess, and taking it slowly in an obvious attempt at not gaining time. At one point he stopped altogether and applied the handbrake and he sat there gazing ahead, his elbows resting on the steering wheel. Suddenly the elderly chap turns at me and he has to lean threequartersway across the damn aisle so you thought he was going to fall off his seat! He gesticulates out the window in the direction of a grocer cum newsagent shop. You see that there, he says, that shop there, he says, you see it?

Yep.

Well there used to be a cigarette machine stood there, right outside the door.

Is that right?

Aye. He nodded, giving a loud sniff of the nose, then sat back again without further ado. From the way he had performed the whole thing he was obviously a nonsmoker. But even this deduction is a boring try at producing something not so boring from something that is utterly beyond the defining pale even as a straight piece of abject boredom. If the old fellow had simply leaned over the aisle and whispered: Cigarette machines . . . just starkly and in a low growling voice and left it at that, well, I would still at this very moment in my life be incredibly interested in just what precisely the full set of implications

The lass returns the lass returns!

Tea or coffee?

Tea please; and make it two thanks, one just now and one during. Mirs, the age of sauce the age of sauce!

She did not reply to that last bit though, mainly because I managed to stop myself saying it out loud thank the Lord.

A player

He didnt want to start in on something else; he didnt; and it was very important that he didnt; it was in the nature of things, being quite close to dying, which was what he was wanting, he was wanting to die, quite soon, he didnt want to wait too long. It was not something he was taking pains to conceal either. How the hell should he? Let it out into the open air, right into the atmosphere and let them see; let it all out and just let them see and then they could know and maybe understand, if that was ever possible but he doubted it. It made his breathing come shallower and it rasped, thinking about how they took it. All of them. So let them just know about it. Not to hide any of it. Nothing.

It was maybe something in the way he had been living since old Fiona died, but that wasnt long ago and he had been operating like that in the playing days anyway, all these last years. He was sick of it, he was right sick of it, sick to death of it. He was good. He was. He didnt need no cunt to tell him. Good or bad. He didnt need it, he didnt fucking care – never had and never would. So he was no about to start in on something else either neither he was, no now. Nothing like that at all. God sake. How the hell should he?

It could have been a thing other folk saw as a character trait maybe, some sort of integral bit of his character or something but he couldnt care bloody less. He just felt himself he was himself, his own man, and that was that, that was bloody that. It made him angry, just to think about it.

The bloke sitting at the table behind him with the plate of

egg and chips. Then the old Chinese woman who served, waiting for him to order his whatever it was – Spanish omelette, egg-and-noodle roll – but he wasnt going to order nothing. Nothing. The very idea made him sick. And them two wee girls that lived round the street were up at the counter buying chocolate to take back to school. Old Fiona had been good with them. All kinds of weans. She had been good with them, she would have made a nurse, or a teacher in the primary schools or if she had had kids herself, grandchildren, she would have been good with them, reading them stories and being patient with them when they done their mischief, no getting ratty the way he would have if it had been him, if he had been a grandfather – which maybe he was because there had been other women besides old Fiona; there still was, there was Maggie. The bloke sitting behind looked at him out the corner of his eye. Because he was talking to himself. His lips not just moving but the vocal chords as well. It was like all of him was moving now out in the world, nothing being concealed any more, out it all went with a snap of the fingers. This was him close to dying at long last bring out the trumpets he felt like bashing it out. But he knew it, he knew it, he bloody knew it. It made him feel good. He didnt fucking give a fuck.

Also the newspaper the bloke had noticed and was gesturing at wanting to borrow, from him, his newspaper, that was what it was. He smiled a polite smile and wet his lips and the sores inside his mouth, his gums perhaps got some disease the way he was always getting them sores, like wee volcano mouths, what was it, he was wanting, the bloke, the newspaper, he was wanting the newspaper off him. It was about something he was being asked also, he was being asked something, what the hell, and he said yes to it, whatever it was, he was asked, maybe no even asked, maybe saying yes and no even getting asked. It was about the horse racing, the newspaper for the horse racing. The bloke was asking him about the horse racing, horses that he was betting.

The wee lassies had went away back to school with their

chocolate, wee Pakistani lassies, what was it he was wanting to know, the bloke, it was about a horse he was doing and was asking him about, he didnt know, didnt know about them, not the first thing, horses, he never had the interest, it didnt was something he did at all, it was politics as well, the horses and the betting, the maharajahs and the billionaires, he couldnt be bothered with it, lot of shite, the way it stopped folk from using their loafs

like in the early days when the promise was there and the whole bloody world would have heard about them except they were just young, just so young, behind the ears, what could they do, getting ripped off, nothing, they couldnt do nothing, not properly, not just by theirselves, if they had had somebody, somebody just to let them know the way things were, somebody that could have showed them how to use their loaf, that would have done them, if they had had that.

He glowered at the bloke, steady, studying him, the way he was reading the newspaper and at the racing page, just the way he was looking at the racing page, reading it while he was digging a chip into the yolk of the egg: he was comfy, he was sitting there comfy. This is what it was. Just sitting there comfy. A lot of blokes as well, young yins especially, that was like what they did, they took things, your newspaper, anything, they took it – they took your stuff, the arrangements, the way you did things, when you did things they took it, you had to learn how no to bother, if they took it and made it for theirselves. You learnt that. He never minded it it was the way of the world, that was the way things were so why worry, young folk and old folk how they watched and just watched, so that you were best laying everything out, getting it all out and in the open and let them see, just let them see, without having secrets, like Bill Broonzy telling Guthrie just to Steal it, Steal it. Because he wasnt going to give it but you could just take it. No time no time, no time, for that kind of thing.

The old Chinese woman at another table clearing it up but waiting, aye waiting, what was she

to order something, he was to order something. He usually had an omelette when Maggie was here. He liked it, omelettes. But with himself maybe just the egg-and-noodle roll. She smiled at him near to his head and it was like she winked at him but how could that be, maybe it could be, her winking because her smile how she did it; she was so wee and the big bum in her trousers like you felt you could smell her the movement, her vigorousness, she scarcely had to bend in the wiping, wiping down the table, her being so wee – plus her breathing as if she was not wanting the sound to be overheard, keeping her breathing low, low; and you felt like telling her, Breathe out Breathe out, it's good for you, good for the lungs, you had to blow out and get them cleared and never mind who heard it it was your body you were to be looking after, your lungs and your breath, nobody else's and you were to play, play. But how come that bloke had the newspaper? that was annoying, how come he had it – had he gave him it? Had he actually gave him it? he couldnt hardly remember. Had he asked? He had. He had asked for it; if he could have it, he could remember him asking: but had he gave him it? or did he just take it, the way they did these young blokes you have to watch them the way they just take things although you have got to give them them, you've got to, else anyway they'll just take, take take take, take take take; had he gave him it? He couldnt remember, he couldnt remember it, giving him it, he couldnt, he would have remembered if he had; he would have remembered, surely to God he would have remembered for fuck sake something like that, unless maybe he had just took it, the way some of them did if they thought they could get bloody away with it it would make you right bloody angry bloody cheek it was right bloody impertinence. Where was Maggie, where in the name of God was Maggie, the bloody hell was she? Poor old Fiona but, that was her there her head on the pillow with her eyes open but rolled up the way poor old soul, her mouth still a bit wet and damp on the brow. Fiona. That was her now. How could it be! His brains werent thinking right. Could it be her? Who else! It couldnt be. It couldnt. No her. Old Fiona. She was good – better than that cunt Maggie, her bad temper. Imagine that, old Fiona. He was to have been the one as well, no her, her being first like that, he was wanting to be first, he was to aye be first, that was the thing; and she was going to get the old squad the gether, she was going to round them all up, the old squad. Maggie would have helped get her it done. If she had wanted, except maybe she wouldnt, she wouldnt want to, that was the last thing

But needed because she was always bloody forgetting, always bloody forgetting, a memory like a bloody hen, a sieve, if you left it to her. If she bloody messed it up. All the boys too all coming, and having a laugh, they'd have a laugh, maybe a drink, smoke a couple of joints, celebrating, the old days, they werent all fucking bad, some of them werent they were good, good.

Ah Jesus but was this him now where was he! He was here. He was just here and he was feeling damn tired and painful – no painful what was it in pain he was feeling in pain he was sick and tired, he was sick and tired of it all, he was damn sick and tired, damn sick and damn tired, of the damn lot. Where was Maggie? Did he just look round for her there over his fucking shoulder? And him at the fucking table behind with the newspaper there how had he got the bloody newspaper, it was no fair him taking it that way how they just took took took. The tears were into his eyes, he was soon going to be bubbling, it was just no fair him taking his paper like that just for reading the horses, bloody horses bloody waste of time and money

the table inches from his face; he was hunching over, he was hunching over

Otherwise how come his face was inches from the table? The pong of that, formica

The old Chinese woman giving him a smile. She knew he was expecting Maggie and that was how come he was sitting there. But he wasnt expecting her, she wasnt coming anymore. She was an old woman too with the big bum, this Chinese, and the smell off her, just sweat; she was an old-timer, like Fiona.

Ach he was finished anyway. And he wanted to be finished as well because it made him right bloody angry sometimes, and angry as well at Maggie she was a pain in the bloody neck, a pain in the bloody neck, a damn nuisance. Where was she? Where the hell was she? That dampness on Fiona's chin, on her bottom lip, the spots of sweat.

He had no time for it.

It was her waiting on him to order now Christ what next what next, she was there now at the foot of the table, smiling but being nosy at the same time, nosy, she was aye nosy, wanting to know things all the time wanting to know things it was just nosiness, nosiness, how these Chinese were no supposed to be nosy but here they were this yin, this old yin, how she was, wanting to poke her nose in he felt like being crabbit with her and telling her just to fuck off and go to another table, away and wash the damn dishes out the road, a bit of breathing space instead of all this crowding in aye crowding in on a person, stuffy rooms and all that smoke engulfing you, right on top and overwhelming you, aye overwhelming you, making you feel, making you feel

It had nothing to do with her anyway. Fuck all. Nothing. What had it to do with her! Nothing at all. People had nothing to do with you although they made out like they did. That's what happened in life, they pretended to have some big say in how you went on. And once he was dead and buried how they would talk about him, chatter chatter chatter, blether blether blether; he knew the way they would go, how they would act like they had all been in it the gether as if they were bosom buddies; just lies, lies lies and more lies. He was going to go away, he was going to go away, he wasnt even going to eat. But he continued to sit there and a sniffing sound came from his nose, he was aware of the chewing noises coming from the table behind. Oh Maggie, Maggie. Maggie wasnt there and he wasnt expecting her. Where the hell was she, where was she, how folk just fucked off and left you, they just went away, that was what happened, they just went away, they went away, they went away and left you, they fucking went away and left you, it made you right bloody angry.

Naval History

I met them in the doorway of a bookshop up the town, just as I was leaving. They were absolutely delighted to see me. Alan and Sheila; I hadnt been in touch with them for years. It was fucking embarrassing. She put her arms round me and gave me a big cuddle and then planted a big kiss on my lips while he stood to the rear, a big beaming smile on his coupon; then he shook my hand. Heh steady on, I said.

Ach but James it's really good to see you.

Come on into the shop, said Sheila.

I'm just out.

They both laughed at that. Aye I know you're just out, she said, but come bloody back in. Even just for a minute.

Are you insisting? I said, trying to get my face muscles into a relaxed condition.

You're damn right we're insisting! said Alan, gripping me by the shoulder and about-turning me.

I'm a small-sized bloke so this kind of thing happens too often for comfort and I shrugged his hand off. He apologised, but smiled as he did so. I fucking hate people doing that, I told him, making a point of brushing my shoulder.

Aye, you've no changed!

Of course I've fucking changed . . . I said, then I smiled: For a kick-off I'm baldy.

You were baldy the last time we saw you, said Sheila.

Was I?

Aye.

I just looked at her although I found it hard to believe. People have a habit of throwing things at you about your past in such a way that makes it seem like they're making this great statement which unites all our experiences into one while at the same time they dont really give a fuck either way, about the reality, how things truly were, whether you were baldy or had a head like Samson and Delilah. You dont need this kind of thing even when it's genuine and this definitely wasnt genuine. Plus these days I find it difficult getting enthusiastic when I meet old acquaintances. I dont know what it is, I just seem unable to connect properly, I can never smile at the proper places – it's like a permanent condition of being browned off with life. And no wonder either, when you come to think about it, with cunts like this always interfering.

Soon the pair of them had started dragging me round the place. They led me to a display table where they picked up a huge big tome. And landed it on my forearms. I couldnt believe it. It was like an absentminded fit of idiocy. I tried to snatch a glance at the title but they led me off immediately, him propelling me by the shoulder. They started lifting other books from here and there, piling them on top of the first one at a fierce rate with this crazy fucker Alan insisting I dont say a word and each time I tried to he did this stupid finger-into-the-ears routine with big laughs at his missis, it was like a nightmare, me wondering if I was about to wake up or what. I gaped at him, unable to open my mouth for a couple of seconds. I managed to speak at last. I dont know what you're fucking playing at, I said, but one thing I do know, I dont fucking want them.

Ah come on! he laughed.

What ye talking about come on?

They'll be good for your home study.

My home study?

You need them, said Sheila.

Do I fuck need them what you talking about? Then I managed to spot a couple of their titles and it looked as if they were naval histories. Naval histories! I said, trying to keep my voice down, What you giving me them for? You think I'm a fucking naval historian? I mean look at this! For christ sake! RECOLLECTIONS OF A FIRST LORD OF THE ADMIRALTY. What would I want to read that for! And look at this yin . . .

It was MISTER MIDSHIPMAN EASY. In the name of god, I mind my auld man and my big brother reading that when I was about five fucking years of age. And then I almost collapsed. What's this! I said, trying to keep my voice down. It was two more books they were trying to land me with: big glossy efforts. Hollywood movie-star photographs. What the fuck's going on! I said, this is definitely a nightmare. Katharine Hepburn and Humphrey Bogart. What yous up to?

Sheila replied, We're no up to nothing.

Aye yous're bloody up to something alright.

Alan sighed in an exaggeratedly amused way; as if we had always been great mates and he understood me from top to bottom. You're a failed scholar, he said, a failed trades-union organiser, plus you're a failed socialist.

Dont be fucking cheeky.

More important, he said, you're skint, and we know you're skint. We bumped into Willie Donnelly yesterday morning and he told us.

Willie Donnelly told you . . .

And anyway James, Sheila was saying, if that lassie who works behind the counter knows what ye do for a hobby, she'll give you a good discount.

What d'ye mean what I do for a hobby, what ye talking about now?

Are ye no still writing your wee stories with a working-class theme?

My wee stories with a working-class theme . . . Do you mean my plays?

I thought it was wee stories.

Well you thought wrong cause it's plays, and it's fucking realism I'm into as well if it makes any difference.

It'll no matter, said Alan with a wink. As long as she knows ye write something plus if you give her a nice smile.

Do you know who you're talking about, I said, you're talking about Sharon! Sharon . . . I glanced quickly across at the counter to see if she had heard. Lovely Sharon! Beautiful lovely Sharon who wears that tight black T-shirt!

Fucking joke man you're crazy, the pair of yous. I stared at him: You must be a headcase, and I'm no kidding ye. That's Sharon you're talking about. A nice smile! What do ye think this is at all a fucking charity shop man this is a fucking classy bookstore and she's a fucking classy woman. Christ! A nice smile! Give her a nice smile! A lovely lassie like that! Look, in the first place I dont want the bloody things. There isni a second place.

Rubbish, says Sheila, who are ye trying to kid? Then she smiled at Alan: He thinks we dont know!

Alan grinned. And he added, So that's okay then James . . .

Okay? It's not fucking okay. It's not fucking okay at all. Come on, take these fucking books out my arms and let me go. Christ almighty yous've landed me with at least fifteen here so it's going to cost a bloody small fortune.

Aye but they're a surprise, said Alan, plus you'll like them. I know you'll like them, because you always did.

I always did?

You were aye the same, back when we were weans the gether.

You're actually mixing me up with somebody else I think. Unless you're just trying to annoy me.

He's no trying to annoy you at all, said Sheila, poking me on the side of the arm, and I had to step forward to balance the books and stop them falling:

Heh watch it, I said, careful.

Well he's no trying to annoy you.

That's a matter of bloody opinion because I think he is. And

I dont know either how you wanted to butt in there and poke me Sheila because it's no got fuck all to do with you there, that last sentence, the statement I made to him because if it had been intended for you I would've fucking done it like that, I would've addressed myself like that, to you I mean.

Sheila grinned. You've definitely no changed!

I stared at her. I've totally changed. Totally. I kept on staring at her because one of these funny wee mental things had happened in my nut where the word totally was sounding like it had changed its meaning or something and if I had been working at the typewriter I'd have probably knocked over the fucking Tipp-Ex bottle – and what was the name of the guy that sang the 'I Belong To Glasgow' song? Because for some reason this is what I wanted to know at that precise moment. Then I was speaking:

Since yous two knew me, I was saying, since yous two knew me . . .

Sheila was nodding, encouraging me to speak on.

I breathed oxygen into my lungs to get myself ordered. Not only have I went totally baldy, I says, I'm divorced. Mary chucked me in for another man.

Mary chucked you in for another man . . . said Sheila in a loud whisper. My God!

Who did she chuck you in for? asked Alan.

After a moment I told him: That eedjit McCulloch.

McCulloch! He laughed out loud then shook his head to put a check on himself. He calmed down and frowned man-to-man. James James James. But that's serious eh? And he winked to destroy any semblance of genuine sympathy.

I dont really know what ye mean, serious. And to be honest with ye, and you as well . . . I said to Sheila, I dont know how come yous are calling me James all the time; friends call me Jimmy and family call me Jim. Ye know what I'm talking about?

The pair of them looked like they were bewildered. I carried on speaking. Aside from that, being divorced and all the rest of it, I've given up all habits of the flesh; that includes alcohol, cannabis, marijuana, masturbation as well. I'm probably heading towards that strange state Charles Dickens mentions once or twice to get himself out of plotting problems, internal combustion.

Internal combustion? said Sheila.

Aye. He was a novelist but. I'm a playwright. Know what I mean, I'm involved in drama. Drama. Because according to yous pair I'm no, I'm a naval historian or some fucking thing, a compiler of Hollywood movie-star bio-pic photographs – mildly titillatory as well by the looks of these cover designs. But it's the naval histories that are the worst, I've never been interested in them in all my entire puff. And in some ways I should take it as an insult that that's what yous think of me because enormous tomes like this smack of an unhealthy fascination with the trammels of empire building and as you were so ready to point out a minute ago Alan, my concerns have aye been communistic at the very right of it, to put it fucking mildly.

Alan smiled. Ye aye had a good sense of humour as well.

Did I?

Aye.

You could've fooled me.

Well it must've been somebody else then.

Exactly.

Somebody awful like you.

Aye. Maybe the guy that saved up books on naval history for a hobby. And I stared at him so he knew I was not kidding. Behind him I could see Mr Moir who managed the bookshop gazing along at us. This was all I needed, my credibility destroyed completely. Look, I said, I would be grateful if yous took all these books out my arms and I'll help yous return them to their proper places. Honest, this is like a bad dream.

I leaned closer to them both and whispered, It's my favourite bookshop. I sometimes get reductions . . . Aye, you're right, the lassie at the desk does know that I write plays. I think she does honestly like me although I daresay she probably just expects me to die young or something and it's romantic, like what she expects out of literature due to the influence of some totally fucking crazed teacher of English. She waits till Mister Moir goes off somewhere else and then I go up and get my purchases weighed in at maybe 33 and a third off.

Jammy bastard! whispered Alan. I knew that was how it'd be. You were exactly the same when you worked on the buses, that wee bird you were shagging over in Gartcraig Garage, mind?

I gaped at him.

I hate that word, Sheila was saying with her eyes closed, it's really ugly.

I looked at her. Come on, my fucking arms are falling off. Get these fucking books off or else I'll have sprained wrists – my tendons have been inflamed for years, fucking tynosinovitis.

Having sex with I meant to say . . . said Alan to Sheila, Sorry love . . . then he winked at me.

Everybody knew! said Sheila, smiling. When yous waited in the office for the last staff bus and then never sat the gether, and then yous aye got off two stops separate as if we didni know yous were going to run into a close as soon as our backs were turned and the bus was out of sight!

Randy buggers! winked Alan.

And then Sheila started that laugh she did – she was famous for it – a hoo a hoo a hoo, a hoo hoo hoo; that was the way she laughed, it would have drove you fucking potty.

Yous two are crazed eedjits, I said, that wee so-called bird you're blethering about me shagging was Mary, the woman herself, her that walked out on me for this dirty evil bastard that she walked out on me for and I'm not a guy to go over the top, if you ever knew me at all you must at least credit me with that. And if her brothers get me I'm a dead man.

Her brothers . . . ?

Her brothers, aye.

Ye talking about McCulloch? said Alan.

What? I'm talking about Mary, my Mary, my fucking ex-wife – scabby bastard. Her team of brothers, I said, they've been after me for fucking weeks.

Aw her brothers . . . Alan nodded, then frowned for a moment: Did they used to play for Brigton Garage?

Back in the bygone days, aye.

Dont start talking football, muttered Sheila.

Alan was watching me. If it's the same ones I think it is then you're in trouble.

Thanks.

Naw but I mean it, fucking bruisers they are, bad news.

Bad news, I know they're bad news, they're evil bastards, that's what I'm saying. Christ almighty. And if I didni know I was so fucking paranoiac I would think yous were here plying me with these enormous big tomes just to weigh me down, because ye know her brothers are outside waiting to waylay me, hiding up a fucking close or something, and I'll no be able to run.

That's no funny, said Sheila.

I stared at the two of them. I could easily convince myself this was precisely what was happening. Here they were helping Mary's brothers. It was a set-up. They were here to do me in. Bastards, I might have fucking known. Fate at last.

And I want to buy these books for you as well . . . Sheila was saying, honestly James I mean it, as a present for old times' sake. Especially if you and Mary are divorced. That's a sin. When did it happen?

I studied her without saying a word. There was something up here and my memory was trying to warn me.

Eh?

I waited before giving her an answer. Five month ago . . .

Five month ago! She shook her head. That's hard to believe.

I kept on studying her.

Hard to believe . . . she murmured, glancing at her man.

Mind you, I says, I would've thought you'd have knew already, being as how yous two were supposed to be so fucking close and all that Sheila, friends I'm talking about, you and Mary, confidantes and all that if I recollect certain parties we attended in a mutual capacity. And I'm talking about you as well Alan unless you've fucking spuriously forgot.

Listen, he said, and I'm being honest, if these headers *are* waiting outside then you'll need all the help you can get. And I do mean handers James handers. Alright? That's all I'm saying.

What?

You've got a hander, I'll hander ye.

Thanks but no thanks.

Dont be daft.

I fight my own fucking battles.

My Alan's a good fighter, said Sheila and she gave me a funny look.

I know he is. I'm just saying I fight my own battles, that's all.

Sheila's nose wrinkled: Well you aye did do didnt ye.

What's that supposed to mean? I said. But I knew fine well the one thing it did mean; Sheila didni like me and probably never had liked me. She probably thought I had been a bad influence on Mary, because aye, the more I came to think about it, these two had definitely been close – whisper whisper whisper! Thick as fucking thieves was a better way of describing it.

Sheila was talking. And then she stopped talking, right in the middle of the sentence. As if maybe Alan had gave her a signal. I tried to think what it was she had said but I couldnt. The next thing Alan says: Come on and we'll get you some more books James, especially now if this wife of mine's going to be doing the buying. Ye know what like she is with money!

Naw, I said, no way, leave me alone, I want nothing to do with this.

The pair of them stared at me.

Cut it out, I says, whispering, and I glanced from them to the cashier's desk and then to the exit, wondering if I could make a quick dash for freedom, beause there was definitely something no right about this. But there was Mr Moir watching me with a funny look on his countenance so I had to speak just to be seen to be acting naturally. I'm finished with all that personal stuff, I says to Sheila, trying to give her a smile but failing: I'm finished with it, women, yous just do my fucking nut in, I just canni work yous out at all.

Heh steady on, says Alan.

Steady on nothing, I says.

You're a bad-tempered so and so, muttered Sheila, no wonder Mary left you for Tommy McCulloch.

Ha ha ha, I said. And Sheila gave me such a look I thought for a minute she was going to wallop me one so I stepped back. Right that's enough, I said, that's just bloody fucking enough! I turned and strode straight along to the cashier's desk – I had just seen Mr Moir go into the back of the shop which meant I had a moment's breathing space. I gave Sharon a quick smile to let her know I needed urgent assistance.

What's up Jimmy? she whispered.

A pair of crackpots out of my past, wanting to dump this huge pile of books onto me – here, help me get them onto the table eh? Naval histories, look, unbefuckinglievable!

But Sharon stopped in her tracks. They had come up from behind me and I felt this hand clamp down on my shoulder like to about-turn me again and I jerked out from under it and turned to face them: Any more from yous two and I'll call the polis!

We are the polis, says Sheila.

What?

You heard, says Alan.

What?

And we could do you for breach if we wanted, but lucky for you we're off-duty and we canni be bothered.

And he was looking straight at me, contempt written all over his face. And here it was all now fitting in. Folk like you give us a pain in the neck, he was saying, we try to do you a favour for old times' sake and look what happens.

That's right, went on Sheila, because you used to be married to my pal when we all shared the same uniform. Whereas the truth is you were aye a bad-tempered wee bastard – you and your bloody union.

Is he giving you any trouble officer? said a voice – Mr Moir it was, coming out from the back shop.

You could say that.

We've had our eye on him for a while, he says, is that right Sharon?

Sharon kept her head lowered and muttered something that wasnt intelligible to me and her face went red because she was involved in dishonest company.

Is that right Sharon? says Moir again with an insinuating voice.

Dont be feart of *him* hen, said Sheila indicating me.

I'm not feart of him.

He's just a wee bully.

He always was, said Alan, even when we were weans the gether in the Boy's Brigade – until he got done for shoplifting.

Well that's a lie for a start, I said, because not only have I never got done for shoplifting, I was never even a bloody protestant and you've got to be a bloody protestant to get into them, else they turn ye down, they dont let you over the door. And I gave a quick smile to Sharon, letting her see I knew she was trying to be on my side and if she wasnt allowed to because of the situation then it was fine, it was fine, and I wouldnt think any the less of her. My da brought me up a good socialist, I said.

Sharon gave me a quick smile back and I knew I had figured her out correctly; she was a great lassie and would always stand by me.

That's the truth, I told her, we used to sing the Red Flag

morning noon and night. Our house was full of books. Piles and piles of them, economic histories, political biographies, the lot.

Rubbish, said Alan.

Rubbish! What do you mean rubbish! I'm fucking telling ye the way it was.

Less of the language, replied Sheila.

Well you're bloody upsetting me. I dont know what the hell's going on, unless these crazed eedjit brothers of my ex-wife have fucking bribed you to find me.

Your mouth needs soapy water, said Alan.

Put the books down on the counter, cried Mr Moir.

With great pleasure, I says, with very great pleasure. But I didnt; I whispered to Sharon instead: This is so bad, I says, it's just so bad. I want you to be my witness to what's happening. I was in this shop minding my own business – I wasni even inside it I was outside it! – and then this pair waylaid me.

Waylaid ye, says Alan, who the hell waylaid ye?

You did, the two of yous.

Did we hell.

Well what's this then? I said, pointing at the pile of books. What did you pile me up with them for except to slow me down or something?

Instead of replying the two of them shook their heads, and Alan gave a weary smile at both Sharon and Mr Moir. What I find so upsetting, he said, is that me and him used to be mates.

Once upon a time, I added. Like all good fairy tales it came to an abrupt end.

What do you know about fairy tales, said Sheila, these wee stories you write are all cheap thrills and sex.

That's no true, I said to Sharon, she's just lying.

You calling my wife a liar? said Alan.

The facts speak for themself.

The facts speak for themselves! That's a good yin. What do you know about facts?

More than you.

Ha ha.

Aye I know ha ha, I says.

That's because you're a joke, replied Alan and it made his wife burst out laughing. He winked at her.

Some man you are, I said.

I know, a man and a half.

You make me want to boke, I said, but I was playing for time, looking to find a way out of what was going on. Sharon was gazing at me. I've always loved you Sharon was what I thought but couldnt get it verbalised, probably because if I had I would have compromised her and I didnt want to do that. She was a brilliant lassie. Then a thought: if I flipped the books up into the air there was a chance I could make it to the door. But they were watching me carefully for just such a move – especially Sheila; it seemed like she was the brains behind the squad. When I knew her she was dangerous as well; in fact it occurred to me that she had always been out to get me, right from the kick-off back in the old days. A crazy idea was beginning to dawn on me: maybe she had fancied me and it had turned to hatred, maybe because I had fell for Mary she had set out to get me, and she had started by poisoning my marriage. And if that was the case then this whole business was just hair-raising. I looked at Sharon. She was the one voice of reason. Yet there standing next to her was Moir, the guy that ran the fucking place. What a smug bastard he was. I had always thought that. Even the way he scanned the books I bought whenever I was unlucky enough to get served by him, it was like he was casting judgements. I stole another glance at Sharon, if I could somehow get her to realise what I was going to try, if somehow she could realise what it was and could maybe create a diversion. That tight black T-shirt too, she always wore it and it was like she had forgot to stick a bra on first thing every morning the way her nipples poked out it was hard to even think what you were buying sometimes, she just rang up the till, gave you the receipt and waited for the dough, it was just too much, too much:

You come with us, muttered Sheila, taking me by the shoulder, and I had to go with them, my forearms cramped under the weight.

That thread

After the pause came the other pause and it was the way they have of following each other the next one already in its place as if the sequence was arranged according to some design or other, and set not just by the first but them all, a networked silence. It was that way when she entered the room. The noise having ceased right enough but even allowing for that if it hadnt it would have – which is usually always the case. She had the looks to attract, a figure exactly so, her sensuousness in all the moves so that her being there in this objectified way, the sense of a thousand eyes. Enter softly enter softly: it was like a song he was singing, and her smile brief, yet bravado as well, that style some women have especially, the face, the self-consciousness; and all of them being there and confronting her while her just there taking it, standing there, one arm down, her fingers bent, brushing the hem of her skirt. She was not worried by virtue of him, the darkness of the room, any of it. Like a sure knowledge of her own disinterest, his non-existence as a sexual being, in relation to her, and he grinned, reaching for the whisky and pouring himself one, adding a half again of water, the whisky not being a good one. She was still standing there, as if dubiously. She was seeking out faces she recognised and his was one that she did recognise, lo, but would barely acknowledge, she would never acknowledge. Had he been the only face to recognise; the only one. Even that. He smiled then the sudden shift out from his side jacket pocket with the lighter and snap, the flare in the gloom, the thin exhalation of blue smoke; he sipped at the whisky and water, for his face would definitely have had to be recognised now, from the activity, no matter how softly, softly and quietly, no matter how he had contrived it. Now his elation was so fucking strong, so fucking vivid man, and striking, and so entirely fucking wonderful he wanted to scream he had to scream he really did have to he had to scream he would have to he wouldnt be able to fucking stop himself he was shaking he was shaking the cuff of his sleeve, the cuff of his sleeve, trailing on the surface of the table, his hand shaking, shaking, now twitching and his breath coming deep, and she would have sensed it, sensed it all, and she would be smiling so slightly around the corners of her mouth, the down there, her thick lower lip how round it was, how round it was and mystifying, to describe it as provocative was an actual error, an error, a mistake. But the hesitancy in her movement. That thread having been long flung out now, though still exploratory, but ensnaring, it was ensnaring, causing her to hold there, so unmistakeably hesitant now rubbing her shoulder just so self-aware yet in that kind of fashion a woman has of rubbing her shoulder at the slightest sensory indication of the thread, feeling it cling, that quiver and he shivered, raising the whisky to his mouth and sipping it, keeping his elbow hard in to the side of his body, keeping it firmly there because that sickness in the pit of his belly and the blood coursing through his cheeks, and burning, burning, everyone seeing and knowing, he was so transparent, so transparent, she just shook her head. What was she going to do? She just had shaken her head that most brief way, and she turned on her heel and she left, left him there. He couldnt move. He would cry out. But his face was controlled, so controlled, although the colour now drained from his cheeks, or else the opposite, was it the opposite? and his hand now shaking, the cigarette lighter on the coffee table.

From the Window

He lifted his grandson from the floor and sat him on his knee; he rocked him back and forth, pulling funny faces, but when the wee boy started wriggling about he returned him to the carpet and glanced across to where his daughter Isobel was sitting: Fancy another cup of tea hen?

Do you?

Well I'm asking you.

Isobel shrugged but she rose from the couch. I'll get you one.

Naw you'll no. I dont want one, I was just wanting to know if you did. However, if you are passing the kitchen, I'll take a can of beer . . . He grinned. There's a couple in the fridge.

Tch dad!

When she brought it to him he pulled off the stopper and drank from it straight off. She said, You'll poison yourself, it's all dirty round the rim.

Ah! He wiped his mouth.

Anyway you shouldni be drinking at this time of the day, no at your age.

What ye talking about, it's one o'clock in the afternoon!

You're too auld for it.

I'm fifty-three, give me a break – you'd think I was a pensioner to hear you . . . He swigged another mouthful then raised his eyebrows: After last night's performance but maybe you're right – see the head I had on me when I woke up this morning!

I've got no sympathy for you.

He smiled.

I'm serious dad.

Ach I'm no as bad into it these days as you think.

Are you no . . . ?

Naw.

She nodded.

Honest, he said, last night as well never mind it being a Friday, I was staying in with all the best of intentions – no kidding ye. Me and your mother in front of the telly and all that then a bang at the door. Frank Smith and Big McArdle, so I says aye okay. First time I've been out for weeks. Your mother didni mind me going.

Isobel did not reply, and he paused, then shook his head: Unfortunately I dont even remember getting home.

That kind of drinking isni good for you.

I dont need you to tell me that hen.

Aye well ye shouldni keep on doing it then. You're just destroying yourself physically.

Thanks.

Ye are but dad.

Thanks.

Ye've got to face facts.

No doubt you'll remind me if I ever forget them.

Well somebody's got to.

That's your mother's job Isobel no yours.

Aye but she'll no approach ye about it so it's left to me.

How do you know what she approaches me about? You dont, you dont know. So dont think ye do.

Isobel reached for her cigarettes and lighted one. Her father was making a point of watching her do it. She ignored him. She blew out the match and laid it in the ashtray. Then he muttered:

Aye you've got a cheek to talk about anybody with all that smoking ye do. High time ye gave it up my girl, for the wee boy's sake if no your own.

She made no response.

D'ye hear me?

I hear ye, yes, I do, I hear ye. She looked at her wristwatch, then at the window. I wonder how long's she going to be ... She's awful late.

Och I've seen her later than this. He smiled slightly, reached to clap his grandson on the head and he sniffed quite loudly, jerking his thumb at the wee boy: Is he smelly?

I dont think so.

Mmm ... Her father pursed his lips, wiped his mouth; he gazed into the fireplace for a spell, before glancing suddenly across at her: So what happened to all that stuff they tried to pap down your throat at Sunday School?

Pardon?

You know what I'm talking about.

Naw I dont, I dont.

He sighed and raised the beer can to his lips, but he didnt drink from it. He stared at the baby, he shrugged eventually. I just like the notion of weans getting baptised.

Aw, so it's that again, christenings.

Naw but I do, I just like the notion.

Dad I dont want to go through all this again.

Dont get me wrong hen I'm just talking about the actual notion itself.

She held the cigarette to her mouth; she puffed twice, not inhaling the smoke, dispersing the cloud with her left hand.

It's like it's a kind of initiation into the human race ... He gestured at the wee boy but before he could continue speaking she muttered:

I dont know what ye mean by that.

Naw hen look, if we just stop and study this wee thing here, just for a minute; what we see is it's neither one thing nor the other, a set of responses and reactions just, that's all it is, give it some grub and it dirties its nappy, dont give it some grub and it greets.

So?

So. He shrugged.

Tch! She shook her head and inhaled, blew the smoke at the ceiling.

Ye dont like me speaking like that . . . ?

I dont care if ye speak like that or no, but he's more than just what you're calling him, a set of responses and reactions – as if he was a machine. Babies areni machines.

Ye could've fooled me!

Seriously dad.

He chuckled. You're too sensitive.

She glanced at her watch.

Ye are.

Oh well, it must run in the family.

He grinned.

I dont mean you, you're like a bear in a china shop! She rose from the seat and walked to the window, taking the ashtray with her.

He watched her as she stood gazing down the two storeys to the street. After a pause he said, Ye know something, you were a smelly wean when you were wee, ye wereni potty-trained till ye were going on five years of age! I'm no kidding ye, it was the talk of the street.

Thanks dad . . . She tapped ash into the ashtray.

The Green Lady thought ye had congenital diarrhoea!

Dont be disgusting.

Her father laughed. So dont get on your high horse, that's all I'm saying.

Isobel shook her head.

Several moments passed. Then he said, It's actually just your mother I'm thinking of.

Dad . . .

Naw but I am.

I just dont want to be a hypocrite, she said, turning to face him.

But ye wouldni be being a hypocrite ye would just be being a mother, and a daughter. Isobel I mean look hen dont get me wrong on this, I couldni care one way or the other – even although I says that about the basic notion of the thing, I dont really care, no really. He shifted on his seat, shaking his head: And as far as the church goes . . . ye know me better than that, when it comes to the church and hypocrites, it's just like Rabbie Burns said it was. He paused, gazing at her. It's your mother I'm thinking about.

Isobel sighed.

It is, it's no me.

Dad, I just wish you wouldni go on about it.

Ho – I didni know that's what I was doing!

We've done enough talking on the subject.

He nodded, studying the label on the beer can. He said: It's just with you being on your own now, I mean, it was his idea – about no getting the wean baptised – in the first place; when it was born I'm talking about, it was his idea, no yours.

Dad, it doesni matter whose idea it was, mine or his; it doesni matter. I'm just no getting it baptised and that's that.

Fair enough, it just strikes me as a wee bit selfish.

She stubbed out the cigarette.

I dont mean selfish . . .

She stared at him for a moment, then leant her elbows on the window-sill and gave her attention to the street below.

Eventually he called: By the way hen, did I tell ye, they're trying to get me to stand for re-election again. I telt them naw but they'll no listen.

Oh well you've just got to insist.

I know. I'm gonni. Cause I just dont have time. Me and your mother are supposed to be doing up the house at the end of April. She's wanting the front room wallpapered and she's talking about getting new points put in as well! So I mean we'll be upside down here, I'll no have time for anything hardly.

When is it?

What?

The election.

Five weeks.

You'll just have to tell them then wont ye.

I'm going to. I mean God love us it's high time some of these young yins got into the act. They need a good bloody shake-up. See when I was that age! I mean ye had to go cloak-and-dagger ye know, even just to pay your dues. If the management found out you were in the union you would've been out the bloody door, pronto. No negotiating table then ye know. They'd have bloody shot us if they could've got away with it!

Isobel made no answer. She was still peering out the window.

Honest hen they would've. That's what like they were. I'm talking about back when I started out in the job, when some of us were trying to get things organised. He continued gazing at her; he raised the can of export to his mouth and after a pause he drank from it. He dried his lips on the cuff of his shirt-sleeve, and frowned at her: You listening?

Yeh.

Ye sure? He smiled.

Och dad I was just away thinking.

He nodded.

Och . . . I was just remembering Saturday mornings. I used to hate them. She smiled.

You used to hate them?

Isobel turned to him. Because I always used to think something bad had happened to mum, an accident, I could never stop myself thinking about it and it was awful because I would think too that just me thinking about it might make it happen. Tempting fate, ye know. And she was going to get taken into hospital. On her way back from town with the messages, her with all these enormous shopping bags. I was always expecting to hear the siren and then the ambulance would come hurtling round the corner, bringing her in it . . . Isobel looked at him and smiled. I mean when I was wee dad.

Oh aye.

That corner of the street along there, when you stare and stare and stare, if you're waiting for somebody . . .

Isobel turned away from her father. He could only see the back of her head. He glanced at the baby who had managed to get the ornamental brass poker from where it was kept by the side of the tiled fireplace. He stared down at him for a few moments, then shrugged, When you're wee . . .

Isobel said: I used to watch out for you as well. Especially on Tuesdays and Thursdays when you were working late.

I mind that . . . aye.

She stared out the window.

Listen hen dont get me wrong, I worry like hell about your mother as well but I know she'll be here sooner or later I mean tempting fate like ye says, I think you're better just showing a wee bit of patience, a wee bit of patience. He gestured with the beer can: Come away from the window.

She turned her head sharply, but did as she was told. She got her handbag from where she had left it beneath the coffee table and she snapped it open, took out her cigarettes.

Her father sniffed. Ye angry?

No dad, I'm no angry; I just wish you would remember I'm an adult sometimes.

He nodded. Sorry.

Putting the cigarette packet down on the table she quickly took the poker from the boy's hands, she lifted him upwards, chuckling, her eyes closed, gently rubbing her forehead in his face; and she sat down on the couch, sitting him on her lap. Her gaze went to the table and the cigarette packet.

Want your fags? he said.

No.

Ye sure?

Yeh.

Ye still angry?

No.

Good.

She sighed. I'm just a bit worried.

There's no need to be. There isni. You know your mother, she'll have met somebody. She'll be gabbing away. She'll have forgot the time. Ye know the way she goes hen I mean sometimes I'm feart to let her out the house in case she canni find her way home again! He chuckled, then he groaned. That's me making it worse eh!

She looked at him. His forehead had creased as if he was anticipating a smile from her; she smiled.

Sarah Crosbie

The big house was standing empty for years before she came back. She came from America. But according to the newspaperman she had owned the house long long before. The big house stood at the end of the street, less than a hundred yards from the river. There was not much the people in the street could tell him. The old woman never spoke to them at all. She had always lived alone surrounded by cats and dogs. *Sarah Crosbie*. It turned out that the house had been there about two hundred years. This bit of the river had been a ford at one time. The foundations were much older than the rest of the building. Somebody called Rankine had rebuilt it and the date 1733 was discovered above a side door at the back. This Rankine was famous. The newspaperman was looking for people called Rankine to see if they were related. He thought the old woman might have been a descendant. But nobody knew. People kept away from the big house. If a neighbour or somebody ever had to go to her door she always kept them waiting on the front step. When the McDonnell Murders were going on back in the '20s a group of locals barged their way inside the big house door. They found a body behind a bricked-up chimney-piece down in the basement. A man's body, dead for many years. Nobody knew a thing about it and neither did the old woman. She had not been in the place long at the time. The police thought he might have died from natural causes and judging by the tatters of clothes he could have been a building worker or something.

When she went into hospital the newspaperman tried to gain

entrance to the big house but he was refused on certain grounds. Workmen arrived the next day and they barred the place up.

It was eighteen months ago she turned up at the police office. She was in a bad state. She told them people were in her house, they had done things to her. But she would not say what things. Policemen returned to the big house with her but saw nothing suspicious. Next day a health-visitor called on her and she was admitted later on to the geriatric ward at Gartnavel Royal. A few women from the street took a bunch of flowers up to her but she just stared at the ceiling for the whole visiting hour. And it was after this the newspaperman began coming around. He goes to see her in hospital as well once or twice.

That's where I'm at

Then there's that other case. I'm talking about the hopeless one we can all get into at some stage or another. Usually it's with a pal we've had for years, when he's pissed drunk and you're no; and you notice everybody's all staring, they're staring at the two of yous. It's when that happens the bother starts and things get quite interesting. You get the boost. It's exciting, it's the excitement, the heart starting to go and it affecting the whole body; you feel the shoulders going and if you're a smoker you're taking the wee quick puffs on the fag, sometimes no even blowing out the smoke, just taking the next yins rapid, keeping it buried deep down, letting it out in dribs and drabs, a wee tait at a time. It's because you're trying to occupy yourself. You're no wanting to seem too involved otherwise it all starts too quick; you want to calm things down, because you know what like you are. That's how as well that you can try and kid on you're no aware of what's happening. When it's a betting shop you're in you act as if you're totally engrossed in the form for the next race. If it's a pub you stare up at the telly. The broo, well ye just stare maybe at the clock or something. But all the time you're keeping that one eye peeled, watching your pal, if he's making a cunt of himself and getting folk upset. Bastards. You're just waiting, trying no to notice, trying to concentrate on other things. Fucking useless but you know it's going to happen; there's nothing you can do about it. Sometimes the waiting doesni even last that long. You're so wound up ready to go you just burst out and fucking dig up some poor cunt who's probably no even been involved in the fucking first place! And you're at him ranting and raving:

You ya fucking snidey bastard ye what's the fucking game at all?

And he's all fucking taken aback: What d'you mean, he says.

Dont fucking give us it, you says.

But I'm no doing fuck all.

Ya lying bastard ye you're fucking on at my mate there you're fucking out of order.

What? he says.

And you start shouting: If ye fucking used your fucking eyes you'd see he was drunk ya bastard!

What! What d'you mean!! I'm just standing here having a pint minding my own business.

Minding your own business fuck all, you shout at him. And the poor cunt now can hardly speak a word cause he's bloody feart, he doesni know what you're going to do, if you're going to fucking batter him. And he looks about the boozer for support, for somebody that knows him to defend him maybe. But nobody does. They dont actually know what happened. They never saw fuck all and dont really want to get involved. They're no really that interested anyhow, when it comes down to it, especially if it's the betting shop it's happening in because they're just waiting for the *going behind* call so's they can rush over and make their bets. In fact they're probably just watching what's happening to pass the time. There again but some of them will be interested, they maybe know the bloke you're digging up. They might even be the guy's mucker for all you know! But you're no caring. You dont actually give a fuck. It could even make things better. What also happens with me at a certain point is how I suddenly step out my skin and I can look down at myself standing there. Only for a split second though, then I'm back inside again and so fucking wound up I dont notice a single thing, nothing. I wouldnt even notice myself, if I was standing there and I actually was two people. One time I turned round and gubbed a polis right on the mouth. I didnt even fucking notice he was there. He tapped me on the shoulder and I just turned round and fucking belted him one, right on the fucking kisser man and he dropped, out like a light, so I just gets off my mark immediately, out the door and away like the clappers, and poor auld Fergie – that was my mate – he wound up getting huckled; and what a beating he got off the polis once they got him into the station! Poor bastard. But that's where I'm at, that kind of thing, the way it seems to happen to me. It never used to. Or did it? Maybe it did and I just didni notice because I was young and foolish and a headstrong bastard whereas now I'm auld and grey.

the Hon

Auld Shug gits oot iv bed. Turns aff the alarm cloak. Gis straight ben the toilit. Sits doon in that oan the lavatri pan. Wee bit iv time gis by. Shug sittin ther, yonin. This Hon. Up it comes oot fri the waste pipe. Stretchis right up. Grabs him by the bolls.

Jesis christ shouts the Shug filla.

The Hon gis slack in a coupla minits. Up jumps Shug. Straight ben the kitchin hodin onti the pyjama troosirs in that jist aboot collapsin inti his cher.

Never know the minit he was sayin. Eh. Jesis christ.

Looks up at the cloak oan the mantelpiece. Eftir seven. Time he was away tae his work. Couldni move bit. Shatird. Jist sits ther in the cher.

Fuck it he says Am no gon.

Coupla oors gis by. In comes the wife an that ti stick oan a kettle. Sees the auld yin sittin ther. Well past time. Day's wages oot the windi.

Goodnis sake Shug she shouts yir offi late.

Pokes him in the chist. Kneels doon oan the fler. He isni movin. Nay signs a taw. Pokes him ance mer. Still nothin bit. Then she sees he's deid. Faints. Right nix ti the Shug filla's feet. Lyin ther. The two iv them. Wan in the cher in wan in the fler. A hof oor later a chap it the door. Nay answer. Nother chap. Sound iv a key in the door. Door shuts. In comes the lassie. Eywis comes roon fir a blether wi the maw in that whin the auld yin's oot it his work. Merrit hersel. Man's a bad yin but. Cunt's never worked a day in his life. Six weans tay. Whin she sees thim ther she twigs right away.

My goad she shouts thir deid. Ma maw in ma da ir deid.

She bens doon ti make sure.

O thank goad she says ma maw's jist faintit. Bit da. Da's deid. O naw. Ma da's deid. Goad love us.

Unlucky

It was early evening when Lecky came along the road, already dark; the chip van was parked across by the chapel, puffs of blue smoke drifting up from its funnel. He joined the queue. The van was a converted single-decker bus; as somebody made an exit the others waiting moved up one by one onto the old platform. He bought two single cigarettes and tapped a match from a boy he knew standing behind him in the queue. When he struck the match along the metal floor the young woman working the friers frowned at him, so did a couple of the other customers. Outside on the pavement he exhaled a mouthful of smoke then took another long drag, keeping the smoke in his lungs, letting it out through his nostrils. His belly didnt feel good but being out in the breeze and away from the fumes in the van made him feel better. He smoked about a third of the fag before nipping it, and continued along and up the steep hill. When he passed the gable end of a building some drops of water landed on his face. If it was actually going to rain, that would be good; he felt like it raining because of the freshness. There was plenty of cloud about – the moon hidden and a redness making it a bit supernatural till you realised what it was, a reflection, the lights of the city.

It took twenty minutes to reach John's close. He walked up the stairs to the top storey, flapped the letter-box on John's door. There came an immediate thumping from inside and the door came swinging open, a wee lassie hanging onto its handle with both hands, one sock on and one sock off, her toes wedged into the crevice at the top of the bottom panel. She continued to hang there, the door creaking on its hinges. She shouted: Daddy.

Behind her a boy stood staring, he held something clutched to his mouth, a toy or something. Then John was there: Give us a minute, he said, showing Lecky into the kitchen.

I thought I was going to be late.

Nah you're okay.

John's wife was sitting on one side of the settee holding a teacup against her cheek. A baby lay beside her not wearing anything except a big cotton nappy, a dummy tit in its mouth. But it was awake and its eyes were taking note of what was happening. Lecky shifted his stance a little so that he was facing the television.

Minutes passed. John's wife reached up to the mantelpiece and extracted a cigarette from the packet there. A comedy show was on and something happened which got her smiling. She said to Lecky, Do you ever watch this?

Aye, sometimes.

It can be quite funny.

He nodded. He put his hands into his jerkin pockets. The door opened while she was replacing the box of matches onto the mantelpiece. John peered in. Then he came to the fireplace and got himself a cigarette. He stood smoking for a time gazing at the television. When he moved to leave his wife said, Will you be late?

Nah, doubt it.

Lecky walked ahead of him down to the front door. The two children came out of the bedroom to watch. Time yous were in bed, said John.

The two of them stared at Lecky. He opened the door and stepped onto the landing. John paused a moment behind, he closed over the door; I'll no be a minute, he said.

Lecky nodded, leaned his elbows on the banister, gazing down to the next landing.

There were two other doors on this top storey; one was boarded up and without a nameplate. Smudges of paint and whitewash covered the walls; a lot of initials had been scratched or pencilled in. Lecky was deciphering some when the door opened and John reappeared. Needed a slash, he said. He winked and jerked his thumb at the boarded-up door: You and your woman no looking for a pad yet?

Eh . . . Lecky grinned, scratched the side of his head.

John laughed. Aye well you dont want that yin man the roof's liable to cave in any moment. He slapped Lecky on the shoulder as they walked downstairs, gestured back up at the other door. That yin's empty as well but. Get in and squat!

Lecky chuckled.

They continued down. At the foot of the close John told him to wait while he went through and out the back.

There was a terrible smell of cats' piss about the place. Lecky strolled to the front close and poked his head out. It still wasnt raining.

Then John's footsteps. Heh Lecky . . . John winked and tugged back the right sleeve of his anorak; he was holding two circular steel bars about half-an-inch in diameter; their ends nestled inside the palm of his right hand. I've had them planked in the fucking didgie all week, he said, fucking midden men – I was worried in case they found them.

Lecky grinned.

Did you mind the busfare?

Aye, the auld man.

For me and all?

Aye, I knew you'd be skint – as usual! Lecky laughed and dodged off when John tried to land a punch on his chin. As they started walking he turned the collar of his jerkin up and gave an exaggerated shiver: Fucking freezing!

It's your nerves!

My nerves . . . !

Aye your nerves ya cunt ye.

So? Lecky grinned after a moment. Doesni mean I'm no cauld. What about you? Trying to say you've no got any!

Who me? Ye kidding? I've just been for a shite twelve times since I ate my supper.

Lecky laughed but it sounded too abrupt. He shivered again, rubbed his hands together with a smack, his shoulders hunching. They crossed over the brow of the hill and turned the corner, and could see the lights of a double-decker bus stationed away below at the terminus. John yelled: Ya bastard! And they raced off down the slope.

The guy they were meeting was waiting in a pub near the Saltmarket. He was older than John, he looked nearly thirty, he had a moustache drooping at the corners. The two of them used to work in the same bottling factory a while back. His name was Ray. He had an almost-full pint of lager sitting in front of him. John made the introductions then started in on a yarn about this bloke who drove a forklift and smoked dope all the time. But Ray interrupted him by gesturing at Lecky: Did you fill the boy in?

John paused. Aye, he said.

Ye sure?

John frowned.

I've got to fucking ask, muttered Ray.

John nodded. He said to Lecky, Did I fill ye in?

Aye.

Ye know what you're doing then? asked Ray.

Aye.

Ray nodded after a moment.

Run over the details with him if ye want to fucking check, said John.

Ray frowned at him. Aw aye, in here – that would be a good idea.

John said nothing, his right hand was in his pocket. He raised his left hand to his mouth and he chewed at his thumbnail. He looked at Lecky who looked back at him, then he looked at Ray.

Ray shook his head slightly and said, I just mean there's aye some cunt with big ears John, that's all I mean . . . He sniffed: Did ye mind the equipment?

John grinned suddenly at Lecky and he nodded at the nearby wall: Nice decor in this place innit!

Lecky smiled.

Soon Ray was swallowing down the rest of his lager and was leading the way through the bar to the exit. Down the street he stopped off at a shop and bought a packet of chewing gum, unwrapped a stick and shoved it into his mouth. Then he ripped the cellophane off a ten packet of cigarettes and withdrew one, shut the packet.

Thanks mate, said John.

Ray opened it again and gave him one, and he gave one to Lecky without a word.

No chewing gum? said John.

Ray sighed and brought the packet back out.

They walked steadily, Ray always a stride or two ahead of the other pair. The place was way along east, not far from the river, a sort of minor industrial estate which had been created mainly by renovating old warehouses and other disused buildings, but there were also newer buildings, long one-storey structures. The area itself was old, the streets still part-cobbled; most of it now in total darkness.

Lecky wasnt sure what the time was; the last he had seen was the clock on the mantelpiece in John's kitchen. By now it had to be getting on for eleven o'clock, maybe after. Turning down a wee side street they continued along parallel to the main road. Three blocks on Ray halted before another corner and carried on alone. Lecky glanced at John but John stared after Ray, not making any comment. Ray stood in from the corner, gazing round it; then he waved them on, whispering just loudly enough for them both to hear: Come here and see this . . .

He was pointing to one of the one-storey structures across the other side of the street. All its lights seemed to be switched on inside. Plus there was the sound of machinery coming from it, a dull throbbing noise. It's a fucking nightshift, he whispered.

They stared across at it for several moments. Ray was shaking his head. A fucking nightshift, he muttered. Then he pointed out the building facing it, on the same side as they were now standing. It was an older building and looked like an ordinary three-storey tenement. That's our gaff there, he said, down in the basement. We're supposed to go in from the front shop above. Look, it's right across from that main entrance.

John said, Jesus Christ.

Fucking unbelievable.

Did your mate no tell ye like?

Naw Christ, he couldni have known.

Surely he could've fucking found out?

He probably didni even think about it John.

Fucking dickie.

Ray stepped away from the corner and he leant against the wall. He brought out his cigarettes and passed one to each of the other two, flicked his lighter. When they were smoking he said, It's a bastard. Anybody could come walking out and they'd see us a mile away. Even if they just looked out the fucking window.

Lecky frowned. He said, D'you mean ye didni know there was a nightshift on at all?

Ray glanced at him then glanced away.

And John replied, Naw Lecky, that's what he's saying.

Wh! Lecky shook his head: No knowing they were working a nightshift man that's mental.

Ray turned sharply to John: What's up with your mate, has he got a problem?

John sniffed, he started chewing on his left thumbnail.

Fucking mental, said Lecky.

Ray looked at him: D'ye think I'd brought yous if I'd fucking knew? Eh? Do us a favour.

Lecky didnt reply. John now walked to the corner, the cigarette cupped in his left hand. He stood peering round for a while, then he looked back and said quietly, We can still go in. Come here . . .

Both Ray and Lecky went to the corner.

There's nobody came out since we've been here, he said.

Aye but, Ray was shaking his head, Christ sake John that's no even five minutes.

Five minutes – fuck sake man that's all it takes.

I dont know.

It's all it takes.

Ray was still shaking his head.

What do you think Lecky?

I dont know.

We can definitely do it . . . John turned from the corner to inhale on his cigarette, he blew the smoke away before peering back at the one-storey building. Eh . . . ?

Eventually Ray whispered, Fucking chancy.

John continued to stare in the direction of the low building, and at the old tenement facing it. Lecky took a last drag on his fag before nipping it and sticking it into his jerkin pocket. Some more drops of water landed on his face and he squinted upwards. Fucking raining, he said.

John was frowning at Ray: Listen man I've been going about sweating for days cause of this; fucking wife and weans man they're feart to come near me.

I'm just saying it's chancy, that's aw.

Chancy! I know it's fucking chancy. John shook his head, cleared his throat and spat the spittle to the gutter. I know it's fucking chancy.

Aye well that's all I'm saying.

John looked at him, and then he was walking out from the corner and down the street across from the one-storey building.

And Ray followed immediately, the pair keeping close in to the shadows at the side of the old tenement wall. A moment later and Lecky set off at the rear, aware of a funny feeling in his legs. The other two had gone about ten yards beyond the doorway of the shop they were entering and when Lecky reached them they both waved him on to where he was to position himself, down by the corner of the street and the main road. Immediately he arrived he struck a match against the wall and got one of his nips burning, sucking the smoke deep into his lungs and trapping it there, staring to the right and to the left, and back to the right, and nothing was coming thank fuck, nothing. John was staring at him. He signalled it was okay: moments later he could hear the chinks of the steel bars, and then a really loud racket of a noise, a rattling it was, really really loud, a really really loud rattling noise. It was coming from down the way and across and he pressed himself back against the wall, sidled round the corner to the pavement on the main road; he tossed the fag into a puddle then peered back round the corner. It was actually a mechanical gate, it was getting hoisted up across in the place where the nightshift was working. A chain seemed to be hoisting the fucking thing. A big wide entrance. Inside a big lorry was getting loaded up. A couple of men doing it. They were talking away about something, their voices carrying. And the driver was in the lorry and switched on the starter, the engine revving up, the headlight beams. And then other headlight beams away in the distance of something coming on the main road, a motor car, travelling fast. Lecky kept tight into the wall. After it passed he peered round the corner again, seeing the lorry now being guided out by a big skinny guy in dungarees and specs, and if he was just to walk another twenty yards or something he would be right into the shop doorway and they wouldnt be able to hide from him. Lecky stepped back out of sight, his eyes closing but opening almost immediately – it was the last thing to do – he glanced round the corner. The lorry had turned now and the driver's head was at the window, he was exchanging words with the big skinny guy. Lecky stepped into the shadowiest bit of the wall. Soon the lorry appeared at the corner, the driver turning the wheel hand over fist, and breaking a moment to shift gear; and it was out onto the main road, picking up speed. Lecky stared after it until the red tail-lights were no longer visible. Another motor car was coming. He stayed where he was until it too had gone. When he peered back round he saw John away along at the far corner, beckoning to him. Across at the nightshift building the entrance gaped open but the workers had disappeared. Lecky stood a moment; again John beckoned: this time he went quickly, not running but trotting as quietly as he could.

Okay Lecky . . . ?

Aye – fuck. Lecky grinned: Close, eh?

Aye.

Fucking close alright, muttered Ray. Fucking lucky.

Aye.

John winked at Lecky. We're aye fucking lucky, int we?

Aye.

John was smoking. He exhaled and jerked his thumb at Ray: He wants to wrap it.

Fucking right I want to wrap it, said Ray.

How come? Lecky asked.

Cause it's fucking wild.

Lecky glanced at John, and John handed him the fag. Lecky took a couple of drags on it.

Ray shook his head. Fucking wild, he said to John.

John took the fag back from Lecky before replying: Away hame then.

Ray brushed the tip of his nose with his right thumb, he sniffed, spat out the chewing gum he had in his mouth. John started rubbing his hands together and he hunched his shoulders up and down. He said to Lecky: What about you man ye into it?

Lecky shrugged.

Eh?

I dont know.

Ye want to do it?

I dont know man.

Eh?

Lecky shrugged.

It's fucking wild, muttered Ray. He turned sideways and stared along the street; he turned back: Look John there's always fucking the morrow know what I mean . . . Why take risks.

I need the fucking dough, it'll no be there the morrow.

Ray gazed at him.

Lecky? said John.

Lecky shrugged. I'm easy.

Fuck sake . . .

Well what d'ye want me to say?

What do I want ye to say I want ye to say if you'll fucking do it, that's what I want ye to say!

Lecky looked at him.

Just fucking say it, if ye want to fucking do it, if ye dont fucking dont, dont fucking say it, ye just fucking do what ye want.

Lecky said nothing.

I mean ye make up your own fucking mind, it's your own fucking opinion, that's what fucking counts Lecky.

Lecky frowned.

Innit?

Lecky stared at him.

John shrugged. Just do what ye fucking want to do.

Lecky's mouth was dry, he swallowed saliva. I'll do it, he said.

Dont do it for me.

I'm no . . .

Ray peeled another stick of chewing gum; he gestured with it at the other two but they didnt respond. When he took out his cigarettes Lecky glanced at him and he gave him one. Ray was looking at John.

The three of them waited another few minutes but nothing arrived and nothing departed; the entrance still gaped open. Ray led the way, Lecky continuing on to his position at the corner of the main road. When he reached it and looked back the other two were out of sight. From somewhere he could hear a vague whining sound like the engine of a bus revving and straining in too low a gear, then it had died into silence.

A clank. Coming from the shop doorway. Another clank then a crash. Really fucking loud. Lecky stepped back against the wall, squinting across at the windows of the nightshift building. The faces looking! But there werent any. Nobody was there at all. Thank fuck for that.

And now silence. The two of them were inside. Lecky edged out from the corner, seeing both ways into the distance. If he did see a squad car he would fucking whistle. No he wouldnt that would be fucking mad, fucking mental, he would just stay still, he would wait, he would wait till it had passed. No he wouldnt he would whistle, he would have to, unless he just ran down, he would have to run down, he could run down quick before they came, he would have to tell them, otherwise they wouldnt fucking know, they wouldnt know they were fucking there. He had smoked the whole of Ray's fag. He had nothing in his pockets. Even a bit of chewing gum! He walked a couple of paces away along the main road, turned back. No sign of the moon anywhere. It was funny how it disappeared. Clouds were so fucking thin but they could hide the moon. He got to the corner and looked round and there was the man in dungarees, the big skinny guy with the specs, he had seen Lecky; he was smoking and had taken the cigarette from his mouth while staring over; now he was staring into the shop doorway, now back to Lecky. And Lecky stood still. If the guy didnt actually see him but was just staring in the general direction. He wasnt, he was watching; you could tell, just by the way he was standing, he was obviously fucking watching, the fag sticking out his mouth. Lecky stepped back behind the corner. A moment later he peered round again: the man in the dungarees continued to stare at him. What to do. He walked a few paces away from the street, along the main road. What was he to do? He stopped and turned. What. Back to the corner. Fuck. Right round it and along to the shop doorway, that fucking bastard still standing there staring, fucking staring bastard, skinny big specky-eyed bastard standing there fucking staring as if he was a fucking sentry on guard duty, fucking Buckingham fucking Palace. Lecky stopped opposite him and he stared across, the big skinny guy staring back. He wanted a smoke, a smoke would fucking be good. And then the man about-turned and went in through a door and Lecky moved smartly into the shop and the interior, pitch-dark till his eyes got accustomed and there was another room; stairs down to the basement: John! John! Lecky yelled: John! Fuck sake!

Silence.

John! Quick! Right now! Move!

Then a loud banging sound and foosteps rushing and Ray was in view below. That big bastard, cried Lecky.

What?

He saw us, he's away to fucking do us. Quick!

What? Who ye fucking talking about?

Him, the big skinny bastard – the one that reversed out the lorry.

Ray was gazing up at him.

Honest man I'm no kidding ye, he's away to fucking grass us, yous better fucking come . . .

But Ray was off before he finished talking and he felt like going right after him, gubbing him one on the fucking mouth, ignorant bastard, he was a fucking ignorant bastard – a good bit aulder than Lecky but so what: Lecky was bigger and he was fucking harder, he knew he was fucking harder, and he would knock fuck out him. So fucking ignorant. Lecky stared down into the basement, so gloomy and dark. Where the fuck was John?

He glanced back at the doorway, walked towards it, then stopped. What was he to do. Another room to the side, also in darkness. He stepped a pace and his heel crunched glass, a lot of it. Sounds from the basment but quite vague and far away. Bloody smell of dampness too, like fungus or something – it was as if the place hadnt been used for years. So dark. He stood still. The very last thing was to close his eyes, no even for a moment.

Was that a thump! He crouched. It was like a thump. He stood very still then dashed to the top of the basement stairs and shouted, John! John! Fuck sake come on!

Nothing. They didnt answer.

There were no sounds at all. He needed a pish. Fucking desperate. He went a step while unzipping his fly, started peeing, there was steam, a steady ssssss, it was calming; ssssss. If there werent any sounds from below it meant they had stopped and were in through to the other place, they had made the breakthrough. He stepped back. A dribble of urine down his leg. He walked a few paces, again crunching glass. He bent to the floor and picked out a long sliver which would act as a weapon, a knife – and there was that good feeling when he held it tight; it was knowing it was dangerous just by that alone, by the way you held it tight in your hand without any gloves to cover it, its ragged edges, how they would cut into you. And what was that was that a thump? it sounded like a big fucking thump! Lecky had crouched and now he stood perfectly still and there were footsteps. It was a polis standing in from the front doorway wearing one of these big fucking black coats; funny how they always fucking wore them. Lecky flashed the sliver of glass in his right hand. Dont come fucking near, he said, or I'll cut your face.

The polis watched him. Then disappeared. Away for handers. Them and their fucking handers they always had fucking handers, you never knew how many there were going to be, dirty bastards.

Another pish, it was desperate, he moved quickly, into the room he had last been, to the far side, doing the pee immediately.

Then back to the top of the basement stairs, the sliver of glass back in his right hand. But he didnt want to go down the fucking stairs because he would be trapped. Where was fucking John? And that other cunt. Where the fuck.

Plus the voices, footsteps. Trying to be low; keeping things low – as if he was fucking stupid or deaf or something. Bastards. Fucking funny polis right enough. Lecky felt a dampness in his hand like blood or sweat or something, a stickiness. What would he do would he just fucking drop it and just let it go and get down into the basement man if there was a place to get out, a fucking hole maybe – where had they went? The glass, getting crunched, their big fucking feet now, there wasnt going to be time.

A woman and two men

Some folk would think it was her keeps them the gether, without her who knows what they would do, making sure they get their grub, whatever it is, the bowl of soup, the sausage and egg, whenever she gets round to making it. But it's all an illusion, it just isnt true. It's sentimentality. It isnt a true picture at all. People just like to think that because they dont want to think something else. You see her, she hardly talks at all. And she never walks in the middle. There is something but right enough, you dont quite know what it is about her. Plus the fact she never seems to hear what the other two are talking about. She has a set look on her face all the time. Probably she knows everything they have to say anyway, their conversation's probably the same all the time. The older guy is about fifty years of age, the younger one about thirty-five, maybe even a nephew, because their relationship appears to be to do with family rather than friendship, but this is guesswork. It looks like the older one has been the longest with the woman, that the younger one just came along and decided he wanted in on the act. Unless it was a case of being invited in by the other two, or just the man, because this nephew, you dont feel he's really up to doing things for himself and neither do you get the feeling about her, about the woman, that she ever gets a say in the matter either, unless maybe she doesnt want one; she has such an inferior way of going about you can hardly imagine her ever saying much at all. But this might no be true, maybe she does, maybe she just gives the impression she doesnt. Whenever they walk down the road people stare at them, and they're open about it, because of the way they look, as if they're full of their own lives, as if what they do concerns them to the exclusion of everything else. Not only does that make them interesting it means folk feel able to stare at them without them noticing which is just as well maybe because the older guy is quite aggressive; you get the feeling about that, there's a nastiness about his face, he's always got a girn. He's definitely the chief. But then one time right enough she was on her own and she walked normal, she was swigging from a can of stout, so she might not be as docile as people think. Somebody looked at her and she looked back. The person had just came out the baker shop near the Botanic Gardens and maybe was having to step out her road – whatever, but the woman just gave her a 'look'. Somebody told me, apropos of what I dont know, that she 'liked the men', meaning she liked to go with men. But that makes it seem she's got choices. It makes it seem like she's been able to make up her mind about things some of the time but maybe she doesnt, folk just like to think about other folk, especially women, they like to think they make up their minds about everything. But they dont, it's a fallacy.

Except I suppose there's the swing of her skirt. That lurching movement makes you think of a piece of material just thick with dirt and that is what you think of that skirt it's like you can imagine the sperm of quite a lot of men. Having said that it's important to say about her how you always think she is the one who is reflective, that it is her who reflects on what is happening roundabout; she's the one that notices what people are signifying when they look at the three of them. Plus if ever you're confronted by them, it's her eyes that stay with you; it's her you see eventually, the one who makes it hard for you. It can start you thinking about things, probably about men and women I suppose, the different types of relationships they have, how you think the women it is who carry the burden yet in such a veiled aggressive way you never feel sorry for them. They know the score. It's as if it's always them that work out the percentages. Even her, this one, the weight of her skirt, you dont for a minute think she is a hopeless victim and you dont think she is as passive as she makes out. Right enough she is a victim in the way she is just one woman having to face up to two men and you dont know quite what goes on in that situation, even if she sometimes has to find a punter if they're in trouble. That time she was overheard when they were seated on the bench down by the Kelvin, just over by the kids' swing park, and she says something that showed how she felt on her own in the company, what she said wasnt heard by the two guys – or else they didnt pay it any attention, they never 'heard' her. They were on the paving stones at the edge of the flower beds, the two of them involved about something or other, or maybe nearer the point, the guy with the permanent girn on his face was talking and the nephew was listening, and then the woman says. It's no like that. Her hair straggling down her shoulders and her mouth gumsy. I think the nephew heard her and the other guy didnt because he just never expected her to speak unless spoken to, something like that. But again you know there's that way you can tell when somebody isnt very bright, maybe just how he sometimes smiles for no reason anybody can see and that nephew was a bit like that, I dont think he was the full shilling. So girny, the older guy, he turns to her: Did you speak there?

Naw.

Aye you did.

I didni.

Aye ye did.

I didni.

Ye fucking did.

Then she just shut up. Girny stared at her and you would have expected him to hit her one. I think he would've if she had said anything more. He was daring her, that's what he was doing. But she never says fuck all. She just stared at the other women, the ones with their kids playing on the swings and you wondered about that, if she was away thinking about them and relating it to herself, the way she was. It was sad. You felt as if there was this terrible awful gap between them but there wasnt really. It was all a bit weird. I just wish she could have washed her hair. I felt that for her. I felt if she had done that then the gap wouldnt have been so bad and so big, all them with their weans playing in the wee swing park, all standing there having their wee chin-wag the way women do, enjoying the sun and all that, while there was this other one, their comrade I suppose in solidarity, there she was, but they werent bothering about her, trying no to see her, then there was girny himself getting up off the bench and giving her the wire, Come on you, he said, not in actual words but just the way he jerked his thumb; the nephew as well, giving her a look, and then they went away down towards the old dummy railway.

Lassies are trained that way

The lassie came in on her own; she glanced roundabout then continued on past the *Ladies*, heading into the lounge. Minutes later she was back again, squinting this way and that, as if letting it be known she was only here because she was meeting somebody. When she arrived beside him at the bar there was a frown on her face. She asked the woman serving for a gin and orangeade, stressing the orangeade, how she didnt want natural fruit juice or the diluting stuff. She was good-looking. She had on a pair of trousers and a wideish style of jersey. Eventually he spoke to her. He gave her a smile at the same time:

Has he gave you a dizzy?

The lassie ignored him.

Has he stood you up? he said, smiling. Then he drank a mouthful of lager. In some ways he hadnt been expecting any response, even though he was just being friendly, taking her at face value and trying to ease her feelings; get her to relax a bit. This wasnt the best of pubs for single women, being frank about it – not the worst, but definitely not the best.

Her eyes were smallish, brown, nice. He liked her looks. Okay. What is there to that? There can be strong feelings between the sexes. He was attracted to her. Fine. But even more than that: probably if something bad was happening he would have been first there, right at her elbow. It was a big brotherish feeling. He used to have a couple of wee sisters. Still has! Just that they are no longer wee. They are married women, with families of their own. He used to be a married man with a family of his own! Which simply means, to cut the crap, that him and his wife dont see eye-to-eye anymore. If they ever did. She doesnt live with him. And he doesnt live with her. They separated a year-and-a-half ago. He spent too much time boozing down the pub. Too much time out the house. That was the problem, he spent too much time out the house. The work did it. The kind of job he had is the kind that puts pressure on you. And what happens but you wind up in the pub drowning your sorrows.

The lassie with the brown eyes, she was standing beside him. He didnt know what she was maybe she was a student. Although she was older than the usual. But some of the older students came round here. Even during the day, when you might have expected them to be at their class getting their lessons, here they were, having a wee drink. He thought it livened things up. Other folk didnt. Other folk didnt think that at all. They thought it was better to have things the opposite of livened up – deadened down – that's what they thought it was better to have, that was their preference. When they went into a pub they wanted no people, no noise and no laughter, no music, no life, no bloody fuck all, nothing, that's what they liked, nothing, to walk into a pub and get faced by nothing. How come they ever left their place of abode? That was the real question. How come they didnt just stay put, in their bloody house. Then they would give other folk a break. If they were actually interested in other folk then that's what they would do, they would stay fucking indoors and give them a bloody break. But they didnt do that. Out they came. He couldnt be bothered with it, that kind of mentality, he just couldn't be bothered with it. They were misanthropes. The very last thing he ever wanted to be. No matter how bad it got he would never resort to that way of behaving. He genuinely thought people should help one another. He did. He genuinely did. Something that was anathema nowadays right enough, the way things were. But so what? There's aye room for variety. Who wants everything to be the same? Imagine it: a whole regiment of folk all looking the same and then thinking the same thoughts. That would be terrible, absolutely bloody horrendous. You see some blokes going about, their faces tripping them. You wonder how come they ever set foot out the door, as if they just left the house to upset folk. A pain in the neck so they are. The kind that never does somebody a turn unless it's a bad yin. His wife's people were like that. They used to talk about him behind his back. They spoke about him to her, they carried tales. She believed them as well. Plus they did their chattering in front of the wee yins. Bad. If you've got to talk about somebody, okay, but no in front of the wee yins. Bringing somebody down like that. It's no right. There again but his wife didnt have to listen; nobody was forcing her, she could have ignored them, she could have told them to shut their bloody mouth.

The lassie was staring across the bar to beneath the gantry, to where all the bottles of beer were stacked, as if she was comparing all the different labels or something. Because she was feeling self-conscious. You could tell. And there was a mirror up above. She was maybe wanting to look into it to see if she could see somebody but she wasnt able to bring it off in case she wound up catching somebody else's eye. That was probably it. He gave her a smile but she ignored it.

He didnt want to feel hurt because it would have been stupid. Not only stupid but ridiculous. She hadnt ignored him at all. She had just no seen him. But she was no seeing anybody. Which is what lassies have to do in pubs. It's part of how they've got to act. He had a daughter himself and that's exactly what he would be telling her next time he saw her. You just cannot afford to take chances, no nowadays – different to when he was young. Aye, he said, young yins nowadays, they have it that wee bit harder.

And he glanced at her but she kept her stare fixed on the bottles beneath the gantry. Which was okay really because he had said it in such a way she would be able to do exactly that, ignore him, without feeling like she was giving him an insult at the same time. That kind of point was important between the sexes, between men and women, if ever they were to manage things together. He gave her another smile and she responded. She did. Her head looked up and she nodded. That was the irony. If you're looking for irony that's it. Plus as well the way things operate in conversation it was really up to her to make the next move, whatever it was, it was up to her.

The woman serving behind the bar was watching him. She was rinsing the glasses out at the sink. Her head was bent over as if she was attending totally to the job in hand but she wasnt, it was obvious. Probably because she knew he was married, thinking to herself: So he's like that is he; chatting up the young lassies, I might've bloody guessed, they're all the bloody same!

And that would make you laugh because he wasnt like that at all. No even just now when he was separated, when he was away living on his own. It was a total guess on her part and she was wrong. But women like to guess about men. They get their theories. And then they get surprised when the theories dont work out. She had seen him talk to the lassie and she just assumed he was trying to chat her up. It can be bad the way folk jump in and make their assumptions about you. And apart from his age what made her so sure he was married anyway? He had gave up wearing the band of gold a while ago and she was new in the job, still feeling her way; she was still finding out about folk and as far as he was concerned what could she know? almost nothing, it was just guesswork.

The woman was wearing a ring herself but that didnt even mean *she* was married. As far as a lot of females are concerned a band of gold's a handy thing to have pure and simple for the way it can ward off unwelcome attention. There again but let's be honest, most men dont even see a ring, and even if they do, so what? they just bloody ignore it.

The woman stopped rinsing glasses now to serve an auld bloke at the far end of the bar. He said something to her and she said something back and the two of them smiled. She had a quiet style with the customers, but she could crack funny wee jokes as well, the kind you never seem to hear at first – no till after the person that's told you has went away and you're left standing there and suddenly you think: Aye, right enough . . . This is the way it was with her. And then when you looked for her once it had dawned on you she was off and pouring the next guy's pint, she had forgot all about it. It was actually quite annoying. Although at the same time you've got to appreciate about women working in a pub, how they've got to develop an exterior else they'll no be able to cope. This one for example had a distracted appearance like she was always away thinking about bloody gas bills or something. Mind you that's probably what she was thinking about. Everything's so damn dear nowadays. He said it to the lassie. He frowned at her and added: Still and all, it wasnt that much better afore they got in, the tories.

She looked at him quite surprised. It was maybe the first time she had genuinely acknowledged he was a person. And it made him think it confirmed she was a student, but at the same time about her politics, that she was good and left-wing. He jerked his head in the direction of the woman serving behind the bar. Her there, he said, I think she's a single parent; she looks like she goes about worried out of her skull because of the bills coming in – she'll have a tough time of it.

The lassie raised her eyebrows just; and that was that, she dropped her gaze. In fact she looked like she was tired, she did look like she was tired. But it was a certain kind of tiredness. The kind you dont like to see in young people – lassies maybe in particular, though maybe no.

I'm forty going on fifty, he said and he smiled, forty going on fifty. Naw but what I mean is I feel like I'm fifty instead of forty. No kidding. In fact I felt like I was fifty when I was thirty! It was one of the major bones of contention between me and the wife. She used to accuse me about it, being middle-aged. She used to say I was an auld man afore my time. No very nice eh? Accusing your husband of that.

He smiled as he shook his head, swigged a mouthful of beer. Mate of mine, he said, when I turned forty, at my birthday, I was asking him what like it was, turning it I mean, forty, and what he telled me was it took him till he was past fifty to bloody get over it!

He smiled again, took his fags out for another smoke although he was trying to cut down. The lassie already was smoking. He lit one for himself. I noticed you come in, he said, the way you walked ben the lounge and then came back here, like you were looking for somebody. I'm no being nosy, it's just an observation, I thought you were looking for somebody.

She had two brown moles on her cheek, just down from her right eye. They were funny, pretty and beautiful. It made him smile.

That was how I spoke to you, he went on, because I thought you were in looking for somebody and they hadnt showed up. I'm no meaning to be nosy, it was just I thought the way you looked, when you came in . . . He finished by giving a nod then inhaled deeply on his cigarette. He was beginning to blab and it was making her uncomfortable. He wasnt saying it right, what he was meaning to say, he was coming out with it wrong, as if it was a line he was giving her, a bit of patter.

She was just no wanting to talk. That was it. You could tell it a mile away. Then at the same time she wasnt wanting to be bloody rude. It was like she maybe didnt quite know how to handle the situation, as if she was under pressure. Maybe she would have handled things better if it had been a normal day, but for some reason the day wasnt normal. Maybe something bad had happened earlier on, at one of her classes, and she was still feeling the effects, the emotional upset. He wanted to tell her no to worry. She wasnt at her classes now.

Unless she thought he was acting too forward or something because he was talking to her – though as far as pubs go surely no, it was just what comes under the heading of being sociable.

And we have to live with one another. Come on, if we arent even allowed to talk! Nowadays right enough you cant even take that for granted; it's as if you're supposed to go about kicking everybody in the teeth; you're no supposed to be friendly, if you're friendly they go and tell the polis and you wind up getting huckled for indecent assault. There again but folk have *had* to get that wee bit tougher nowadays, just to survive. He said to the lassie: Do you know what the trouble is? I'm talking about how things have got harder and tougher these past couple of years.

She kept her head lowered. It made him smile. He glanced over the counter but the woman was off serving other folk. He smiled again: You obviously dont want to know what the trouble is! And that's your privilege, that's your right. But I'm going to tell you anyhow!

Naw but seriously, he said, the way things are – society I'm meaning – it's just like auld Joxer says in that play by Sean O'Casey, the world's in a state of chassis. I'm talking about how capitalism and the right wing has got it all cornered, so selfishness is running amok, everywhere you look, it's rampant – no just here in Scotland but right across the whole of the western world. It's bloody disgusting. Everybody clawing at one another. Nobody gives a shit. We just dont care anymore about what the neighbour next door might be suffering. It's true. They can be suffering. That auld woman up the stair for example, take her, you've no seen her for how long? a week? a fortnight? a bloody month? So what do you do do you go up and keek through the letterbox? naw, do you hell; nothing as simple that, what you do is go and phone the bloody polis and get them to come and do it for you. That's the way it is. So you come to rely on people like the polis as if they were angels of mercy – instead of what they are, the forces of law and order for the rich and the wealthy, the upper class.

The lassie frowned.

Sorry, he said, am I talking too loud? I know you're no supposed to nowadays. When you talk about something you're really interested in you're supposed to bloody keep it down, the noise level I mean. So so much for your interest, if it happens to be bloody genuine . . . He shook his head, sighing; he drank from his pint of lager, glancing at her over the rim of the glass, but she was managing not to look at him. Funny how that happened. He could never have managed it himself, to not speak to somebody who was speaking to you. He would have found it extremely difficult, to achieve, he would have found it really difficult. Maybe some folk were mentally equipped to carry that kind of thing off but he wasnt, he just didnt happen to be one of them – not that he would have wanted to be anyhow. Mind you, if he had been a lassie . . . But lassies are trained for it, in a manner of speaking; it's part of the growing-up process for them, young females. It doesnt happen with boys, just if you're a lassie, you've got to learn how not to talk; plus how not to look, you get trained how not to look. How not to look and how not to talk. You get trained how not to do things.

My mother was a talker, he said, God rest her she was a good auld stick. I liked my father but I have to admit it I loved my mother. She used to sing too. She's been dead for fifteen years. Fifteen years. A long time without your maw eh? I was just turned twenty-five when it happened. A long time ago.

The lassie smiled.

You're smiling, he said, but it's true. He tapped ash onto the floor and scraped the heel of his shoe over it, then inhaled deeply. He had loved his mother. It was funny to think that, but he had. And he missed her. Here he was a grown man, forty years of age, and he still missed his mammy. So what but? People do die. It's the way things are. Nobody can change it. The march of progress.

I dont believe in after-lives, he said, and I dont bloody believe in before-lives. Being honest about it I dont believe in any of your bloody through-the-looking-glass-lives at all. And that includes whatever you call it, Buddhism or Mohammedism or whatever the hell. There's the here and there's the now. Mind you, I'm no saying there's no a God, I'm just no saying there is one. What I will bloody say is I'm no very interested, one way or the other. What about yourself?

O . . . She smiled for a moment then she frowned almost immediately; she dragged on her cigarette and let the smoke out in a cloud. Then she dragged on it again but this time inhaled.

He shrugged. It's alright if you're no wanting to speak, I know how things are. Dont worry about it. Anyway, I'm doing enough chattering for the two of us! One thing but I will say – correct me if I'm wrong – your politics, they're like my own, we're both to the left. Eh?

She nodded very slightly, giving a very quick smile. Probably she was a wee bit suspicious. And if she wasnt she should've been; especially nowadays. Because you just never know who you're talking to. He gazed at her. There was something the . . .

And then he felt like giving her a kiss. It was so sudden and what an urge he had to turn away.

And he felt so sorry for her. He really did. He felt so sorry for her. How come he felt so sorry for her? It was almost like he was going to burst out greeting! How come? How come it was happening? He gulped a couple of times and took a puff on the fag, then another one. God. He bit on his lower lip; he stared across the bar to where a conversation was on the go between some guys he knew – just from drinking in here but, he didnt know them from outside – and didnt really want to either. Nothing amazing, he just found it difficult being in their company, it was a bit boring, if he had to be honest, nothing against them, the guys themselves. What was up? What was wrong? He blinked, he kept his eyelids shut for several moments.

A tiny wee amount of gin and orangeade was left in her glass. She was obviously trying to make it last for as long as possible. And she wouldnt allow him to buy her another. That was for definite. It was a thing about females. She was looking at the clock. That was another thing about them! Women! God! Strange people! He grinned at the lassie: Yous women! Yous're so different from us! Yous really are! Yous're so different!

She gazed at him.

Yous are but honest.

In what way?

O Christ in every way.

She nodded.

I mind when my daughter started her period if you dont mind me saying – I felt dead sorry for her. No kidding. Know how? Because she wasnt going to be a boy! He shook his head, smiling.

That's awful.

Naw, he said, what I mean . . .

But she had looked away from him in such a style that he stopped what it was he was going to say. Along the counter the woman serving was setting pints up for a group of young blokes who had just come in. He said, I dont mean it the way it sounds. The exact same thing happens with a pet, a wee kitten or a wee puppy, when it's newborn and it's just like any baby . . .

I dont want to hear this.

Naw but . . .

She shook her head. I dont want to hear it.

Aye but you dont know what I'm going to say.

I dont want to hear it. She smiled, then set her face straight, stubbed her fag out in the ashtray.

He had just been wanting to tell her how the things he liked as a boy he had wanted his wee lassie to get involved in, because he knew she would enjoy them, that's all; nothing else, things like football and climbing trees, jumping the burn; nothing special, the usual, the usual crap, just the things boys did. Of course she would go on and do the things lassies did and she would enjoy them. He knew that. That was what happened. And it was fine. But it wasnt the point. It was something else, to do with a feeling, an emotional thing. Surely you had to be allowed that?

He indicated her near-empty glass. D'you want a drink?

No thanks.

He smiled.

I'm going in a minute.

He smiled again. There's barriers between us, the sexes. But what you cannot deny is that we're drawn to one another. We are: we're drawn to one another. There's bonds of affection. And solidarity as well, you get solidarity between us – definitely . . . That's what I think anyhow – course I'm aulder than you . . . When you get to my age you seem to see things that wee bit clearer.

She looked at him. That's just nonsense.

I'm no saying you see everything clearer, just some things.

She sighed.

I was reading in a book there about it – it was a woman writer – she was saying how there's a type of solace you can only receive from the opposite sex, a man from a woman a woman from a man.

It's nonsense.

It's no nonsense at all.

She paused for a moment, then replied, Yes it is. She looked away from him, off in the direction of the group of young blokes, one of whom stared at her. So blatant too, the way he did it. He just turned and stared at her, then he turned back to his pals. And the lassie shifted the way she was standing. She looked up at the clock and checked the time against her wristwatch.

They keep it quarter of an hour fast, he said. Common practice. A few of the customers complain right enough. But it's so they can get the doors shut on the button else the polis'll come in and do them for being late and they might lose their licence. So they say anyway. Mind you it's bloody annoying if you've come in looking to enjoy a last pint and then they start shouting at you and start grabbing the glass out your bloody hand. My auld da used to say it was the only business he knew where they threw out their best customers!

She didnt respond.

He grinned. I mean it's no as if they open quarter of an hour early in the morning! Look eh . . . are you sure I cant buy you one afore you go?

No, thanks.

He nodded.

I'm just leaving.

He never turned up then eh!

No.

Was it your boyfriend?

She shook her head.

D'you mind me asking you something. Are you a student?

Why d'you want to know?

I was just wondering.

Why?

Aw nothing.

She continued looking at him. He felt like he had been given a telling off. For about the third bloody time since she had come in. He swallowed the last of his lager and glanced sideways to see where the bar staff had got to. And then he said, Do you think it's possible for men and women to talk in a pub without it being misconstrued?

She paused. I think people should be able to stand at a bar without being pestered.

O you think you're being pestered? Sorry, I actually thought I was making conversation. That's how come I was talking to you, it's what's commonly known as being sociable. I didnt know I was pestering you.

She nodded.

Sorry.

It's just that I think people should be able to stand at the bar if that's what they want to do.

So do I, he said, so do I. That's what I think. I mean that's what I think. My own daughter's coming up for seventeen you know so I'm no exactly ignorant of the situation.

The woman behind the counter had reappeared and was looking along in his direction, like she had heard the word 'pester' and was just watching to see. He shook his head. It was like things were getting out of hand; you wanted to shout: Wait a minute! He frowned, then smiled. When he was a wee boy him and his brother and sisters would be right in the middle of a spot of mischief when suddenly the door would burst open and mammy would be standing there gripping the handle and glowering at them. And they would all be on the confessional stool immediately! She didnt have to fucking do anything! They'd all just start greeting and then cliping on one another! What a technique she had! It was superb! All she had to do was stand there! Everybody crumbled.

He grinned, shaking his head, and he called for a pint of lager. For a split second the woman didnt seem to hear him. Then she walked to the tap, started pouring the pint, staring at the lever very deliberately, as if she was making some sort of point. It was funny. Maybe she was a bit put out about something. Well that was her problem. If you've got to start safeguarding the feelings of everybody you meet on the planet then you'll have a hard time staying sane.

The lassie wasnt there.

Aye she was but she was across at the group of young guys. They looked like students as well. He didnt have anything against students. Although the danger was aye the same for kids from a working-class background, that it turned you against your own people. How many of them were forever going away to uni and then turning round and selling themselves to the highest bidder as soon as they'd got their certificates. Then usually they wound up abroad, if no England then the States or Canada or Australia, or Africa or New Zealand, it was all the same. Then they spent the rest of their lives keeping other folk down.

One of the young blokes laughed. It would have been easy to take it personally but that would have been stupid. Getting paranoiac is the simplest thing in the world. A gin and orangeade was on the counter in front of the lassie but she was paying for it out of her own purse. A young guy glanced across. Another one said something. But there was no point seeing it directed at yourself. The woman behind the bar was away serving another customer. The change back from the money for the pint of lager was lying on the counter. He put his hand out to get it.

Real Stories

So because she couldnt get doing her own work she occupied herself in other ways. What happened is she stayed in her room and started telling wee stories to herself. She did. That was what she did. Wee stories about her girlhood with outcomes that were different from real life. Usually it was her that was the heroine whereas in real life she had never been the heroine, and none of her pals had ever been the heroine either. But that didnt matter. Not to her. She never deluded herself. She always knew them for what they were so so what is what she said to herself as soon as the criticism started, they're my own stories and nobody else's so why should I worry about them being true or no, just to suit other people. She did enough worrying without having to worry about that as well. And with the spare room being hers she could shut the door tight and she could have put a bolt on if she had wanted to. But there was no need.

When her husband was there he tried to get into her mind. It was like he started needing solace or a comfort or something like that. It was funny. As if he thought he would maybe manage it through her stories, as if he thought that was how to do it, by getting inside her imagination. Because he didnt like his own imagination. That was what he said. But there had to be more than that even although he said there wasnt.

At first what he did was he started getting her to tell the stories out loud. But that never seemed to work properly. She couldnt do it right except once or twice, and even then, when she felt she had got close to succeeding he wouldnt believe her. He thought she was making it up, he thought she was just saying the stories succeeded because she was wanting to keep the real ones secret. He thought there were 'real stories' she was keeping secret from him and that was where the solace lay. But this was happening at the stage where there was a coldness in her towards him anyway so she was quite happy to let him believe she was cheating if that was what he wanted. She felt really that he could believe anything he liked. She was then stopping all her interest in him. But leaving that apart her stories just werent for him. She didnt like having to share them, especially no with him. It was not like he had been a good man to her. She had always preferred it when she could go away into her own room and shut fast the door, for he would at least respect that, he would never try to enter unless she invited him. And she stopped inviting him. By then it had got so she just couldnt abide the idea of him at all, it was excruciating and she couldnt cope with it. She couldnt, she just couldnt cope with it. It was awful. She felt clammy. It was a creepy feeling. Him sitting there the way he did.

And as well as that if she was not to be allowed to do her own work well she just wasnt going to put up with it, with him being there, not if she wasnt going to be allowed to do it. She needed to be alone, she needed to shut fast the door and even bolt and snib it if she wanted, if that was what she wanted. But there was no need since he respected it. If he had been a true bosom partner to her then none of it would have mattered she didnt think, none of it. Even the stories would have been to share. It was just him. Not everybody made her feel like this, just some.

And she didnt care about his job. She had never cared about it. It was just a dreadful thing and she couldnt hardly imagine it it was so dreadful. Yet in the early days it was funny how she seemed to spend most of her life dashing about trying to get things right for him. That was really so funny. But she was daft back then, she was young. She used to go all his messages. She did all the things for him. He always had things needing doing and she used to do them for him. She didnt mind doing them for the reason that she used to like just being outside the house plus as well what it included, the change of clothes, because she used to put on a new set of clothes when she went outside. She would wait till he was out the road, then she would sneak away with a hat or a scarf or a nice veil, she would have them tucked in at her elbow or else under her coat.

What was the meaning of these messages? That was something that used to make her wonder. Sometimes it was like he just dreamt them up to get her. She wondered what she was doing it for and if it was just him and nothing to do with his actual business at all. To her he was a rascal the way he was needing to have everything. He was like that from the start. He was never going to be content, he was always going to need everything. Some men rule your life and he was one of them.

It became it wasnt any good just shutting herself in the room because she knew he was hovering about outside the door, and it started preying on her mind if she allowed it. Every time she let her mind go she would see him, there he was; and with that look on his face like a smirk. It was creepy. Then she found a way of working it so she could get it all into her stories. That was how she coped. She got it all into her stories. Next thing she started making him feel funny. That was a scary thing for him. A point came when he discovered he was thinking morbid thoughts all the time. He wanted to tell people. He didnt though because he thought they would think he was daft. That was the kind of folk he knew, that was what like they were. It would have drove her crazy to know people like that. She would have wanted her own work. Always being stuck with these kinds of people and no space and no time for yourself. That was what he had to put up with; and she was glad. It was what he deserved. And him being filled with these new anxious feelings, morbid ones. She knew fine what was happening. But she didnt care. She was finished with it all. Him and his bad thoughts. She didnt care what happened to anybody. She once used to like her nephew. He was a nice boy. But she never saw him now and it didnt matter.

All of that. Nobody could have forced her. She would just have stopped up all her senses. Her eyes and her ears and her smell and her touch, everything. When I was a wee lassie about ten years old and this after the first war had took place, I went to play with my dolls with a wee boy who was my wee pal I told you about whose daddy was a docker down Charlie Connell's yard. This was the night his grannie died. She had got took funny when they were listening to the early wireless and Billy and me didnt notice because we had out his toy soldiers made of cardboard boxes his daddy had cut up for him and I had my dollies and we were playing at wars, his was the British Army and mine was the Kaiser and all his uncles were there in the house it was just after my daddy had got killed I mind because my mother's greeting still hadnt let up and she was down the stairs that was how I was up because I would do anything no to be there with her it was awful.

She could tell worse things if she wanted. She could. She could have started making it so's he heard the very very worst things imaginable for him, because it was like he was just a wee schoolboy who had never been out in the world, as if he had come from a well-off family with a nice big house over in the southside and apple trees in the garden. He was just plain stupid. When I was a wee lassie and Billy McDevitt's uncles were there in the house with me just after my own daddy had got killed and my mummy scarcely even wondered where I was was I out or in and that was me just by myself ten years old, and I just didnt have anywhere to turn and I was so scared with all the noises hiding there behind the coal-bunker with the wind outside howling round the chimney tops till you thought they were going to come crashing down onto your head through the window.

He listened to her and all the things she told him. He listened to it all, everything. It was like he had never heard anything like what she could tell and never ever thought anybody he knew could know such things, especially her never mind it was back when she was a wee lassie, as if it was her to blame as well, them being true in reality. You could imagine him there with his hand on his forehead close to staggering under the news, the burden of that just. It was enough to make her smile but she kept it to herself and just carried on telling him all what she felt like, she just didnt care. And then as well was the time she never left the room but just stayed there for as long as she liked, and he was outside and she could hear him listening there, wondering, if she was sitting maybe on the side of the bed staring into the wallpaper and the shapes from the design, a thick wallpaper which caused shadows on itself and you could see the world there or part of it, the bits that hide underneath where folk are dead and dying, getting killed and there they are all bleeding with their bits and pieces oozing out there on the grass, the dirt, and nobody to see.

She could have worked in an office and had a career. That was what she should have done, if she had got the chance, a career-woman. She would have been better than him and she wouldnt only have had terrible folk to know because she would have been different. And she wouldnt have been with him. She wouldnt have been with anybody maybe, maybe no anybody at all. She would just have kept her own door. She would have had it nice, she wouldnt have had him. Not him and not nobody. If she had wanted one she would have took one, it was easy, men looking at you, that was easy. But she just wouldnt want one, she wouldnt. She would just have had her own friends. She would have made a man up if she wanted one. That's how she would have done it. All clumsy and sweating. Her man would have been small, small-boned; he wouldnt have made a noise, he would just have been there when she wanted, and when she didnt he wouldnt, because he would have known. And he would have respected her. And he would have admired her and maybe liked her and loved her. He wouldnt have thought things. He would have been good to her. You think of men who respect a woman. They would be there. That was what she always thought, she believed it.

A decision

When she told him she was going he stared at her, stupefied. Instead of shouting and bawling he asked her to repeat what she had just said. She did so, stepping back a yard, though by the set of her face and demeanour generally she wasnt at all scared for any physical reason. He looked at the carpet and frowned. Then while fumbling a cigarette to his mouth he offered her one but she declined, gesturing at the ashtray on the coffee table where she had one already, it lay smouldering; he stared at it, an Embassy Regal.

She was lifting a suitcase in the direction of the door, a grey suitcase. He was puzzled. Where the hell had she got it from? He had never seen it before. Dark grey it was, with green trimmings all round the edge.

And she was taking care not to meet his gaze. What did that mean?

But what was she playing at altogether?

She was at the door, hesitating but there, standing the suitcase upright between her feet.

Suddenly he knew what it was. They had turned her head. It's them, he said, they've turned your head. But he was so aware of how doleful he sounded. But he battered on talking to her. I knew it would happen. You aye said it wouldnt but I knew it would. I knew it, right from the start. I did. I knew it. I mean did I or didnt I?

She nodded slowly. You were right, I was wrong.

Aye but I dont want to be right, I dont want to be right . . .

It's no your fault, dont think that – it's me. I'm just . . . I'm just . . .

Naw, he said, dont go blaming yourself because it's no you it's them, it's down to them.

She didnt answer. She was looking at him in a way hard to describe. It was probably a mixture of things, feeling sorry for him was one, feeling disloyal would be another. What else? Oh she was just fucking probably feeling sick, sick in the belly. He nodded and inhaled on his cigarette. He didnt care if he died of bronchitis, or cancer. If he was going to be alone he was as well dead anyway because he couldnt live on his own – he would be dead in a week, he would go mad, he had to have people, he needed them, he just needed them. Her. He needed her. So how could he just stand there staring at her leave, he couldnt, it just wasnt fucking a possibility.

I've been growing away from you, she was telling him.

God! She was sounding like she was bloody pleading! He felt like bursting into floods of tears. She was pleading. He could see it in her eyes.

I have been for a while, she said.

Jesus Christ she was going to break his heart at this rate because she was telling what was the whole truth and nothing but the truth and he sucked on his fag once again, getting the smoke and holding it and sucking on it again and shutting his eyes, clenching the lids shut there for Christ sake. She was talking to him:

I wanted to wait and tell you . . . I could've went this afternoon but I decided I wanted to wait and see you face to face.

I appreciate it, he blurted out and meant it, he meant every word.

It wouldnt have been fair otherwise, she said.

Naw.

Just going I mean . . .

How come she had tacked that bit on the end, just going I mean, what had she said it for? Could she no just have shut up? Why did she need to bloody add on these wee bits. Why did she no just shut up! Her fucking mouth! Why did she no just shut up!

Just going I mean, she said, it wouldnt have been fair to you, to us.

O God. To us! If he was to let her go on still she was going to make it worse and worse and worse and bloody fucking worse again. He shook his head and sighed. He stared at her: Do you expect me to take ye back if you decide you want to come back? Eh?

The suitcase there between her feet.

Eh? he said, his voice that bit louder.

She just stared at him and the implication was: Have we sunk to this? that you could accuse me of that?

Come on, he said, I'm just trying to be realistic. To be practical. You might want to. It happens. People split up, they walk out on their partners and then decide they want to come back – the grass turns out to be no so green as they thought . . .

She was already shaking her head but he continued on, okay, a stubborn bastard: No but how do you know? he said, you cant know for sure. And I mean do you expect me to just take ye back if it does happen?

I dont think it will though.

Aye but how do ye know I mean I like the way you say that as if ye know for sure but how the hell can ye I mean ye bloody cant. He stared at her. Eh? Ye cant for sure.

God, she was getting impatient and he had to play for time Christ because otherwise she was right out the fucking door, she was just right out and away. Look, he said, it's a simple question I'm asking.

What is?

It was lost. He stared at her. He couldnt think of it. His mind was blank. She was really truly, really truly, she was leaving. You're leaving, he said. And he rushed on: All I'm saying is do you expect me to take ye back if you come back? If ye come back.

What do you mean? she said, and there was terrible sadness and worry all intermingled, he felt like sitting down, so tired right at that moment, the force of what she was doing, of what was happening right here and now between them for what now seemed to be forever, permanent separation, a permanent separation . . .

The tears were there in her eyes.

But do you? he said loudly, getting angry with her for this and her fucking pity, pitying him. Dont fucking pity me, he said, just dont fucking pity me.

I'm not pitying ye. I'm not.

Aye ye are – just go if you're bloody going; but dont you fucking pity me. And who are ye going with anyway? Is he waiting down the stair? Is he? Down the fucking stair?

There's nobody.

Ya liar.

She shook her head.

Ye are, ya bloody liar ye.

Now she frowned at him. I didnt have to wait ye know I could just have went this afternoon when you were out at the E. T. I could've.

How come ye never then?

Because it wouldnt have been fair, to just leave.

Okay, he said, thanks. Thanks.

She reached for the remains of her cigarette from the ashtray on the coffee table. There was only a puff left in it. She stubbed it out; her other hand settled onto the handle of the suitcase. He stared at it, grey and green coloured trimmings, he had never seen it before. It looked brand new.

So you've decided then, he said, that's it final? When did ye decide?

Does it matter?

Aye.

For one isolated solitary moment in time she stared straight at him, then she sighed and it was a sigh of pure relief. It was a sigh of pure relief. There she was. That was her. Whatever it was he had said was enough for her; to know she had done right, that the decision she had made was the right one. He frowned because he was puzzled. What had he said? What was it? It should have been there in front of him so clearly but he couldnt bring it to mind. What was it? What had he said, just there, a minute ago, that had set the seal on her leaving?

The door had closed. He studied it and he thought about it, her leaving. But the when didnt make one bit of difference, unfortunately, she had just gone, she was away; he thought of running to the window to maybe shout down at her but what was the point of that, it just wasnt him, it wasnt the sort of thing he did; he looked at the door, he studied it.

the chase

The first thing to do is walk slowly and dont look either way, you keep the hands in the pockets, the jerkin pockets, the shoulders hunched a little. Folk watch you. The police are there as well. It's nasty. There is a thing not good to the mind. But you have to keep going. It is a vice, and the way of all vices, that compulsion. It isnt even of interest. The heads dont turn. They notice though. They notice. They just dont hardly bother because it is so expected. That predictability. Yes, okay, which is a relief. If the predictability did not exist the thing would become the more burdensome, the more destructive to your mind. Not your mind, your soul. Minds are just too uninteresting. But souls. Souls are interesting: they are of interest. Note the irony. Souls are of interest. If you live in an atmosphere that is religious then they are not of interest, but our atmosphere is irreligious, not to say sacrilegious, so, the existence of souls. My own soul . . .

Well now, the unfinished thought, the pregnancy of it. We dont know. That is to say, we are unable to tell. But, the duty to the thought: my own soul is, not to beat about the bush, lacking in effervescence. What do we mean by that. We mean that my soul is in a state. The state is one of trauma, though trauma is too harsh. My soul is the soul of a depressive, manic perhaps, even maniacal. A hundred years ago the notion of manic depression was not in play. I banged my eye. I put up my hand to my face, to maybe rub my brow I cannot remember, but my finger went into my eye! It damn well nips and water streams from it. There is a heatwave too. It is three a.m. I was not able to sleep because of the heat. My partner's body was sweating. Each time we closed we stuck, or I stuck. My partner seemed not to stick. It was me who stuck and had to dislodge myself and I could almost hear the sound of it, the slight smacking noise. A car starts up below. A neighbour is mysterious. I hear the car start on other mornings also. The stickiness of my partner's body. I went to the wardrobe and got some clothes on. Three a.m. and I needed to get out. I felt like I was sweating severely. I filled the washbasin in the bathroom with cold water and then dunked in my noggin and let the cold water drip down my neck and down the hairs on my chest so that it was slightly uncomfortable underneath the shirt I wore, but it was worth it to get a feeling of freshness. Besides, I like the night, the depth of it – except that at this time of year it only lasts for something like two hours say, half-midnight to about 2.45, and after that you've got the navy-blue/charcoal-grey tinting the sky.

It was nice being out, I felt that for my soul. I am fond of my partner but it does my soul the world of good to escape, to escape into the air, the still of the dark part of the night. Solitary motor cars. Where I live a couple of shops open right into the late night so it's good, especially good having a place to walk to, you can just stroll as slowly as you like, and if the police stop you you've got the readymade excuse. But if you have a vice, a compulsion – even just walking the street, if that's your compulsion – then they stare at you. They are not at all certain. You look so normal and natural an individual, so normal and natural, that they cannot gauge you, what it is, the police, they cannot think that about you. Therefore what happens next is always tinged not by despair but the utmost nervewracking excitement. I know the district you see and in knowing the district it is a fantasy of mine that the police are trying to capture me. I am standing giving answers to certain questions and they look one to the other, suspicious of me, I see it in their very faces, their gestures, the way they stand ready to grab me if I so much as make a move. But that split second prior to them reaching out to get me I sprint suddenly sideways and through a close, down the steps and out by the dunny there or else into the dunny except I hate the idea of being trapped there and them entering with their torches, flashing on my face. I sprint instead beyond the dunny and across the wall, leaping down into the next backcourt and out through the gapsite down Brown Street and to the waterfront, down the steps and rushing headlong, but quiet, controlling my harsh breathing, the moonlight over the ripples of the Clyde, the tremendous elation of that, and maybe hearing the harsh sounding breaths of the chasing policemen, the slap of their boots on the tarmac, the concrete paving. This is my area and there is the old tunnel too and there is bound to be some old forgotten side entrance I can slip through, clattering down and down and down, my knees almost caving with the force of my movement. God.

it's the ins and outs

While she was telling the yarn she kept her eyes away from me, just pausing now and then, her head to one side, trying to work out if I was still listening. Of course I was still listening. But she was beginning to annoy me. It was to do with her humility, not really humility, something else, a kind of Uriah Heep deceit maybe; I felt like she didnt rate me. I listened because I had no real option. Duty called and I was having to be polite. It was the occasion of my first cousin's wedding and our two sides of the family were supposed to be close. I concentrated hard. She had lines all round her eyes and she was squinting. What the fuck was it? Something about Uncle Boabby and my da. I stood looking at her. I should have taken ice in the cherry brandy. It was a habit I was trying to get into. The ice freshened you up. An old guy in the pub told me that once. He wasnt wrong.

But what the hell was she rabbiting on about? Da was sitting just across the room from us. It was crowded but I could see him, him and the brother, the two of them, having a quiet blether.

And Uncle Boabby; it was strange to think she knew Uncle Boabby at all let alone what she seemed to be implying – carnal improprieties. The last I heard he was somewhere on the west coast of Ireland, and that was years ago. He had been quite an exciting figure for me as a boy and this wee woman wasnt. She looked wizened as well. But Uncle Boabby and his wife used to be continually fighting and splitting up and then getting back together again and then starting to fight again and all that sort of predictable stuff so maybe at a time where they had fallen out and were away from each other this wee woman had appeared on the scene or else it was a time they had got back together again and here it was I was meeting an illicit affair of a former hero. Big deal. Then the da. But who knows with him, he's aye been a dark horse.

I stepped to the window and looked down at the row of cars on the street below. I was needing to get away from here, fucking claustrophobic, family everywhere, it was doing my nut in, I just needed a couple of minutes peace, a breathing space. I felt like going for a big pint of lager – all that cherry brandy man it gives you a drouth, but there was fuck all else to drink, it was as if they were trying to stop the men getting pished, the women, as if they had set it up, in case of trouble, they had planked the fucking whisky and vodka. And they were carrying the bacardi about with them in their fucking handbags. Predictable shit.

The wee woman was watching me.

Maybe I had misunderstood the gist of what she was telling me, maybe I was reading the signals all wrong. I'm famous for that. All these interconnected relationships of the older generation. You never know what they were up to. You listen to them talk and you can never make any sense of it. Useless wondering further. I saw her lifting a cigarette from a packet on the mantelpiece and I hoped the packet belonged to somebody else. In this company that was death although if she was just a gatecrasher then all would be explained. But imagine gatecrashing a wedding like this. Different if it was the type of event you get in other countries and people enjoy themselves, a carnival atmosphere and so on, Brazil or someplace, the Samba, women doing their dances in all-revealing blouses, Ah Chicita, but no this kind of one, pouring rain outside, everybody getting wet from the run up the steps into the fucking close: one of the wee nieces doing her bridesmaid had crashed into a fucking puddle on the way.

The wee woman was looking at me. She came over and started talking. I told her to keep her voice down in case some of the family heard. What she was saying was definitely suspect. No two ways about it. Maybe she was involved with the DSS, just here checking up on the precise whereabouts of certain parties for some sort of future reference, a new legislation maybe. There was a black stone in a brooch round her neck. Probably if you stared at it too long you got mesmerised. Or else it had a microcosmic tape recorder charged inside. Naw, I said, I dont stay with my parents, we've got our own place, me and the wife. We're married as well, know what I mean, it isni a cohabitation deal.

She nodded.

Just in case you're interested.

I'm not.

Good.

She tugged on the cuff of my suit sleeve. I brushed her hand off. I just want to tell you, she said, your mother's never liked me.

Ach that's nonsense.

It's true.

I looked at her.

It is.

Naw it's no.

She never passed on Bobby's messages.

How do you know she got messages?

Oh I know.

How could ye if ye didni get them?

Hh. She smiled.

Maybe my Uncle Boabby didni send ye any. I know for a fact he's a bad letter writer. Ask anybody.

Tch, dont be so stupid.

I dont like being called stupid.

Well ye're saying things you know nothing about.

So what?

She tugged on my sleeve again: Sssh . . .

So what? I whispered.

It interferes with people's lives.

You're the one that's interfering hen. This is a family occasion.

Ye've got no right to speak to me like that.

Look I dont even know ye and ye're telling me all this gossip.

It's no gossip.

Aye it is; that's exactly what it is.

It's factual information.

I sighed.

You dont know anything.

What ye talking about?

She smiled and turned away, staring across at where my Uncle Dan was sitting with one of his auld cronies; the new bridegroom was there as well. The wee woman had started her whispering again: I tried to have a word with your father but he looked right through me.

Are ye sure ye've got the right family?

What's that supposed to mean?

Just what I say.

What do ye say . . . ?

I gave her a look. The way she spoke was really beginning to annoy me. And she wasni even looking at me. She was actually staring at my brother now, I mean just staring at him, as if she was seeing him for the first time – dont tell me he was bloody involved! The woman was out of order. She carried on talking some sort of rubbish to do with wartime situations. What fucking war was she talking about? Then she finished up saying: You're too young anyway so ye are: you wont understand.

I'm a bloody married man missis.

Hh. She glanced sideways, shaking her head.

Look, I said, the maw's ben the kitchen, go and have a word with her. She'll fill ye in.

We dont communicate.

Is that right. Aye well there's no point dumping it all on me, I'm no her first lieutenant. This sort of crap, personal gossip and aw that, I dont understand the ins and outs – thank Christ. If ye have got a grievance she's the lady, her herself, go and see her.

The wee woman turned to squint about the room.

She's no in here I'm telling ye she's ben the kitchen, holding court with the female team. Away through.

Maybe I will.

Good.

Maybe I'll just do that.

Aye well on ye go.

Maybe that's just what I'll do.

Good.

And then we'll see.

I sipped at the cherry brandy, looking across at the brother and my da, kidding on I hadnt heard the last bit. Behind them I could see my grannie in a corner, sitting on the usual stool; she refused comfortable chairs at all costs, scared she could never climb out them again. A wee niece stood next to her, whispering into her ear. One of the brother's lassies. I wish to Christ I could just have went for a pint. No wonder Uncle Boabby had fucked off to Ireland.

The wee woman started again: Yer mother just wouldnt want to hear what I've been saying to ye.

What are ye saying to me? I mean I dont bloody know what ye're saying to me.

Yes ye do.

Naw I dont.

Ye do so.

Look I dont. It's all nudges and winks.

People should see what's under their nose.

Exactly. I swallowed the last of the brandy and wanted another. This kind of rubbish drove ye to drink. Where was the wife? Fucking hell, she was being chatted up yet again. I glimpsed her through the throng. A guy with Grecian 2000 hair, dwarfing her. I knew the bastard. Big Tojo. Kidding on he was having to really stoop as well, so's he could see down the cleavage. Fucking dress she was wearing, I told her no to wear it. When she stood sideways ye could see everything, it was bloody disgraceful.

The wee woman said something else which I didni hear. I said yes to keep her happy but the nod she gave me was like I'd confirmed her suspicions. Maybe I had put my foot in something. I stepped to where the drink was lying and replenished the tumbler; I took another quick look at her while I was pouring: about five foot nothing in height. When ye come to think about it but, the clothes she was wearing, they looked reasonably smart. They did. Probably I had been misjudging her. What do ye call these things, a stole or something, fur; smelling of mothballs but it was fine on, probably hell of an old but she would have taken good care of it over the years; you could picture it. Expensive and fashionable for somebody that knew the score, somebody the same age as herself – the maw for instance, she would have clocked it immediately, that sort of deal. What the fuck age was she? At a guess, late forties – maybe even younger.

She had stopped looking at the brother now, she was back looking at Uncle Dan. That was all we needed, him to be involved – fucking scumbag, tightarsed bastard.

Aye she must have been attractive in her heyday but no doubt about that. She was probably much sought after. Uncle Boabby might have had to chase and chase to get her. I caught sight of da saying something quiet to the brother. Who knows what he was up to. I was never his confidant. The idea of putting a word in maw's ear about the wee woman and her marching in to confront him. But would she fuck. She wouldni care one way or the other. Her and da had been bored with each other for years. Their whole relationship was sarcasm centred. It ran in the family. Everybody. I'm a sarcastic bastard myself. Just ask the wife. And where was she now in the name of fuck she had disappeared. Naw, she had just moved to a more private corner, I could see her with Big fucking Tojo mafioso, he was right up close to her, stooping over her. Dont worry son just stand sideways and all will be revealed.

The cousin walked by, still in the bridegroom suit. He was one of us as well; we were all sarcastic bastards. But with malleable personalities. Even the hero, Uncle Boabby, he was a malleable personality. Plus his wife ran him ragged. Women dominated us completely. None of us were cut out for relationships at all. Fuck knows how the species survived. It was families like ours made sperm-banks a necessity.

The wee woman was giving me a frown.

Sorry, I said, I was away thinking about other things. Actually, to be honest, I was wondering, would you say my Uncle Boabby was a firm sort of guy, in your own experience, I mean to us boys he aye seemed to be, the strong silent type and aw that, but maybe he wisni. Any comments on that?

She gave an ironic chuckle.

That surprises me, I said. And the reason it surprises me is because to the best of my knowledge it was my auntie who was the dominant figure in that particular household.

Mmm. She frowned. People are different with people; they're basically chameleons as far as I'm concerned. It was the same when we stayed up in Perth, before him over there ruined things.

She was pointing directly at da. I glanced sideways to see if anybody had seen. And there was the wife. We stared at each other.

To tell the truth me and her have always had a special relationship. I tend to know when she needs me and vice versa. Just now was one such occasion. I fucking love her and that's that. We were just going through a bad feud at this point in time. The whole family was. I left the wee woman immediately and went to see if Mr 2000 was bothering her. He was a sharp big bastard in a mohair suit, flash dresser, a lot of patter. A bit of a gangster in fact. His family were noted in the drugs and money scene round a certain side of the city. He had certain connections one is not able to talk about. But it was easy to put a word in his ear. Come on, I said, whispering: This is a wedding, no a funeral, know what I mean, a wee bit of fucking respect.

He stepped back with a big smile: Boabby my man.

Aye, fucking Boabby my man!

I wisni meaning nothing.

Well ye know she's the wife man eh?

Aye but I thought she came alone.

What?

He laughed and poked me in the ribs.

She came alone but she's still my wife.

Can ye no take a joke?

Behave yerself for fuck sake ye're a guest. I mean I dont even know who invited ye.

The other side, he says, I know yer cousin's new wife's people. I know them quite well in fact.

Aw aye?

Aye.

Aye well I knew it wisni fucking our side ye knew.

Naw. He smiled. Excuse me a minute will ye . . . He winked at my wife and left.

Did I see that? Bastard. Big fucking bastard. Kidding on he was relaxed about everything as well. I would have done him in a minute if I had felt like it. The wife had stepped a couple of paces away from me now. She lifted a chicken drumstick and started nibbling at it; a dod of tomato sauce stuck to her upper lip. If you didni wear those bloody low-cut dresses, I whispered, smiling.

My dresses have got nothing to do with it.

Nothing to do with it! The tops of yer thingwis are showing.

It's a wedding.

So what it's a wedding, does that mean every man that looks at ye's got to see yer bloody boobs?

You're neurotic about my boobs.

I smiled. I brushed her left nipple. Remember when we got married, that night on our honeymoon.

Yeh yeh yeh, it was nice, ye were friendly. She knocked away my hand. Take yer paw off, she whispered.

Thanks o wife. I drew her into me. See that woman in the fur collar I'm talking to, I'm beginning to think her and the big brother have had an affair.

What?

Aye.

My wife smiled, she glanced at the wee woman who seemed to be engrossed in a world of her own. Naw, she said quietly, I dont think so.

Not only him my Uncle Boabby as well, the family hero, the guy I'm called after.

You're havering.

I'm no havering, that's what she's been telling me. Plus my da's got something to do with it.

Yer da?

Aye.

Mm.

Ever seen her before?

Never.

Neither have I. Think she might be a Sheriff Officer spy?

You're bloody paranoiac. By the way, yer grannie wants ye to drive her home, she told me a wee while ago. I told her ye were drunk and incapable.

For fuck sake, imagine telling somebody's grannie that.

Are ye?

Ye kidding? Yous fucking females man yous've planked the fucking booze.

Nonsense.

Anyway, I said, if she wanted me to drive her home she would have asked me hersel.

She's been trying to. She's been trying to attract yer attention. But you've been talking to *her* for the past hour.

What? Ye're no serious . . . She's in her bloody forties, maybe even fifties.

It never stopped ye before.

Take it easy baby.

Well, ye've done nothing but ignore me since we left the church, that's how Tojo asked me to go for a drink.

Pardon?

If ye had been here like a husband's supposed to.

Am I hearing right?

I had to put him off myself. And that's no easy.

What d'you mean it's no easy?

When ye're in amongst a crowd like this.

You telling me he actually asked ye to go for a drink with him?

My wife smiled and turned away. She was wearing a beautiful dress and it clung to her. I put my hand on her bum.

Take yer paw off.

What d'ye mean I was ignoring ye? I never ignore ye as well ye know, I can never take my eyes off ye, I'm aye ogling ye for Christ sake. That's how I clocked big fucking dyed skull chatting ye up.

Tch.

Standing there trying to look down yer dress into the bargain. And you were letting him.

Dont be bloody ridiculous.

Well how come ye stood sideways? Ye can fucking see everything when ye do that.

Dont be so bloody stupit jealous.

I'm no jealous, ye kidding? – I dont actually care.

Naw, you dont care.

I dont. I took hold of her elbow and breathed into her ear. How come ye're so truly beautiful? That's what I really want to know.

There speaks a smug husband.

Thanks very much . . . I stared at her, then shook my head; I left her standing and made my way back to the window. I needed to be alone. The wee woman joined me. I told her I was sorry for being away.

Oh that's alright, she said.

It's my wife I was talking to, we've been having problems recently, marital stuff.

It happens.

It bloody happens alright. What were ye saying about my brother again?

Yer brother?

I waited.

I wasni saying anything about yer brother.

Aw.

If you must know it was yer Uncle Robert.

And my da.

Och him, she said.

On ye go anyway, I said.

I dont want to talk about it anymore. Not in the present company.

D'ye mean me? Because it's just me that's listening.

Mm. Families are families.

Ye dont trust me in other words?

It's not a question of trust.

I just want to know.

Sssh. She hit my hand.

I looked at her. I dont like people doing that.

Well no wonder. It's what yer mother ought to've done years ago.

Is that a fact.

Dont be cheeky.

Did it come down to sex? I said, That's what I want to know, cause the rest's just fucking bullshit, know what I mean.

Sshhh.

Nobody cares in this company.

That's what you think.

They dont.

How do you know what people think? It strikes me you're the kind that's naive about relationships.

That's a joke for a start.

Hh.

I stared at her. Christ missis ye can be hell of an irritating at times.

She smiled. She shook her head slowly. There was definitely something attractive in her. Even although she was wizened her face had firm outlines. I got a sudden notion of her body. I hadnt thought about it before, but I could imagine it now. She would be one of these women that give ye a battering when they kiss ye on the mouth; right aggressive; hard as nails. Fucking hell.

Now she was frowning at something.

What is it? I said.

She whispered, Is that yer grannie?

What of it?

Thought so. What's she doing here?

Pardon?

The wee woman was staring across the room at her.

She's my cousin's grannie as well. She's got more right to be here than any of us, I mean it was her that fucking started it all.

Mm.

Do you know her like?

I havent seen her for years. She was watching us.

Watching us?

Yes.

Ach it disni matter, she's blind as a bat. Anyway, she never minds what I get up to, I'm her blue-eyed boy

– which is true. I could sleep with every woman in Glasgow and she wouldnt mind. But she would mind if I stopped discussing what I'm doing on a day-to-day basis, how I'm living my life generally. She enjoys hearing me speak. She lives in one of these sheltered housing places where it's all old folk and it drives her daft. So she likes to listen to the young folk. She says she doesnt but she does. Up to a point I've always confided in her.

I know about yer grannie, said the wee woman, she's mean-spirited.

I beg yer pardon?

It's true.

Naw it's no she's an auld woman. Her view of life's old-fashioned, she thinks men have got one thing on their mind and one thing only and she just puts up with it. As long as it disni involve her. She stopped having sex when she was twenty-eight. She told me. She never liked it very much except one experience she had in her mid-teens when she worked on a farm and she met this aulder guy who turned her on behind a haystack in the month of June. Apart from that no, it was just a chore to do with evolution. She's an atheist but she's got a humanitarian outlook; if people want the world to continue and develop then fair enough, that's her opinion, she's no going to stop them, even although personally she's a pessimist, I mean a real one.

Is that yer wife over there?

D'ye want to have a word with my grannie like?

No thanks. I dont think it would be appropriate somehow . . . She spoke out the corner of her mouth.

Appropriate?

The big tall man with her. God he's a beast . . .

What! I turned to follow her eyes. Bloody bastard! Soon as my back's turned! Fucking Tojo, there he was, bending over her yet again. A mental age of twelve the bastard. Mind you but I mean that's how me and her were going through a bad feud at the present moment in time. Women dress the way they dress and it's us get provoked. That's the problem with summer weddings as well, ye get all these females parading around with their bodies everywhere. The cousin's wife man what a cracker! Fuck knows how he managed to get off with her, weedy wee cunt. A lassie from Balornock. I used to see her quite a lot. She ran around with a team that thought they were heavy. One of them was a guy from the Milton I used to play football with. We knocked fuck out each other at all grades, Boys' Guild to the fucking Juveniles. I bumped into him recently in a pub up the town, he tried to click my ankles on the way to the fucking bar. What was I saying. The new sister-in-law. When we were boys and that, playing football, her and her mates on the touchline, she used to wear these jeans and her figure was something to behold, it drove ye fucking potty with that shirt blouse thing tied at the ends and her waist so slender and then the beautiful hips and the tight creases under her bum and at the front too like it would cause her extreme uncomfort vagina-wise; that's how women get thrush – but even now in her wedding-gown Christ almighty it hid everything and revealed everything because ye knew precisely what she looked like below, there she would be standing in her bra and panties just I mean that's all – silk too because it's her wedding night and ye can imagine yer hand on the hem line it drives ye fucking bananas.

But ye wonder how yer cousin gets off with women like that. When we were wee he wouldni say boo to a goose. Now he can patter any woman he meets. Wee fucking bastard so he is, smug wee cunt. There's a side of life that's hard to work out. Sex is right at the root of it, it's right at the very soul. That's how I think my grannie's got her head screwed on. I just personally think she shouldni have given up on it when she was twenty eight which is only a year aulder than the wife.

I saw the cousin leave the room. Probably away to change out the bridegroom suit. I noticed as well before the cake was cut all the close relations, we were all lined up for the photographs, and she was to give us all a kiss, the new bride, all the men; he wisni too pleased, ye could see it on his coupon, the cousin, trying to kid on he was hearty or somefuckingthing. The same when I got her up to dance later on. We did one of these stupid waltzes and it wound up we were gonni chuck it because folk were looking and she was getting embarrassed. But they were just looking cause she was the bloody bride. So we started doing one of them stand-on-the-spot-and-wiggle numbers, and her wedding dress man, beautiful, all silk and just fucking gorgeous, I got a semi immediately, I had to leave the floor, and who's staring at me, wee fucking weedy chops man the cousin, staring at me.

Fuck him.

Just nature anyway. Maybe he thought I was taking the piss cause I left her standing. Fucking eedjit.

A wee nephew came walking by in his kilt, pulling a clockwork lorry on a bit of string, a big piece of slabbery chocolate cake in his hand. I grabbed his shoulder. Heh you, get a plate for that cake else it'll fall on the carpet.

Uncle Boabby, he said, I need the toilet and there's somebody in.

Well just wait at the door.

But there's a big queue.

Well just bloody go to the front and skip in first.

I canni and I'm needing.

I'll take him, said the wee woman.

– I had forgotten all about her. Ah he's alright, I said, let him go himself.

I'll take him, she said.

Look missis, the truth is you're a bit of an interloper here I mean it's a family deal know what I mean, know what I'm talking about?

There's family and family.

Ye can say that again.

I'll take the boy, she said.

Whatever ye like, I dont fucking care. I'm going for a pint anyway.

D'ye no think you've had enough to drink?

Naw.

She turned her head and went off with the wee nephew. I knew her game. Fucking obvious. Taking the wee yin to the lavvy man it let her kid on she was tried and trusted. Ye could see through it a mile away. All the yarns she'd been handing me. Maybe I just hidni made myself clear. I couldni give a fuck what she did, or thought for that matter – I didni give a fuck what any of them thought. All except the wife. And big fucking mafioso was still all over her. Definitely out of order. I should just have walked across and let him have it, just banjoed the bastard. Charles fucking Atlas. Steve fucking Zchwasenbacker or whatever his fucking name is, Arnold or something. Either that or I should've got a return bout with the bride, but she had disappeared as well now, probably through with the rest of the women, the aulder generation – fuck them all. For some reason but I wanted to gub my Uncle Dan.

The small bird and the young person

– as for example were a Small Bird to thud into your face. Consider the following: a Young Person is chancing to stroll upon an island somewhere in the Firth of Clyde. THUD. A Small Bird crashes onto the bridge of the nose of the Young Person. The day has been fine, a mid-afternoon with an Autumnal sun warm enough to enable the coat to be discarded should the breeze die. Now, the idea of ducking to avoid the collision will never have occurred to the Young Person for quite often you will come to find that birds do fly on courses indicative of just such a collision. At the last possible moment, however, they will dip a wing sufficiently to swerve off. Not this time! While the Young Person is staggering the Small Bird will drop to the ground and lie still, its feathers stiffly spread. Having covered face with hands the Young Person will, in time, withdraw the hands for an examination of the person. But effects to the body will almost certainly be minimal; a little blood, the slight cut, a possible temporary swelling. And nothing else, apart from the stunned Bird. While the view hereabouts will be extensive the Young Person can see nobody in sight. After a moment the spread feathers begin fluttering; soon the Small Bird starts rising in helicoptereal fashion. Staring at it with furrowed brow the Young Person will turn suddenly and yell, before dashing headlong in the direction of the shingle shoreline.

the Christmas shopping

That obelisk thing I was talking about, it was lying stranded down the back of Argyle Street. Most of the folk passing stopped to look at it but they didnt wait long, they carried on walking. They just werent that interested. Even if they had thought about lifting it I mean it was just too big, they would have needed a block and tackle. A couple of guys from Molly's Bar passed and that's obviously what they were thinking too, there were four of them but they wouldnt have been able to handle it, one of them was fucking pished anyway but plus as well as that they would have got spotted, busies everywhere. Then the teenagers. They were laughing. Quite right as well at their age. Maybe they were laughing at the obelisk thing I'm no sure, a case of the king's clothes or something who knows, I couldnt quite make it out. Teenagers, you're never quite sure – there again you would expect to, because unless you die young everybody's been one I mean it should be bloody predictable, but it's no, you're never quite sure. They also had one of them music machines on loud and a boy started dancing round it. Then there was this posh cunt with a bowler and a brolly came along, the striped shirt and waistcoat, the works, he was probably cutting through by the old library to the Buchanan Street Stock Market, the old yin. He was annoyed but, you could see it a mile away; cause of the lack of respect they were showing it, the teenagers, maybe because it was Christmas, if it was a religious symbol, a Catholic one maybe or something, I dont know. But he was annoyed anyway. But these bastards are always fucking annoyed, they're never anything else. He probably had it figured they were taking the mickey out of life and history because it was a symbol from the past and here they were laughing like fuck. That's our history he was thinking but being a coward – probably afraid of public opinion – he kept his eyes to the front, doing his fucking city gent march on past. Another one of the teenagers, a nice-looking wee lassie, she wanted to paint it! Let's get a hold of some paint and we'll give it a coat! But after a bit more laughter, about nudity and naked bodies and that off they went down the street to do a bit of shoplifting from the Argyle Street shops, them big department stores. Ya fucking dancer, that's what I would do if I was their age.

Then the genteel little old lady. Classic. Straight out an English movie, one of these comedy-type ones. Along the pavement she came with a really determined walk, the word's 'dignified', and smartly dressed as well but there was something about the way she went that made you think she was on the look-out for folk's big feet in case she tripped over them, cause that's a problem for senior citizens. Her clothes were right old-fashioned, just like you'd expect. She had a shopping bag into the bargain, you dont see many like that nowadays, real leather probably, plus the tweed coat and that all buttoned up to the neck, and a bit of flimsy stuff poking out – lace? – something anyway. Quite a crookit back, bent over a fair way. And poking out her shopping bag was a bunch of yellow-topped flowers, tulips maybe or else daffodils. She saw the teenagers, she put one hand up to her neck. Old women like this hardly see anybody at all when they're out walking except weans or teenagers, because maybe they think there might be trouble with them, as if they might start playing some sort of rowdy game and wind up they knock them flying, you canni fucking blame them, the old folk. But then when she saw the teenagers were just going off down the road, the music machine blaring, that was when she spotted the obelisk thing. She just walked right up to it. She did, and she looked at it. It was like she was examining it, with no worries about passersby thinking she was daft. Totally unselfconscious. You notice that about a lot of old folk. Seen it and done it; that's the picture; seen it and done it. She stood in close up to it with what you might call a dreamy look on her face as if it was reminding her about her childhood or something, her old grandpa with a tale about the Indian Mutiny or something, maybe her sweetheart who emigrated to New Zealand, something like that. A real throwback, she put me in mind of Mrs Lafferty, an old biddy used to live where I grew up. God love us she must have been about eighty one, eighty two. And in a funny way she seemed fucking older – no because of her health because she was probably fit as a fiddle, she was just bloody christ I dont know what it was. It was then that the woman with the red hat stopped and the two of them smiled at each other. She said something to the old lady but maybe she was a bit corn beef because she just smiled for a wee minute and then she started walking, leaving the woman with the red hat just standing there with what you would call a bemused look on her face. I was wondering what would happen next. But nothing did. So I just walks up to the thing myself and I stared at it, and it wasni even a real obelisk, it was more like a Celtic Cross. The woman with the hat was just standing there no knowing what to make of it. I felt like asking her if she fancied going for a coffee or a cup of tea or something but then I noticed something in her face when she sees me so I says to myself, Fuck that for a game, and I just crosses ower into Ingram Street and I carried along the way I was going. Some women are funny, I wisni taking any chances.

events in yer life

Last year a 36 year old guy dropped dead while playing a game of football. Derek knew him a wee bit. They drank in the same pub down near the docks. Quite a nice guy, a lorry driver. He liked Scottish people and once or twice let Derek know he was making a trip north on the off chance he wanted a hitch. Married with three kids. What can ye do? There's nothing ye can do. Except to stop laying blame on yerself, it's nonsense, self-indulgent shit; as if ye're centre of the universe. Probably the guy's wife had blamed herself; why had she no told him to stay home that Sunday afternoon, any excuse, make him mow the lawn, they coulda gone shopping or something, anything, it wouldni have mattered, it just wouldni have mattered, to stop him collecting the football boots, just to stop him from playing, from going to play.

Fuck.

The phone rang. It was his sister Linda. She was coming round later on to pick up a few things. Will I bring ye in something to eat? she said.

Naw, I'm fine.

Ye sure?

Yeh.

People cared about ye. They looked after ye. Even when they needed looking after themself. It was amazing. What had he ever done to deserve it? Fuck all really. He hadni really done anything.

He turned off the television. He never usually watched it, he had been out the habit for a long time. Watching it in the morning was especially awful; it was only the Scottish accents made it interesting. He felt like going out for a walk but apart from a couple of shops there was nothing to see except houses – houses houses and houses. What was he going to do with his life, that was the thing. Although after Linda went he could go for a pint. But he didni want to, no to that fucking local anyway. Either they stared at ye or they didni so much as look at ye. Twice he had been in. He hadni met one person. Not one. Thank fuck. He felt like phoning Audrey, the girlfriend. She would be at her work but that wouldni matter, he could still talk to her.

He wasnt going to, he just wasnt going to.

What was he doing what was he doing . . .

Oh christ, oh fuck sake, oh fuck, fuck fuck, oh fuck. His eyelids had been clenched shut; he relaxed himself, fixed a cushion at the end of the sofa and lay down, then curled up on his side, staring at the gas fire. There were these three things in his life: his old man getting killed; doing the stupid thing at art school; now his mother dying, his mother dead. He was thirty one. He was thirty one and he didnt feel like he was making a good job of his life. He kept getting tearful, he kept getting tearful. But that was alright, that was alright. It was alright. It was just

christ. He got up. He went over to the mirror and looked into it. There was the pad and the pen, he started sketching. He had a bit of a sore head. He wasnt sleeping, he just wasnt sleeping. It was being here, he just wasni comfortable. Too many fucking ghosts. That was the problem, too many ghosts.

Nor were his sockets red rimmed, they were not; the tears just ran like from a tap and he wasni wiping them. There was nothing to convince himself about. Grief. He was not at the con. It was just grief.

He needed a shave. He was not going to shave.

He sketched quickly. There was nothing wrong with his eyes he just was tired, tired. Mum was dead. Never mind she was too young she was dead. She hadni even reached 70 and that was bad and it was unfair. But so what, it had happened. If he had phoned more often. He could have phoned. He coulda kept more in touch. He shoulda kept more in touch. Ye just get out the habit, that's all, there was nothing really to reproach himself about. It wasni his fault. It wasni anybody's fault. She had just died. That was that. Everybody was prepared for it. So it wasni a shock. That side of things was fine, there wereni any grumbles, not as such –

– what the fuck does that mean? as such, what does it mean? Ye say these things.

The first real adult experience of death.

Shut the fuck up.

He laid down the pad, continued staring into the mirror. The sockets were not red rimmed. They were not.

He returned to the sofa; switching on the television as he went.

Up until the funeral he had been staying in Plymouth. He had a job there he quite enjoyed. He wrapped it before leaving. Not unusual for him. But he was also needing a break. Necessary in fact. He liked Audrey, he really did, but still and all, he needed to get away. He couldni have brought her anyway. She would have had to go back to work. It woulda been hard for her getting the time. But he coulda asked her. He didnt. He didnt ask her. He didni want her here. He wanted to be on his own. He needed to get here and be on his own. That was how he would handle it. He needed to handle it. He needed to know.

What did he need to know? He needed to know he could make it. He needed to know he was fine. That was it, he just fucking needed to know he was fine.

Because he didni know what he was going to do next. That was the crux. He might even sign on the dole. Or head off somewhere else altogether once the business was sorted out. He was getting sick of Plymouth; he was, he was getting sick of the bloody place. There was a lot of his stuff left in the flat but so what, she would keep it for him. Or else just dump it. What did it fucking matter. It didni fucking matter at all; it was just junk; all the stuff he had, it was just junk, fucking junk.

Ah mum. Mum mum. A weeish sort of woman with a surprised look on her face. No wonder, no bloody wonder. He wiped at the wetness round his eyes with the knuckles of his right hand.

Of course there were all these memories everywhere. A whole stack of things she had kept. When he saw them it was her he was seeing, because it was her had kept them. Although the actual things came from other folk they were hers. Ach but they wereni, no really. They were just there. They were just there waiting for somebody, somebody like him, family, just to come along and see them – he was the ideal person. One or two to do with the old man himself. Not just photos but mementoes, his Royal Marine bunnet and belt; some other stuff from Burma and places, medals. He had even forgotten dad was in the Royal Marines. The stuff lay in a cardboard suitcase. There wasni much but christ it was good, poor old bastard – well he wasni even old at all christ almighty he was young, fifty-four, getting killed outright, a tragedy, but there you are, life's full of them.

Funny that was what he remembered, the surprised look on her face. It was definitely from way back. The world did things to ye. The world just did things to ye. It killed yer husband. Yer son went away. But there were still the sisters. They had all stayed.

Fuck.

He made a cup of tea. All this wallowing. He needed to eat as well. He shoulda let Linda fix it for him.

Still a reasonable-sized lump of cheese in the fridge. He had been eating his way through the stuff in the pantry, all the tins. That would have pleased mum anyway, the lack of waste. O christ she wouldni have fucking cared, known, known or cared, just nothing, nothing, just surprise, surprise surprise surfuckingprise, my god.

He had been rooting about the house. Looking in cupboards and drawers. He hadni done it for years so it was all a bit weird. A lot of his own stuff was there as well. Christ! He kept finding these 'things'. An armband with all his badges from the Boys' Brigade, the B.B. – or the B.B.'s as Mrs Cassidy used to call it, the auld next door neighbour, a Catholic. The B.B.'s. And some lassies at school. The B.B.'s! They just did it to annoy you.

And the bible.

Bible. What does 'bible' mean? He got it for regular attendance. That was him as a boy, sure and steadfast, safe and sorry, a slight lack in imagination. Rubbish, he wasni like that at all. Then the photos from primary school. All the faces. Poor wee bastards. From another world. Probably half of them would still be staying roundabout here. Never having went anywhere. Never having really done fuck all, no even to look back on and tell their kids. But what had he done? That's the problem with memories, nostalgia, sentimentality, ye end up on a downer because of yer own life.

Three of his pictures lay propped against the back wall of the walk-in press. Glazed efforts. He knew they would be here. They were amazing. He used to be the Great White Hope of the family. Being the only male was the major part of that of course. He painted them early on at secondary school, two portraits and a landscape, part of his portfolio. Where was the fucking rest of it? At the bottom of some dusty cupboard probably, or else shredded.

They were bloody good as well. Christ. Mum and dad were really chuffed when he showed them. The landscape especially was good. A view from the bedroom window. He did it a few times at different ages; it was a nice thing with a garden fence, all these pointed stakes, all different sizes, all individuated. The guy it belonged to had painted the top bits red and the bottom bits white and they always looked really good against the sharp cut hedges. Mr Fleming was his name. Christ, Mr Fleming. Him and dad were in the church bowling club or something. Poor old bastard, he hated a ball landing in his garden. Boys playing 'rowdy' games outside in the street, that kind of stuff, it really pissed him off. What was he doing now? The fence had gone. But probably he was still alive and kicking. Crabbit auld bastards like that, they usually lived to a hundred.

But it was nice seeing them again; rediscovering what he was doing at 13, 14, it gave him hope for the future. Maybe he wasni a fucking waster after all. Maybe his life would change! Maybe this was a turning point! He would now become a real artist. His destiny was about to be fulfilled!

The doorbell. Linda.

Elizabeth and Marilyn were his other two sisters. Marilyn lived in Ayr, the other two still in Glasgow. Linda was the eldest and Marilyn the second, Elizabeth being next up from himself. In other words, apart from everything else, he was the fucking baby of the family, the wee pet; he got spoiled rotten, that's how come he was the half-wit ye saw today.

She came in with two cups of tea while he was kneeling on the floor; he was rummaging through a shoebox collection of old photographs. He had finished a cup before she arrived but it woulda ruined the image to tell her. She knelt down beside him. It was cheery and sad, really sad. He never quite felt there in the family, no as far as these kind of memories were concerned. The same with all the talking after the funeral; too many of the stories were early, they didni concern him except as a spectator. So much had happened either before he was born or when he was too wee to have any say in the matter.

I was just that bit young, he said. I mean you were married when I was at primary school.

Yeh. Linda was smiling at a photograph showing him up on dad's shoulders. It was me took this one, she said.

Mum, Marilyn and Elizabeth were also there, everybody hand in hand; dad's shirt open at the neck but smart-looking in a way that seemed ancient. Derek was wearing a strange white hat which he seemed to remember. Was that possible? He could only have been about 3 at the time. Mum smallish and carrying a bit of weight – that smile on her face; he knew that smile; and the coat she was wearing, he knew that as well. How come she carried that bit of weight though? She never seemed to eat. Funny. That whole world, whatever it was, totally gone now, vanished forever. Ah christ. He sighed and put his left arm round Linda's shoulders: Ye're wearing perfume.

I'm no past it yet you . . . But her concentration was on the photograph: Ye were petted as a baby, she said.

Och away.

Ye were.

Petted . . . !

A bit. Linda was smiling . . . That holiday, she said; that was the time Elizabeth fell off the bike and skint her knee. She was always a moaning-faced wee besom – ye shoulda heard her scream!

I remember.

Do ye?

Yeh. It was a caravan we were staying.

O God it wasni half a caravan! Linda chuckled. The toilet was miles away, they called it a latrine. We all had a potty!

Each?

No each! My God though Derek that holiday was one in a million.

I mind we had to go across the Forth Bridge on a train.

That's right.

Although I dont know whether it's me or just yous all talking about it I remember. Yeh . . . He took the photograph from her. The pad and the pen were in the living room. He studied it. What would he have got from it? Ach, just something, there was something there; beautiful wee lassies his sisters, mum and dad, him as well, the wee boy, beautiful. He shut his eyes; what ye should do is drip yer tears into a cup and then dip in yer pen.

Linda had lifted another one out.

But it was these group studies. They were the ones. They were the real thing. The mysteries. I'll get it, said Linda; the phone ringing, she got up from the floor. Whatever it was it was the group studies. When he was a hundred and thirty six he would be ready to start on them. Up until that point, up until that point.

It was for him, the phone. He frowned. It's Bill Finlayson, she said.

Christ . . . Derek grinned and strode through to the living room. Fin! Hullo?

Mister Hannah.

How ye doing?

How ye doing yerself?

Fine christ. Good to hear ye.

I wasni sure ye'd be back?

Coupla days ago.

Good.

Yeh.

I was sorry to hear about yer mother. I saw it in the *Times.*

Yeh.

I thought about going to the funeral . . .

Ye shoulda.

Aye.

So how's life treating ye?

Aw fine, alright.

Good, that's good.

Aye. Listen d'ye fancy a pint or something, when ye going back?

A pint'd be great, great.

Him and Linda in the kitchenette eating toast and cheese. She had cleared the photos away and started making it while he was on the telephone. It was a tiny space but there was a pull-down table joined to one wall. Dad had done the joinering. He used to be quite good with his hands.

Yeh, said Linda, when mum got him going.

Ye mean he was lazy . . . Derek smiled.

I dont mean he was lazy; just he had been out at his work all day.

Yeh, yeh, of course.

Saturday morning then he'd go to the match: ye only saw him on Sundays; sometimes he worked them as well.

Hard for mum.

It was.

It wasnt all good fun.

Linda looked at him.

It wasni easy, he said.

She reached to the oven and lifted across the teapot. Ye aye had a sharp tongue Derek, she said.

Did I?

She shook her head. She flicked her lighter to light her cigarette. She blew out the smoke, sipped at her tea.

I didni think I was that bad.

Linda raised her eyebrows.

Smoking does ye damage, he said.

She pointed at the spare slice of toast. That's for you as well.

Feed the man. I've been looking after myself for a while now ye know I mean I'm no exactly handless.

Shut up and bloody eat.

Sexist.

Sexist? She frowned.

He hadni been going to stay long anyway. Even during the funeral, he had known it then. But now the decision was final. That was definitely it. Two more days. He would get drunk tonight with Fin; they hadni seen each other for a coupla years. That would get the other thing out his system. What other thing? His fucking life.

Maybe Sammy would turn up as well. Him and Derek had

started as students the gether. Fucking hell, nearly thirteen years ago.

He finished the toast then ate the half-eaten bit on Linda's plate. That was definitely sexist. Maybe she had just left it there and was coming back to polish it off later. But she had gone to phone a taxi and pack a few bags. It occurred to him she really was hoping he would stay. It was nice. It was nice. If he could maybe keep on the house or something, get it put under his own name. His sister Elizabeth had mentioned that at the funeral. It was a good big four-apartment. Mum never went to the trouble of buying it so it didni actually belong to the family, not as 'property'. It wasni political, not as such, she just never got round to doing the business. She mentioned the idea in a letter to him once. Maybe the sisters had suggested it. But they wouldni have put her under any pressure. Ye never know though. Ye just never know. What sort of pressures other folk are under, especially if they're short of money. Ye could end up doing anything. What was Linda putting in her bags for instance, what sort of stuff was she taking?

What a thought. What a thought. He smiled and got up from the stool, he walked to the kitchenette window and stared out for a moment then sat back down and drank a mouthful of tea. None of it concerned him anyway, it was none of his business. A dispassionate bastard. He had been too long on his own. Maybe if he had settled down and was rearing a family. Linda had been a mother for twenty years: twenty years.

Down in the back a woman was hanging up washing, a toddler playing by her feet, now hanging onto her leg.

Plus Elizabeth could be a bit pushy in some ways; it was noticeable at the funeral. But she didni have an easy time of it either; she had to be practical, her own man was a bit of an idiot where money was concerned. It mighta suited her if mum had bought the house. So it could be sold later on.

Who the fuck cares. Past history. All of it.

The taxi arrived. No a hackney, just an ordinary car.

The driver got out and opened the boot and Derek helped him lift in Linda's bags.

Here you, she said.

Derek glanced at her and smiled; she was holding her arms out. They cuddled tight. She was crying. Yeh. The feeling that when he left Daneside Drive this time he would never see it again; this was it. A final event. Another final event. He shut his eyes to stop the tears. Poor old mum for christ sake poor old mum poor old fucking mum. He clenched the lids but the spasms shook his shoulders and he knew Linda would feel it but so what she would feel it so fucking what so fucking what.

The driver had returned to his seat and closed the door. His window was down and ye could hear a Radio 1 disc jockey with that horrible jolly voice. He didni want to go back to England either, he just didni want to go back there. Time to get out Britain altogether, he had been back too long, time to get away, a bit of freedom.

Linda was standing beside him. Did I scratch yer face? he said.

Dont worry about it. She smiled. Tommy only shaves once a week. And that's when he's going to play snooker with his mates. Are ye staying the weekend? Have ye decided.

She was holding his arms. I'm no sure, he said.

Tch . . . she sighed.

Ye going to tell me to settle down!

It would be no use would it?

Look Linda I settled down a while ago.

Come back to Glasgow.

Maybe.

Yer girlfriend'll come.

Derek chuckled.

She will. Just ask her. Linda let go his arms and he put his hands in his trouser pockets. She got into the rear of the car and he closed the door; her smile to him was self-conscious.

He waved till the taxi turned a corner, then stood for a minute watching two middle-aged men pass on the other side of the street, they seemed to be arguing about something.

He still had to finish the business details. The undertakers; the wreaths and the entourage, the three motor cars. It was a bit ironic that when ye were dead the cash for yer wreath came out what ye had left behind. I would like to buy some flowers for my funeral. Imagine leaving a message. He was going to leave one, on a postcard, with a seaside view, in with the last will and testament. I want a bunch of red and yellow tulips, I want them placed at the bottom end of the coffin, just above my feet. Pay for it out the petty cash.

He didni mind attending to the business. The sisters had taken for granted it would be one of them doing it but they were glad to leave it to him. Surprised as well, like it had never occurred to them. Quite right, he wasni exactly reliable.

Also the idea it might stop arguments. It happens. Once there's a death everybody starts fighting over the goods. Mum didni have a great deal of stuff but whatever there was would have to be disposed of. He had no especial interest; most of it seemed to be linen. Although some of the mementoes would be nice to hang onto. Plus there was a hat he found in the cupboard where the gardening tools were kept, he quite liked it. But apart from that and a couple of photographs he didni want nothing; nothing; that was what he was entitled to, fucking nothing.

The idea of staying on in Glasgow. Even if he couldni get the house put into his own name. He could rent a flat somewhere. He still had a couple of quid. Audrey might come up. She might no right enough. Did he want her to come up? Whatever. It was the idea she wouldni want to. He just wasni sure. Given the choice she probably wouldni; she would stay where she was. Yeh, that was the reality. She would stay; she had her own people; it wasni so much the place but she had her own people. And the job, she liked the job. In his experience that was what women liked, jobs, they liked their jobs. That was a fucking funny word, job; what does that mean? job.

But how would he get by? Living away from Scotland for so long he was totally out the scene. Could he handle it? Who knows.

He had the pad by the bedroom window and was sketching, a hand-mirror propped in front of him; one continuous line, if it didni work in one continuous line . . . The sky had got dark, big heavy clouds full of rain. He was leaving as soon as the business was done. They could do what they liked with the house. And everything that was in it. Including his three paintings. Fuck it. There's no escaping the facts of life.

He was wearing the hat he had found. Maybe dad had worn it. He couldni remember, but whose else could it be? It was a most unGlasgow hat.

The Hannah resemblance was definitely there. Weird. Fucking hell but he was a strange bastard; he was, how strange, how strange people are, people are so strange, doing these things to one another, to themselves, they do things to themselves, a kind of masochistic quality. He sketched fast. But his face was straightforward – what's a straightforward face? silly bastard, but no, straightforward, nothing startling, a face, a man's face, bits of mum and bits of dad; bits of the sisters – my god these photographs where mum's self-consciousness, having to put up with the camera, the tension, these signs of strain, just the way she looked. How come he hadni phoned more regularly? He could definitely have phoned more regularly. He nudged up the hat so it lay to one side. He took it off and went to the bathroom, washed his face in cold water. Back in the bedroom he closed the window. He would definitely keep wearing the hat. It was appropriate. Quite gallus as they used to say. Monsieur Gauguin s'il vous plaît, the one with Anthony Quinn. He would have to pluck up courage to wear it outside on the street though. The weans would laugh at him, little bastards, they'd fling stones at it. That's what happens in Glasgow, it's the opposite of an attitude problem. He lifted the hat off the bed and looked at it. There's no escaping the facts of life.

That seemed to be becoming a motto of his. What did it mean? Facts of life.

It was a pub down by Charing Cross him and Fin were meeting, which would take him a good hour to get to, by the time he waited for a bus. And he needed two of the bastards; one into the city centre then another one out. Unless he walked it. He could walk it, depending on the weather; it would be nice to walk it, see the city. He was well used to walking anyway, the number of times he landed skint and options there were none. The price of another pint or yer bus fare home, that was an auld yin. There's always tomorrow. Fucking banalities, ye just say them.

The thing that was irking him was Sammy; no irking him a lot but it was still irking him. If Fin had phoned then he coulda phoned. Unless he had left Glasgow. It would be good to see him again, see how he was doing – that gallery he was getting involved with. Maybe he was back painting again. Fin was a close mate but Sammy had been closer. But he was a bastard, these social formalities, they just never occurred to him, things like phoning people. Untrue. They occurred to him, he just fucking ignored them. Unless he didni know. No everybody reads the death notices. Maybe he should give him a bell later, just say hello, see how he was doing.

Mum used to like Sammy, she thought he was a well-brought-up boy. He came from Stonehaven and had a nice accent, that made him exotic. People like exotica, it makes a change. Plus his parents had money; if yer parents have money folk think ye're well-brought-up. Derek had never wanted money. What a lie. How come ye say these things, ye just seem to open yer fucking mouth. Sammy used to call Derek his associate. Imagine calling yer mate an 'associate'? So what, eighteen years of age, ye were just a boy. No big deal.

As it turns out he didni walk it from the scheme into the city after all; he was going to but eventually he couldni be bothered, he took a taxi. Fin had arrived first and set him a pint up immediately. A big pint of heavy; beautiful. The pub was just round from the Mitchell Library, near enough the old stamping ground but without being one of the campus boozers as such. It was okay. Quite busy. A young crowd but mixed, business-type people plus a few that looked arty, students maybe; torn jeans and a coupla shaven nappers; some of the women were beautiful. When Derek went for the next round the woman behind the bar ignored him. Eventually a tall skinny boy took the order. At least he smiled. But maybe it was the hat. He had stuck it on at the last minute. So he now stood revealed as one more arty farty bastard. Unless the barmaid remembered him being drunk in the place years ago and was bearing a grudge. Glasgow pubs. He shifted his stance. He could see Fin sitting at the table, footering with the near empty pint glass. Fin was good. He hadni really got to know him until the end of the second term. Without him phoning there woulda been nothing. And there wasni anything else. Fucking weird. Life is fucking weird.

He got his change and carried the drink to the table. Heh Fin, he said, some great-looking women in this place.

I know.

Is that how ye chose it?

Who me?

Bastard.

I'm a married man.

Does that make a difference?

Unfortunately yes.

Heh, mind that time we did the walk at Glencoe?

I do aye.

That was a real highlight for me ye know.

It was a nice weekend. That wee pub down Kinlochleven.

The climbing itself I mean.

Well wait till ye get the rope on. Pity ye wereni staying a few days longer, ye coulda had a crack at it. I could aye get ye a pair of boots . . .

I could get a pair myself.

Sure. But if ye couldni.

Derek nodded. Sounds good.

It is good, keeps ye sane. Cheers . . . Fin sipped at the new pint.

So ye dont see anybody these days?

Nah. Apart from Matt, but he never talks.

I had this idea ye'd all meet regularly for reunions.

Aye!

Ye forget the world doesni stand still.

Fin licked the tips of both forefingers and smoothed the lines of hair round the top of his head: It's alright for you, he said, I'm gone baldy.

Naw ye're no.

Aye I am.

Naw ye're no.

I am.

It doesni fucking look like it to me.

Dont be nice, I've known ye too long.

Derek took off the hat and laid it on the table, scratched at the crown of his head: I'm losing it as well.

Are ye fuck. Fin lifted the hat, he examined it. Nice hat. They're in style ye know. Glasgow chic. I've got one myself; I didni shove it on in case ye laughed. It's sharp as fuck but, unlike this yin!

Derek smiled. He took it back and put it on. He sipped the top of the new pint while glancing round the pub.

So: how did ye land in Plymouth?

Uch fuck long story; long boring story; it's a short story in fact it's no a long story at all. What about you though, how come ye chucked the Parks Department?

A fit of pique. I had a row with a gaffer.

Derek grinned.

He was a cheeky bastard.

All gaffers are cheeky bastards.

My da's a gaffer. Course he's a cheeky bastard too.

Ye just signing on then?

Aye. I'm looking after the wee yin though. A full-time job in itself that. I quite like it actually, changing nappies and all that, it's aesthetically pleasing. I've found my métier.

Ye doing anything else?

Like what?

Derek shrugged.

Ye talking about *art*!

I'm talking about anything.

Nah. Fin lifted the pint tumbler. I'm just a Monroe freak. Ye know what a 'Monroe' is?

What?

A 'Monroe', it's a hill over three thousand feet; any hill over three thousand feet; that's what they call it, a 'Monroe'.

Where?

Where? Scotland, where d'ye think?

Well how the fuck do I know? I was thinking ye were talking about one actual place – Glencoe or something, Aviemore . . . I dont fucking know.

Nah, it covers the whole country.

Christ.

It takes fucking ages to do the lot, sometimes years. I used to get away every weekend, me and a coupla mates; no so much these days. But we'll come again, we'll come again.

Good.

Aye. Fin shrugged. So what about you?

Nothing really.

Ye were in Spain?

Aye but that's a while ago, a coupla years.

Aw.

Plymouth the now but before that it was Bristol. Spain was

before that again – in fact I think I'd left there the last time we met. Ye know the name of the last place I was working? the Jolly Roger, a bar in Fuengerola; the Jolly Roger! The name sums it up.

Fish and chips and pints of lager?

Just about.

I had these visions too, you with a band of rebels, shifting munitions over the mountains in southern Andalusia, on a mule. George Orwell. Or Hemingway.

Yeh.

So it wasni like that?

Naw.

Ach well, I never did trust that cunt, him and his big-game fishing. Mind you, being honest, I canni say I ever really fancied the country that much, a bit touristy for me.

No it all. Derek shrugged. Parts of it are good. If ye like climbing too I mean . . . They're fitba daft as well, the people. Some good teams.

No as good as here.

Nonsense.

Fin grinned. Ye were saying ye were up last Christmas?

I was, yeh.

Ye shoulda phoned.

I was only here a coupla days.

Still . . .

Ah ye know what like it is; by the time ye see the family . . . And ye canni miss one out, ye hurt their feelings. I didni stay for New Year.

Ye didni stay for New Year!

Naw.

New Year? The famous Hogmanay!

I had just started in the job.

Some Scotsman you are!

Give us a break.

Fin chuckled, raising the pint tumbler to his lips. So ye like England I take it?

Plymouth, yeh, I suppose I do, yeh . . .

Fin drank a mouthful of beer.

Yeh, it's alright. I like being near the sea. Sometimes it reminds me a bit of this place. I quite like the people.

How come ye dont go to a place like London?

There isni a place like London, it's a one-off. Anyway I spent a bit of time there. It's alright. I might go back. I dont think so but. A wee bit enclosed for me – no horizons.

Fin sat back on his chair and folded his arms: Yes my man, ye've been leading a bit of a life.

No really.

Aye ye have.

I've no; it might seem that way: it's just called 'being rootless'. Derek got up suddenly: I need a piss. He paused and muttered, See what I mean . . .

Three females were sitting at a table he had to pass to reach the gents'. One especially looked beautiful, wearing stretch black tights and a short skirt. No the best place for women to be sitting. At some point in the night there could be a smell of urine. Maybe no. Two of them glanced up as he pushed open the door. A stupid thought: were they wondering about him in the act of pissing? what his prick would look like? Did women think these things? He wasni that much older than them. The door creaked loudly on its hinges. Or was he? Maybe he was. They were nice.

There was a mirror immediately inside; he paused a moment, stared at himself, the hat and the unshaven chin. What did he look like? A fucking idiot. Plymouth was alright and so was Bristol, so was London and so was Spain. Maybe he should try and phone Audrey. He wasni feeling that good. He wasni. He was feeling fairly awful in fact. No physically, mentally. Mentally just fucking fuckt. For a start he shouldni have left the job; that was just silly.

But he was silly. He was stupid, he had always been stupid. He had always been stupid.

The urinals were clean, cakes of the blue deodorant stuff. His first piss of the night and the suds were a healthy yellowish brown; later on it would be a greenish white. Unless he pissed blood. Maybe he would piss blood. Maybe he was going to die tonight. Maybe this was it. Poor Audrey, waiting down there. Who would contact her? Nay cunt. Naybody would tell her. He would just have vanished. She would have to make her own inquiries. There wasni anybody up here. No unless Linda, unless Linda did it. Maybe she would. She was alright, good sister. They were all good sisters. Good family. It was a good family. Oh fuck sake. He zipped the fly then washed his hands. Why the fucking hell had he wrapped the job? He was just fucking foolish, that's what he was, foolish. There are facts of life and ye've got to face them. A stupid bastard.

He washed his face, wiped it dry with his shirt, set the blow-dry going for his hands. The blood into his cheeks. He was growing a beard, he was growing a beard. A stone-cold face; greeny white with a dark beard; yellow and red tulips.

It just wasni fair. It wasni a life. No wonder ye fucking looked surprised, no fucking wonder.

He waited in behind the outside door for a few moments, not looking at the mirror, he had his eyes closed. He heard somebody approach. He didni look at the women while exiting. Some guys laughing too loud at the bar. A stupid joke probably. Ye could understand these guys that took a mad-turn and grabbed somebody and let them have it. As he sat back at the table he gave a smile to Fin and he drank some beer straightaway but the swallowing was difficult and he gulped to get it down; a bad moment and he just needed to get through it, he just should never have put the hat on, he should never have fucking wore it, it wasni his it was his fucking da's it was his da's and his mother had fucking nursed it man he should never have fucking wore it it was just fucking wrong; he took another drink. These bloody weird things that happen, bloody weird things, if ye had took another path in life, if ye had went another way, if he hadni went abroad, stayed in Glasgow, if he hadni done the stupid thing at Art School, if he had stayed and finished his fucking course, these things ye do, who knows what effects ye have, these things are a mystery.

Fin was looking at him.

I never fucking asked her ye know.

What?

I just I mean . . . my mother and that. I shoulda come home more regular. Christ ye know I never even invited her for a holiday anywhere. The places I've stayed as well, some places Fin I mean abroad, beautiful, she never seen the likes of it man, no just Spain: Southern Italy, Portugal – I spent a wee bit of time in Portugal; good there, up north, I liked it. Fucking hell man I never invited her to any place. Probably she wouldni have went. But she mighta. I never asked her. I bet ye she woulda. I mean she was never outside Britain in her life. Never!

Fin nodded.

Derek raised the beer to his mouth. I coulda paid her way, he said, if I'd thought about it, I just never thought about it.

Ye dont. Ye never think about these things.

Naw I know.

Naybody does, no till it's too late.

I know.

Unfortunately it's typical.

Yeh.

Fin was watching him. It's just the way it goes.

I know. Derek paused then smiled. I'm allowed to have regrets but eh? am I no?

Aye but I just mean ye're bound to think of the things you coulda done, when ye had the chance – ye're bound to.

Yeh.

It's natural.

Derek nodded.

I know it doesni make it any easier . . . Fin gazed at Derek and when he didni respond he said: Sorry.

Naw.

No exactly diplomatic but.

Fuck that. Derek sipped at the beer; he smiled suddenly. A thought crossed my mind there at the toilet, apropros of fuck all; I could be a father in two countries, three including Britain. I mean I'm no boasting it's just . . . interesting. He grinned: Wee Hannahs running about in foreign countries. Yeh! He glanced at Fin: Must be a good feeling being a father.

No all the time.

Sure.

Sometimes ye just dont feel able to cope. The wife's pregnant again by the way.

Is that right?

Aye. It's a pity ye didni have time to come round for a meal or something. Yous two'd get on ye know, I told her about ye.

Ye told her about me . . .

Aye.

No everything?

Fin shrugged.

Well I'm definitely no going round now.

Dont be daft.

I'm being serious, it's just an embarrassment. Derek shook his head. I wish ye hadni.

Sorry.

It doesni matter. He adjusted the position of his hat then took it off and laid it on the empty seat nearest him.

It was a while ago I told her. She just found it funny.

Yeh, the guy that stole the video equipment, it is funny, funny as fuck.

I'm sorry.

Naw.

Honest, I am.

It's alright.

I shouldni have.

It's no a problem.

Sorry.

It's no a problem Fin it's okay.

Big mouth.

Doesni matter.

It just came out I mean.

Yeh.

Sorry.

No bother.

Naw, I'm sorry.

It's me, I'm sorry, fucking hell, I just over-react. It's a daily occurrence.

I apologise anyway.

I apologise.

Fin chuckled.

Yeh . . . ! So what about Sammy? Ye seen him recently.

I haveni, naw.

Is he still around?

Far as I know. The gallery's still going anyway.

Him and Isobel still the gether?

They are, aye. Time passes but some things stay the same. She had a show on no long ago, a one-woman. Quite well noticed.

Great.

It travelled.

Outside Scotland?

I think so.

She's doing well then eh?

Seems to be.

Ah she was always strong but. She went her own way. I used to like her stuff. I used to like to see what she was doing. She could paint. She wasni feart at all. All these browns and burnt oranges, fucking purple! Derek grinned. Did ye see the show yerself?

I crept in, aye.

What did ye think?

Fin made a movement with his right hand.

Ye didni like it?

Eh . . . half and half.

Derek nodded.

Some of it.

I wonder if it went to London?

I dont know.

Be nice if it did.

Wouldni be that big a deal.

Yeh well . . .

I mean it depends on whereabouts; all these wee galleries they've got down there: New York's the place, that's where they're all going – Berlin. London's down the table. Second Division stuff. So I hear anyway. Mind you it could be the fucking moon for all I know.

Ho!

No kidding. I finished with that sorta shit years ago.

Yeh, well, so did I.

We'll drink to it then . . . ! Fin had raised his pint tumbler. They clinked glasses. No surrender!

Fuck sake dont bring religion into it!

The two of them laughed.

Derek said, I was wondering whether to give him a bell?

Sammy?

Yeh.

Go ahead.

Derek gazed across at the bar, glanced at his watch. It was twenty to eight. What time do the pubs shut?

Midnight around here.

Mm.

Give him a phone if ye like.

Derek nodded.

Does he know ye're in town?

Dont think so, naw.

D'ye no keep in touch?

The last time I saw him was that time with you.

Was it?

Christ Fin I dont keep in touch with anybody – I mean naybody, naybody at all. I dont fucking keep in touch with nay cunt. Derek grinned and shook his head, he lifted the hat from the chair. The original loner . . . He smoothed down the brim of the hat. This musta been the old man's, he said, I found it in a cupboard. I dont mind him ever wearing it though. Ye'd remember something like that eh! He peered inside and picked a hair out from its crown.

One of the three females from the table near the gents' had gone to the bar. She was leaning her elbows there, propping her chin in the palms of her hands, one leg bent at the knee, classic pose. Derek and Fin both studied her. Fin smiled: Time for another round.

She's nice eh?

She is.

She's no the only one in here. Good pub.

Aye it's no bad. Better than it used to be. It was a bit of a dive, mind?

I dont, to be honest.

Naybody went here except the fucking hardened drinkers. It was a man's shop. Spit and sawdust. It's changed owners a coupla times since. They're aye trying to yuppify it. Without total success. So what about the lassie down in England then, been seeing her long?

Nearly six months . . . Derek put the hat back on his head, tugged it down over his brow and folded his arms.

Is it a record?

Ah, fucking record.

Just the way ye said it!

I shoulda brought her with me. I didni ask her but. I seem to be doing everything wrong the now; I dont know what it is.

Ye go through these stages.

Yeh. Derek glanced at his watch. I was thinking about giving her a bell as well.

Ye should.

Ah she'll probably no be in anyway man she'll be out somewhere – gallivanting. He smiled, glancing at the watch again. Fucking gallivanting, soon as my back's turned. He lifted the pint tumbler and studied it, then drank down the remainder of the beer, passing the empty to Fin who still had some to finish: Did ye no say ye were getting a round in?

I did aye. Fin frowned for a moment: I actually bumped into Sammy a few weeks back.

Did ye?

The Horseshoe Bar; we wereni talking, just hello and that. Fin swirled his remaining beer round the bottom of the glass.

Yous two still dont get on eh?

No really.

Yeh, well.

I find it hard to talk to him Derek, being honest, he's so wrapped up in his own head. If ye're no speaking about him ye're no speaking, know what I mean, he never seems to hear ye.

Derek nodded.

He's actually a bit of a prick, ye know . . . Fin swallowed the rest of the beer.

Well he wasni always.

Fin placed the empty tumbler on the table: He is now.

Derek shrugged.

His patter, I canni be annoyed with it – it's alright if ye're twenty one but no thirty one. Gets fucking boring after a while.

Fair enough.

A conversation stopper. Sorry. I'll get the drink.

Doesni matter.

Naw I know ye were good mates.

Yeh, well.

I'm just saying what I think.

Fair enough.

Fin shrugged.

Derek watched him walk off with the two empties, a brief glance here and there as he went. But relaxed. It was his place and he was relaxed. Why not? Glasgow, it was home. But Derek was relaxed too, he felt relaxed. It was his fucking home as well.

The woman was still standing at the bar, now having a word with the big skinny guy who made her smile at something; she returned to her table carrying a tray.

Life.

There was an empty cigarette packet on the edge of the table. He shoulda brought the pad; he had a pen.

Fuck.

It would be good to get on the overnight train, just draw down the blinds, have a sleep, fucking blank it all out. What did he have to do? No much – he had half-told Marilyn he would go and see her. He could phone instead, it wouldni matter. Christ he *could* actually shoot off the night; there was still time; a quick taxi up the road and get the stuff packed; fuck sake.

He couldni. It just wasni on.

The sweater the woman with the stretch tights was wearing was wine in colour, almost no bulge at the chest but ye knew her breasts were probably big the way the bulge protruded lower down, her shoulders hunched slightly. Her and her mates were eating potato crisps. In his experience that's what women did, they ate potato crisps. How come? Just a fact of life. That's what they did. Maybe it was that stopped them getting drunk. Gin and tonic. A different type of drinking they did as well.

Altogether different. They were just altogether different. Sometimes ye wondered why they ever went for a man. They were so beautiful and men wereni. Even the barmaid, probably she was just under pressure. People *are* under pressure. Ye never know what's going on, what's under the surface. Derek slept with this woman a coupla years ago and one night she burst out crying. For no reason. Just life. It was getting to her. He lumbered her from a pub up in London. She was divorced but she had a boyfriend. She wasni crying about that, being in bed with him. She was crying because of life, the things that happen, that's what it was, except she couldni bring herself to tell him. She was really beautiful. She was too thin but and she smoked all the time. Fucking amazing; people; amazing. If Sammy was here just now they'd be moving in on the three at the table. They would. That's what they'd be doing. That time they got off with the two lassies at the pictures along Sauchiehall Street. Fucking hell what a night; paired off in separate bedrooms and the lassie Sammy was with had just come walking in, getting fags or something, no caring, tits bouncing, no even wearing a pair of pants. The men would nevera done that. No way. No embarrassment. Just so relaxed. How come people are so relaxed? Ye wonder. Had mum ever wanted to get married again? Fucking hell he couldni even remember thinking that before. Maybe he hadni: maybe this was the first time he had ever thought it. Maybe she had wanted to. Poor mum, poor fucking mum. People's lives. People's lives. Fin was back. Derek smiled and reached for the pint.

Fin said: D'ye ever smoke a cigar?

Naw.

I was gonni get a couple.

I have smoked them once or twice.

Ye dont like them?

No really.

I sometimes get one.

Ye shoulda.

Fin shrugged. One thing that does occur to me. I was thinking at the bar . . . And dont take it the wrong way. Just yer politics Derek, ye know, they're bound to be different to what they'd been if ye'd stayed.

Ye think so?

Definitely.

Derek nodded.

The way ye mention Britain for instance.

What about it?

Just that there's nay separation up here. It's always Scotland. No just one minute and Britain the next.

What did I say?

Aw nothing really, it's only the way ye say Britain all the time.

I didni know I was saying Britain all the time.

Aye, I mean like it was one country. See naybody does that here. Naybody. No unless there's some sort of qualification involved. I mean that includes the fucking Tories, if they say it, they're being ironic – or sarcastic, just trying for effect. Ye've got to remember when ye're talking establishment here ye know ye're talking Labour Party; they're the reactionaries, that's who we want rid of, no the fucking Tories; they dont count.

Derek nodded.

I mean they dont.

Fine.

Folk dont realise that.

Is this a lecture?

Fin paused before saying: It's no a lecture.

Naw, come on.

It's no a lecture.

Ye talking about Nationalism? Ye a Nationalist?

Fin sighed. Christ Derek that's hardly even a question nowadays I mean it's to what extent. Unless ye're talking about the S.N.P. Is that what ye're talking about?

I'm no really talking about anything. It's you, ye just sat down and started blasting.

Did I?

Yeh.

Sorry.

Ye dont know anything about my politics.

True.

Ye dont. I'll tell ye something but; see down there, people wouldni know what you were on about. To them Scotland's nothing at all, it's just a part of England. No even a county man they think it's a sort of city. Yous are all just paranoiac as far as they're concerned, a big chip on the shoulder.

Oh I know.

I'm talking about the average person. Doesni matter what grade their education is. The average person.

I came on too strong.

Ye did, yeh. I mean I didni even know I was saying Britain all the time!

Fin smiled. Ye were.

I'll watch it in future.

Fin held his hands up: I submit.

In fact it's hard to talk politics at all down there. I tend to keep my mouth shut. Unless I've had a few. Ye know they dont even know geography. They've got this hazy view of the world. See a place like Inverness for instance, they think it's near Yorkshire. Next door to Crewe or somefuckingthing.

Exactly. I mean it's bound to influence ye.

Well I wouldni deny that.

That's all I meant but Derek, ye've learnt to say Britain.

Yeh cause down there it's England, they dont even say Britain.

Aye. So let's leave it.

Naw dont let's leave it.

I think it's best.

Do ye, I dont.

Fin smiled.

Dont patronise me.

Christ that's the last thing I'm doing.

Ye dont know a thing about me.

I'm no patronising ye come on! It's just you've been away so long man – there's a common ground missing.

Yeh well so what?

It takes a while.

What takes a while?

Fin shrugged. Talking. Getting the basics sorted out. Takes fucking ages.

So what?

Fin smiled. We'll just fucking argue.

I dont care if we argue. That's what ye miss christ a good-going debate; I dont get it down there, it's all one-way traffic, naybody to fucking communicate with, no properly, no unless ye bump into a black guy or something, maybe an Irishman. Apart from that . . . It's hard to open yer mouth.

Fin nodded.

Dont just fucking nod.

Well what am I supposed to do? Fin spoke quietly.

I dont know. Carry on talking about what ye're talking.

There's too much.

Ye are patronising me ye know.

I dont mean to.

Well ye are.

Fin shook his head. I dont mean to.

After a moment Derek replied, Okay.

Fin lifted his pint tumbler, drank some beer. They sat in silence for several moments. Fin spoke first: How long ye staying for?

Coupla days. Derek rubbed at his forehead, his eyes closed; Till I get the business done.

Is there a lot?

Yeh. Uch well naw, no really, the undertaker does most of it.

Aw ye do's pay the bills. There's the lawyer right enough. She never left a will, my mother, she had her insurance and that but it's one of these fucking mickey-mouse efforts; this great big certificate; it looks like the kind ye get at the carnival, if ye win a fucking coconut. It just about pays the cost of the wreath and the reception, the wake or whatever ye call it. She had her bank book. Thirteen hundred quid. No a lot eh?

Fin said nothing.

There's furniture and linen and all that; tablecloths, teatowels; that sort of stuff, sheets and pillowcases. It's a case of the sisters taking what they want, then flogging the rest. Or I dont know, giving it away, Oxfam or something; they can figure that yin out. It's sad but. Ye've just got to batter on. Fuck aw else ye can do. That's how I didni want the girlfriend here. I wasni sure how I'd handle it. It's a bit sad, know what I mean.

How was the service?

Aw fine, fine; better than I was expecting, the actual thing itself, quite moving. Some auld biddies turned up I hadni seen for years. An auld auntie! Derek grinned. Ye want to have seen her, christ, beautiful. The ancient of days. Related to my da. I thought it was good, her turning up, I mean . . . Derek grinned again, shook his head. Brooches and fucking . . . ye know, hats and fucking chiffon and all that. I last saw her when I was eight. Stern, christ. Travelled up from Ballantrae or some place. Like an auld Covenanter; ye could imagine her voice booming out in a psalm when the troops were arriving. Fuck sake.

Fin chuckled.

But they aw seemed to be church people. My maw's side too. I mean ye forget people still go to church.

Aw they still go alright!

Yeh . . . Tell ye what I have been doing Fin, sketching, I've been sketching. Myself . . . ! I'm sitting staring into mirrors. Catharsis eh?

Maybe it's necessary.

Yeh, maybe. Listen but I'm glad ye phoned. Sitting up in the house man ye know . . . Good ye made contact.

It wasni a chore.

Uch naw I know but thanks I mean anyway.

Fuck sake man.

Derek grinned. It's just the past, the past; something to fucking hang onti – so's ye can fucking dump it Fin know what I mean, I want the world, the world, capital double-u. Tell ye a plan I've had for a coupla years, saving the dough and going to South America. Getting one of these Volkswagen vans. Getting it kitted out and that.

Mm. Dangerous country. Guy I know was in Nicaragua.

Right.

He was there a year, schoolteacher, says it was fucking amazing, fucking yankee bastards. Central America right enough, no the South . . . Ye did know that eh!

Yeh.

Thought ye did! Fin smiled. Sorry.

Dont mention it.

Fin lifted the beer to his mouth, but paused. Give Sammy a phone. He'll be glad to hear from ye. Dont fucking mind me, I'm biased.

Maybe later. Hey did I ever tell ye when I blew outa here?

Ye hitched across Europe.

Yeh, I was gonni show you bastards, I was really gonni show ye. Art, ye didni know the meaning of the word! Derek stopped and frowned: I wonder what I done it for? That fucking stupid video equipment. It was just lying there. I really fucking done it man eh! Fucking . . . He shrugged, smiled. I went chasing the light. Purity! A certain sky! At a certain time of the morning! With certain cloud formations! Who was I looking at then? I dont know – I think it was Corot. Then that classical stuff, these landscapes with bits of architecture, light breaking through the clouds. What I was really doing was looking for ideal sex! as well as cracking up, because I had disgraced the family

Aw fuck.

Naw, just turned nineteen. The auld man dead five years. I really fucking done it man. I really fucking let them down, my maw and ah christ Fin the lot, ye know, that canni be helped, it's just a fact.

Ah come on.

It's true but, a fact of life. I accept it. The Great White Hope of the Family.

Fin sighed.

I also had this vision right enough; meeting up with a woman at the side of a lonely country road, a shepherdess, or else the runaway daughter of an Arabian potentate, we would disappear into the horizon the gether, knapsacks on our backs.

Fin smiled.

Romantic young fuckers. A misspent youth. It was all these glossy nude prints, that's what I blame . . .

Aye . . . Fin laid his pint on the table: D'ye mind the first time ye slept with a woman?

Yeh.

So do I. I was twenty at the time; quite auld eh?

It's no that auld.

Fin smiled. Aye it is.

I was eighteen.

Better than twenty.

No much.

Still better but.

Derek shrugged.

I mean twenty's auld.

No really.

Anyway, anyway, wait till I tell ye. See it was strange, ye know, I mean it was. It was peculiar, a kind of metamorphosis.

What?

Aye, a kind of metamorphosis, the female's head, when it was on the pillow.

Derek smiled.

Naw, honest, it changed right in front of my eyes, she became a hag, an auld crone. It was like a horror movie. I'm no joking, it was frightening. She had fell asleep and I was looking at her, I was lying up on my elbow, drawing her with my tongue, ye know, on the roof of my mouth – the way us art students are aye supposed to be practising – it musta been roundabout dawn, no quite dark, but no light either. It was after we'd done the business. I think I was still trying to ingrain it in my mind that it'd fucking happened ye know: couldni fucking take it in man. A wonderful experience, ye know, I was trying to capture it forever. That lovely wee feeling when ye press up and ye actually get inside for the first time, all snug.

Shut up!

Naw . . . Fin smiled: Honest.

Derek shook his head. Who was it anyway? do I know her?

Nah.

Ye sure?

Nah. Wait till I tell ye but. She's lying there, right; but see after a wee while, she turns on her back, ye know, her mouth open; I'm just studying her, dead self-conscious man, thinking to myself how it was a magical moment I was gonni have to treasure forever. And then her face changes! Honest! Fin whispered: It had fucking changed! There were all these lines round her mouth and her eyes. And her hair man it was all straggly, and thin like it was really thin. No kidding ye it was fucking frightening. I was wanting to wake her up; cause I was getting scared ye know, but I was waiting for my mind to clear. I knew it was me ye see I knew it wasni her. I shut my eyes a few times but it didni work, I just couldni get myself out it, whatever it was, it just stayed.

The hallucination . . .

Aye.

Ye musta been dreaming.

Naw. A hallucination; ye're right; I was fucking wide awake.

Wow. So what happened?

Nothing. I just musta fell asleep.

Well well.

Naw but fuck sake Derek I mean christ almighty man ye've got to admit . . . ye know, fuck sake.

Did ye tell the lassie?

Naw . . . !

Dont blame ye.

How could ye tell her!

D'ye ever analyse it?

All the fucking time. See back then but Derek I used to think there was something up with any female that liked me, I mean if she didni get bored with my company, there had to be something up with her. Otherwise how come she wasni with somebody else? If she was normal she would be. Ergo she had to have a personality problem. That was how I had it sussed anyhow. I suppose because I'd been waiting so long for the first go it put me off. The longer it went the harder it got. Even after the first yin. It took me fucking ages for the next. Ye used to wonder if it was a figment of the imagination. It was that experience made it real! Maybe if it had all went normal I would still've been fucking waiting! Fin laughed. Naw, no kidding ye. My fucking sanity was saved. Without that brain seizure who knows what woulda happened.

Ach everybody's got problems with women.

Dont spoil it christ.

Naw but they do, everybody.

Aye but they never *saw* me. Know what I mean? I was the type of guy, if I was at a disco, they'd trip over my feet on the way to the cludgie. In conversation or that man whenever one of them was talking to me I knew she was wanting to talk to somebody else. I could aye see her eye roving the company.

It's called sex-appeal.

Thanks.

The spark. Either ye've got it or ye havni.

Aye, thanks a lot.

Hasta la vista, it's true.

That's a boost to my ego that.

It's true but.

You had it I suppose?

Naw did I fuck, I was Mister Hang-Up as well.

No like me ye wereni.

I was – how d'ye think I hung about with Sammy! The cast-offs. I blamed my home-life, being brought up in a houseful of women. I was too aware of the species. See like in the bathroom when I was a wee boy it was always tampons and stick-on towels; perfumes and deodorants; bottles of this and bottles of that; everywhere ye looked – ye went to wash yer hands in the washhand basin and guaranteed ye knocked something flying, guaranteed. Plus all the knickers and bras lying about.

Fin chuckled.

Honest, it's the wrong experience, it throws ye in on yerself. Talking with yer wee mates at school, ye had to kid on ye didni know anything, ye didni want to be disloyal. Maybe if I'd had a brother . . .

I had two of them; we fought like fuck.

Yeh but at least it prepared ye for the outside world, the mysteries of the other sex.

I had a sister too.

Aw, ye were a well-balanced bastard then?

Aye.

So that's that analysis fucked. Naw but seriously, I'm sure it musta had some effect.

In what way?

Who knows? Probably I shoulda turned out gay.

That's what Freud would tell ye.

Would he?

Fin smiled.

It wouldni surprise me. Relationships have all been bad.

Ye still listen to Dylan! Fin laughed.

I thought everybody still listened to Dylan.

I mind the one time I was up in yer house, in yer bedroom, we had the records on; bottles of Newcastle Brown, Dylan blasting it out – Idiot Wind, yer maw brought us up toast and scrambled egg.

That's right.

Me you Sammy, Toby, Vic Edwards . . .

Yeh.

Noisy bastards we were; yer maw musta had some patience.

She was just deaf.

Aw. Was she?

Naw. Derek shrugged, Like ye say, she had a lota patience. A while ago that.

Ten year.

More like twelve.

Twelve . . . aye.

Aw dear. Derek sighed. Fuck. It was good ye phoned.

Give us a break.

Naw, fuck, it was. I mean come on, if you hadni phoned that was that christ, nothing. And that's my life ye're talking about, Glasgow, that's it, that's fucking it.

Fin was silent.

That's fucking it.

Fin had begun playing an imaginary violin. And Derek smiled: Yeh, I know. See I dont want to belabour the point but I'm no in touch with any cunt. When I was up the hill it was all wee cliques. It was like they all knew each other already. As if they'd all went to the same primary school the gether. Honest, that's what like it was.

Derek, it's natural feeling that.

Yeh well. But that's how I fell back on Sammy.

Cause everybody else was avoiding him?

Come on, he was popular. And in comparison to the rest of them I mean fuck sake.

Right enough, he could aye talk a good painting.

At least he had his own ideas, and he was interested.

Fin sighed.

He used to trip up McAllister.

Big deal.

Fuck sake Fin.

Well McAllister: one more chronic ego – fucking tripping him up, that isni much.

Christ what ye expecting off a first-year student?

Sammy's a pseudo bastard. Always was and always will be. Still thinks he's Modigliani for fuck sake. How the hell Isobel stands for it I dont know.

Derek smiled. Ah he's alright.

He's no alright at all.

Derek shrugged.

He isni.

I think ye're expecting too much.

It's no a case of that Derek, ye just spot a pseud a mile away. Fin sniffed. Anyhow, I dont want to spend time talking about him. What's the point, ye know, past tense – it's what folk're doing now that interests me, and he's doing fuck all, fuck all that I'm interested in. Fucking wine-and-cheese parties . . . Fin started rapping his knuckles on the edge of the table, he kept it going for several seconds before glancing at Derek:

But Derek spoke first; It's a class thing with you Fin come on.

I know it's a class thing with me so what?

Ye're sounding awful bitter.

Aw.

Ye are.

Is that right?

It's no his fault his parents had money.

That's fuck all to do with it, the fucking money, I'm no bothered about that. He swallowed a mouthful of beer.

What then? What ye got against him?

I've no got nothing against him.

Ye have.

He's just fucking irrelevant.

Derek stared at Fin, then at the table; he put his hand on the pint tumbler and gripped it.

Irrelevant.

Derek sniffed slightly, he looked at Fin.

Sorry. Fin turned his head away and muttered through his teeth, Fucking class thing! Fuck sake . . .

Derek relaxed his shoulders. He glanced round the room, it was busy, busy; he was gripping the pint tumbler again. He began to say something but so did Fin and they both stopped. It was Fin continued: Dont fucking take this the wrong way Derek right?

Take what the wrong way?

What I'm gonni say.

What ye gonni say?

Dont take it the wrong way.

I dont know what it is yet.

Fin was silent.

On ye go but.

Fin sighed.

I'll no take it the wrong way.

Jesus christ.

Go ahead.

Fin scratched his head, he glanced at a group of people sitting at a nearby table, they were talking loudly and laughing. He waited a moment before speaking: Ye see, what it is . . . dont fucking take it the wrong way now.

I'm no gonni.

See what you done, it was so valuable, so valuable.

Derek watched him.

Knocking the stuff I'm talking about. I'm serious. It was man. For us: us from the sticks, ye know, the ones that thought we were unique.

What ye talking about?

It was a lesson. It put us in our place – put us back in our place. Aye it was a class thing, a total class thing.

Come on.

Ach come on fuck all man they had it drummed into us, the cream of the crop, we were special, so fucking 'special'! Fin glared at Derek. The pride and joy! We were on our way. Fame and fortune. The very worst was if we wound up with some good class white-collar job in an office. All that sort of crap. I'm thinking of my family, the way they saw it. Then for us it was art, ye know I mean *art; art* – that made it even worse. I'm talking about for us, the fucking hillbillies. Because we could fucking be rebels at the same time. We could relax while we were getting on in life; we didni have to feel guilty. Know what I mean?

Derek shrugged.

We were playing games. We were. Fucking pathetic. My maw and da are still like that ye know, they're still expecting great things. Me on the broo; that job in the Parks Department, they think it's all a phase; they're still walking about on a wee cloud of gold, cotton wool or something, candy-floss. They're expecting me to get the call any minute. Our specialness, that's what we had to contend with – we were brought up with it. It drove us apart. Fucking isolated us man, the tip for the top. You're talking about primary school: see in mine, one of the fucking teachers there told my maw I might be up to university standard. Can ye believe it? Fuck sake! Eleven years of age I was. And it fucked me. It fucked me everywhere. Especially with my pals, the wee boys I went about with: word got round. And the gulf started opening then, that was when it fucking happened, the great divide. Conversations used to stop when I entered the company.

Uch away.

I'm fucking serious. There was this wee halo over my head, a golden glow. Plus they thought I was maybe a spy, the other weans, they thought I had to be carrying notes to the teacher – quite right they thought that, quite fucking right. I mean see my maw and da now, see at this very minute, cause I've married a lassie that works in a bank; they're expecting their grandson to wind up fuck knows what, a doctor or something. No kidding ye man it's like they've sired a thoroughbred stallion.

Derek smiled.

Honest. Listen to this too: fucking mate of mine, right, a guy I go climbing with, he went to Uni; know what they told him the very first day he arrived? I'm talking about a first-year student, seventeen poxy fucking years of age: know what they told him?

What?

You're the cream. You're the cream son, that's what they told him; you're the top eight percent in this country. The other fucking ninety two's a bunch of fucking headbangers, that's what they told him; some fucking lecturer, so-called Marxist – specialist in the lumpen proletariat – that's what he fucking telt them! Well I'll tell you something man, I want to fucking go up fucking University Avenue and fucking strangle the bastard, that's what I fucking want to do.

Mm.

No fucking kidding ye; it's pathetic, just pathetic. And then they all go about gawking at each other; they do! Fucking gawking at each other! Total wonder and amazement at their own fucking uniqueness. Whatever crap the lecturers dish them out too ye know they all listen to it, they all fucking listen to it. We were the same man. We all went about with this wee smile on our fucking faces. Predestination. The chosen few. Bound for Glory.

Woody Guthrie.

Woody Guthrie.

No everybody falls for it.

No everybody falls for it, okay. Okay; no everybody falls for it. Fin had lifted his pint tumbler, he paused before drinking from it: But see cunts like McAllister Derek they're the worst. The so-called radicals. They're just Sammys dressed up.

Derek laughed.

They are but. See if Sammy ever became a lecturer up there that's what he'd be, another Joe McAllister, getting all the students following him about like wee puppy dogs, screwing all the first-year lassies, getting all the boys thinking he was the greatest rebel in the world – genuine revolutionary and all that, Che Guevara on twenty grand a year plus perks for a twenty six hour week. Ah for christ sake. Fin snorted, then began chuckling. Fucking crazy. They're the worst but, it's them keeps the system going; straight dialectics; they inject the new energy, they give it the power, the fucking life, the weltenschang whatever ye call it. In fact they dont, they dont, they actually stop it; they stop it; they fucking crush it at birth. You're just lucky ye missed it. I had it for four years.

After a moment Derek said, So what's my part?

Fin nodded.

Ye started off gonni tell me something, I wasni to take it the wrong way ye said.

Aye . . . Fin sighed, smiling: You went too soon man that's your trouble.

I had nay choice.

Och I know, I know . . .

So what is it?

Uch nothing. I mean I've more or less said it. It's no a big thing – although it is, in a way, it is; ye see ye left a lasting impression.

Yeh well.

Ye did. Ye fucking spurred me anyway. No at first but gradually, ye know, I'm dead serious, it's a good kick up the arse I was needing. I mean . . . that's what I was needing, a good kick up the arse. Fin chuckled. They fucking hated what you did. Oh they did man dont fucking kid yerself. The unnameable. Whenever some cunt like McAllister started on with all that crap about how any real artist will aye beat the system, there you were, with the swag bag, getting the boot, artist or no it doesni fucking matter. First it's the economics, then after that it's the economics again.

Derek shrugged.

Dont underestimate it.

I dont.

It got in the way of the propaganda.

That means my life hasni been in vain.

Dont underestimate it.

I dont.

Fin nodded.

Ye just have a habit of sounding as if ye dont think I know fuck all.

Rubbish.

Is it?

Fuck sake Derek.

Ye've been patronising me all night.

I've no.

Ye fucking have.

It was a lesson ye see. For all the would-be revolutionaries; artist as rebel and all that, as long as ye dont interfere with the property.

Yeh.

I'm no patronising ye at all.

That's good.

Christ that's the last thing I'd do.

Anyway, let's change the subject.

Ye keep saying I'm patronising ye man, and I'm no.

Just let's change the subject.

Fuck sake. Fin shook his head.

Just the now, ye know, cause of my mother and that.

I'm sorry.

Derek nodded. Want a whisky or something?

No really, naw.

I feel like one . . . Look Fin it was a fucking brainstorm what I did. Just fucking stupidity, right. That's all it was. The stuff was lying there and it was an empty room. I'm no even sure now if it wasni a prank. A prank, know what I mean. Maybe it was. I canni even remember. Total stupidity.

But what are mothers for eh! I left it for her to sort out. Derek smiled. When I didni know what to do next, I left it for her; the stuff Fin, I left it on the bed. I got off my mark. I couldni handle it. But it didni break her heart. In fact she was quite a wise auld dame. Quite shrewd. Quite shrewd . . . Derek stopped to breathe in. He smiled again, took off the hat and footered with the brim. After she returned them the stuff Peterson went up to see her.

I heard that.

He told her I was a silly boy but they wereni gonni press charges.

Cheeky bastard.

Wish to fuck I'd just dumped the stuff.

That woulda really done it, they only had it on loan.

Yeh! I woulda taken that into consideration! Derek shook his head: Fucking indignity but eh fucking indignity – the whole thing.

Fin was silent for a moment, then he said: Some of them probably still hate ye for it ye know, stealing their thunder as potential rebels.

A legend in my own lifetime eh, Sydney Devine.

Fin chuckled.

Imagine influencing a generation but, think I'll go and impress that lassie in the black tights. Derek put the hat back on his head: Sure ye dont want a short?

Uch okay, if ye're having one.

Whisky?

Aye.

As Derek walked to the bar he could see the phone being used, a guy talking into it. Once it was free he would try Audrey's number again – better now before the drink started hitting. He put both hands on the edge of the bar, shifting his stance; maybe go for a curry after, he was bloody hungry as well.

The barmaid came past and he called for two whiskies. Glenmorangies, he said, would ye make it doubles . . . She turned to the gantry without acknowledging him, sticking the first glass up under the optic.

The phone was now available. He knew the Plymouth code. Would she be home! Of course. Unless she was out. He scratched at his ear, his finger nudging the brim of the hat. For some reason the woman was off serving somebody else. She had the second Glenmorangie poured but she had left it on the gantry shelf.

It was a pint of Guinness she was attending to, she must have been waiting for it to settle before topping it up, at which point he had come in with his order for the two whiskies. So now she was finishing the previous customer. Nothing wrong with that. He reached for the jug of water, poured a fair amount into the tumbler. It looked sickly. He wasni a whisky drinker. That was just that. He shouldni have ordered it. Impressing Fin. Doubles as well. Fucking typical. Foolish. But he was foolish. That's exactly what he was. A foolish young man. Not a boy. A man. At his age and in his situation he was no longer entitled to call himself a boy, not even a foolish one, not even in his own head, especially in his own head. That was another fact of life.

Five pound sixty, said the barmaid, the second Glenmorangie in front of him.

Five pound sixty . . . wwh! He got the money out, gave her a tenner. He raised the whisky to his lips while she was getting him the change. But he didnt drink any. It wouldnt be refreshing. Refreshing is the last thing it would be. There wasnt any drink that would be refreshing now, except tea, a cup of tea. With two sugars. He closed his eyes, smiling, but not at anything in particular.

by the burn

Fucking bogging mud man a swamp, an actual swamp, it was fucking a joke. He pulled his foot clear but the boot was still lodged there like it was quicksand and it was going to get sucked off and vanish down into it forever. He felt the suction hard on his foot but when he pulled, curling his toes as firm as possible, out it came with a loud squelching sound. Thank Christ for that. He shook his head, studying the immediate area, these marshy stalks of grass were everywhere; fucking hopeless. He glanced back across the wide expanse of waste ground and up to where the blocks of flats were. But he had to go this way and go this way right now, he was late enough as it was, he just couldnt afford to waste any time. He continued on, steering clear of the clumps of long weeds, the kind that told you where the worst of it was, but it was bad and each step now his boot sunk in an inch or so, but still not as bad as before. Imagine if he had lost the fucking boot but Christ almighty, hirpling down the road for the train then into the interview office, trying to explain to the folk there how you had just lost your shoe in a fucking swamp. My God, a fucking joke right enough. He stopped to look ahead. Then the rain started again and this time it wasnt a passing shower, the sky was full of dark grey clouds, he turned up the collar of his suit jacket, it was going to get worse, nothing surer. And he would get bloody soaked. What the hell time was it? Aw for fuck sake who cares, he plunged on, veering off towards the banks of the burn. You could actually hear the roar of the water; so it was probably running awful high. So there was no chance of him crossing at the usual stepping stones, maybe have to skirt right the way round through the wood to get to the bloody bridge. Aw dear. He hated having to go that way. By this time he had reached the last of the marsh and there was the ordinary grass and the short clumps of bushes. He passed the wee tree, most of its branches half snapped and trailing onto the ground. A kid's sock dangled off one of them. Then the slope up to the bank of the burn. It was all slimy mud here and he had to steady himself by using his hand as a prop, stepping up in a kind of semi-circle. His hands were all muddy now and he had to pull off a couple of big docken leaves to wipe them clean. The roaring from the burn was really loud now, deafening. He waited a moment up on the bank, staring down at the swollen water, it came rushing, spray flying out, so high it looked set to overflow the banks. You couldnt even see the stepping stones where he would have crossed, probably about two feet of water were covering them. So that was it now there was no chance, the path across the bridge or nothing, that was for fucking definite, he just had no choice in the matter. He sighed, blowing out through his mouth. He felt a wee twinge across his shoulders and that was followed by a shiver. He actually did feel tired although it was only about half eleven in the morning, he felt a bit weak in fact. Then the rain on his head. He felt like going away home again, back to the fire, cup of tea and put the feet up. It was just a joke, the whole fucking thing. Away in the distance he saw a shape looming into view through the trees, then another one. Two blokes. They cut off but, taking a different route to get to the flats, up through the field. The rain now definitely getting heavier. He walked as fast as he could along the peak of the bank without slipping on the fucking mud, arse over elbow into the burn – probably he wouldnt have been able to save himself from drowning for Christ sake. Once upon a time aye, but no now. He glanced down as he went. The water was flowing that fucking fast. It was years since he had had a swim too, years. High time they extended the path along this way for the poor cunts living up the flats, the fucking council, it was out of order the way they didnt bother. They had been fucking talking about it for donkeys. He left the bank at the first opportunity, following a narrow trail into the wood and he took shelter beneath the first big tree. He started shivering again. Just the dampness maybe because it wasnt really cold. And he needed a coat. He really did need a coat man this was just stupid. He had one right enough he just didnt wear the fucking thing, he didnt like it. It was too big for him for a start, it was his brother-in-law's. You could have wrapped it round him twice. But still and all he should have wore it, he could have carried it over his arm and just stuck it on and off, depending on what it was doing, if it was raining or not, he didnt have to wear it all the time. His suit shoulder nudged against the tree trunk now and he moved from it, it was slimy, it was really fucking slimy. He gave the material a good rub but the stain still showed, the mud or whatever it was. He caught sight of his boots, all soaking wet and bits of grass and leaves sticking to them, nettles, the lot. Some picture. The wife would be pleased. Once they dried but they would be alright, brand new – except because of the damp they would turn white probably. They werent that old either, bastard. Just like it when you needed everything to be right, when you needed to be at your best, the way you looked. Fucking Jesus. My God. Never mind. Never mind. They would do for the time being, as long as they stayed damp they would pass inspection. If he ever got out of here! Because the fucking rain was pelting down and thick heavy blotches were dropping through the branches of the tree and landing on his nut. Still another half mile through the wood and he would have to start moving soon, he couldnt afford to wait any longer oh but Christ he didnt want to go he would just have to make a run for it, he would just have to make a run for it, just forget about the rain because it wasnt going to go off now, it was on for the bloody duration. The smell of the tree was in his nostrils, it was like decay or something like it was rotten. A lot of the bark had been cut from the trunk here, peeled off. Somebody with a knife. Wee boys probably. Maybe big ones. He studied the bark that was left, the thick dark green stuff, all crisscross lines and it was like cobwebs inside it, a gauzy sort of stuff; it would be full of beetles, beetles and termites, maggots, all living off it, the bark was there to be eaten, they would eat it. He jumped suddenly out from the tree and started running, keeping his head down. At places the trail got really narrow and it took sharp angles and he had to slow down to avoid the traps, the bent branches and the roots and stumps of trees. It was a joke, it was just a joke. Then he was having to walk, he couldnt go any faster, it was just too thick, it was too thick. He had his hands in his trouser pockets. By the time he arrived in the office he wouldnt be in a fit state for the interview. They probably wouldnt even let him in the fucking door man they would send for the fucking polis, the way he was looking, the suit all fucking mud and the boots turned white because of the fucking dampness man it was just bloody out of order, you just had no fucking chance. He needed a car. Every cunt needed a car. That was what happened when you stayed out in the schemes, it was fine till you wanted to go someplace, once you did you were in fucking trouble. Stupid, it was just stupid. But it was a bastard, it really was a bastard, these bloody fucking bushes and swamps man what could you do, going for a fucking job, just when you needed to look right, it aye happened, that was the way it went, you just couldnt win, you just couldnt fucking win man never, you could never win. He glanced about him. Then he looked back over his shoulder. A funny feeling there. He walked on a few paces then slowed again, he stopped. He stopped and listened, he was feeling a bit funny, like somebody was watching him. It was like there was somebody watching him. He felt the twinge in his shoulders. There *was*. There was somebody watching him. What was it he felt so Christ almighty another shiver, somebody definitely watching him. It was gloomy and dark now with the trees high and affecting what light there was; shadows, all the bushes, all thick. He stood where he was, he just stood there. Then he felt it again, right across his shoulders. It was a chill. He had caught a chill. Definitely. He was damp, he was bloody cold. He was oh Christ almighty and he felt it another time now right across his chest as well a sort of tremor and down his thighs to his knees it was, it was like a tremor, a spasm. But it was his daughter, it was his daughter. Like her ghost was somewhere. He knew it. He knew what it was exactly. Because it was the sand pit. It was right across the burn from where he was standing and if it was winter and the leaves had fell you would see right across and the sandpit was there, it was right there, just on the other side. Aw dear, the wee fucking lassie. Aw dear man aw dear it was so fucking hard so fucking awful hard, awful hard so fucking awful hard. Oh where was the wife. He needed his fucking wife. He needed her. He needed her close. He needed her so fucking close he felt so fucking Christ man the sandpit, where the wee lassie and her two wee pals had got killed. Hiding out playing chases. Aye being warned to steer clear but in they went and then it collapsed on them, and it trapped them, all these tons of earth and they had all got suffocated. Aw dear. Aw dear. He stepped in near a big tree and leaned his arms against it, his forearms, crossed, them shielding his eyes, he was greeting without any sound, he just couldnt handle it. He couldnt. He had never been able to. It used to keep him awake at nights. For ages, fucking ages. He could never get it out his mind. For Christ sake bloody years ago it was, bloody years ago. Oh Christ. She was stronger than him. The wife. She was. She really was. She could handle it. He couldnt. But she could. She could handle it fine. She got by on it. But he didnt. He couldnt; he just couldnt handle it. He never could. He had never been able to, he had just never been able to. He opened his mouth to breathe fresh air. The insides of his mouth ached. Throat dry. A wetness at the corners of his lips: he wiped them with the cuff of his suit sleeve. He had just never been able to handle it; he couldnt come to terms with it at all. These years. All these fucking years. And that wee fucking lassie oh God man he just could never fucking handle it. Plus as well he would have wanted to be one of them that carried her out. No just her but the other ones, her two wee pals. But he wasnt there. He didnt know. He just heard about it later. Him and the wife man they never fucking knew it had happened, no till too late, it was too late when they knew. It had been firemen done it and some other folk who went down. But him and the wife never knew about it till too late, there was nobody telt them. But it was nobody's fault, they didnt know who it was that was buried, no till they got them out. The firemen came and cleared out the rubble, then they found them, the wee souls, they lifted them and carried them. He would like even to have seen it. He telt the wife that at the time as well, just from a distance, it would have been fine as long as he could just have seen them, the wee legs all spindly and them broken like that, their wee bodies. Ah dear, ah dear. He swallowed. The tears were running down his face again. He shut his eyes tight to stop it. He could feel rain down the back of his neck; his throat was so dry. He flexed his shoulders. Just seeing her would have been good, smoothing her head and hair, just smoothing her head and hair, that was all. God. Ah God he was feeling better, it was passed. Poor old wife but it was a shame for her, the missis. She had to carry on. She had to cope. Different for him. Different. He wasnt stuck in the house, he had a job at the time, but she was, she was stuck in the house. Plus she had to look after the other one. That was what kept her going. Christ almighty he could do with a drink. All this rain and he was dying of fucking thirst. It was past now, finished. He felt better. Aye he could do with a drink, of water just. The feeling was away, it had gone. There was another twinge now at his knees but it went as well. He shivered again. He was alone. He had to carry on now. He started walking, following the trail. One thing he did know but, see when he died, he was going to die of a heart attack, he was going to die of a heart attack and he was going to be alone, there wasnt going to be no cunt, no cunt, he was going to be fucking alone, that was the way he was going to die, he fucking knew it, it was a fucking racing certainty.